WHY
SHE DIED

BOOKS BY J.G. ROBERTS

THE DETECTIVE RACHEL HART SERIES
1. Little Girl Missing
2. What He Did

As Julia Roberts
THE LIBERTY SANDS TRILOGY
Life's a Beach and Then…
If He Really Loved Me…
It's Never Too Late to Say…

Christmas at Carol's
Carol's Singing

Alice in Theatreland
Time for a Short Story

One Hundred Lengths of the Pool

WHY
SHE DIED

J.G. ROBERTS

Bookouture

Published by Bookouture in 2020

An imprint of Storyfire Ltd.
Carmelite House
50 Victoria Embankment
London EC4Y 0DZ

www.bookouture.com

ISBN: 978-1-78681-922-2
eBook ISBN: 978-1-78681-921-5

This book is a work of fiction. Names, characters, businesses,
organizations, places and events other than those clearly in the
public domain, are either the product of the author's imagination
or are used fictitiously. Any resemblance to actual persons, living or
dead, events or locales is entirely coincidental.

PROLOGUE

6.25 a.m. – Saturday

Abi Wyett pulled her waist-length blonde hair up into a ponytail, securing it with a bright yellow spiral band before perching on the edge of her bed to tie the orange laces on her trainers. She smiled. *The only thing bright about me this morning is what I'm wearing,* she thought, checking her watch. It was twenty-five past six. She shuddered. Abi had always been a night owl and before February she would only ever have seen 6.25 a.m. on her way back from a night out, but since she had agreed to help her best friend Hannah with her training programme, lie-ins were a thing of the past. It wasn't so bad now that the mornings were lighter and warmer, but there had been times in the depths of winter when her exhaled breath formed clouds in front of her and her cheeks were numb with the cold. At those moments, she had regretted agreeing to help Hannah with her hare-brained plan to be the youngest British woman to conquer Mount Everest.

Abi tucked her mobile phone into the zip-up compartment on the waistband of her leggings and pulled the lead of her earphones out from under her vest top, leaving them dangling from the neckline. Although the two girls ran together, both found that the time passed more agreeably if they were listening to music. They rarely spoke after their initial greeting until they finished their run. *She probably won't even say hello to me this morning after I pulled out of working at the club last night,* Abi thought as she closed the door to her room and jogged along the corridor to Hannah's. She continued jogging on the spot to warm up her muscles while she waited for Hannah to answer. After a few moments she knocked again and called out, 'Come on, Hannah, time to get moving. I've got a Leavers' Ball meeting at half past nine.' There was still no reply.

Hannah hadn't missed an early-morning run since she had started her training regime back in February, even going on her own on the few occasions when Abi had cried off. Checking her watch, Abi realised she was a few minutes later than their usual 6.30 a.m. meet-up. *Surely she would have come and knocked on my door, unless she was madder with me than I thought.* She knocked for a third time, but when there was still no response, Abi presumed Hannah had left without her. After a moment's hesitation when she seriously considered returning to her room and getting back into bed, she decided to try and catch up with Hannah. The girls always followed the same route, past the university football and rugby pitches and into the woods beyond. *If she left at the same time as usual, I can catch up with her before she gets to the trees,* Abi thought, putting her earphones in and hitting the play button halfway along the lead nestled against her chest.

The morning was crisp and fresh, but the blue skies overhead held the promise of another warm spring day as Abi ran down the steps towards the playing fields, her eyes scanning the perimeter path. There was no sign of Hannah. She quickened her pace. Abi hated confrontation, and hoped any awkwardness over her last-minute decision not to work the previous evening could be defused more effectively if she could catch up with her friend and fall into step at her side.

Abi had been faced with an impossible choice. Phil, her boyfriend, was supposed to be travelling to an away game for the university rugby team on Friday, but he'd been injured in the final practice session on Thursday evening and they'd taken him to hospital for observation. When Abi visited him on Friday afternoon, he'd asked her to stay until visiting hours were over and she'd felt she couldn't refuse. Hannah had made out it didn't matter after Abi messaged to tell her that she wouldn't be going in to work, although the final line of her reply – 'he and Jamie would have a photo finish for most jealous boyfriend' – had suggested that she thought Phil was deliberately preventing her from working.

Maybe Hannah has a point, Abi thought. *It was Phil's plans that changed, yet he expected me to just drop everything to be with him. I doubt if he'd have done the same if it had been the other way around.*

The ground felt hard and unforgiving underfoot. Abi tried to remember the last time it had rained as she pounded the cinder path at the side of the rugby pitch, already breathing quite heavily and beginning to perspire. April was renowned for showers, but she couldn't recall any significant rainfall the previous month and certainly none at all so far in May. It was more pleasant for running but not so kind on her joints.

There was still no sign of Hannah up ahead when Abi veered off onto the hardened mud path, strewn with twigs and dried leaves, that led into the woods. Before the trees became too dense, sunlight was able to force its way through the leafy canopy overhead, creating a dappled effect on the ferns and bracken growing in abundance beneath, but the further into the woodland Abi ventured, all sunlight was extinguished. In the gloom, she had to concentrate more fully on the path to ensure there were no branches obstructing her way that might cause her to trip and injure herself, particularly as she was running alone. From past experience she knew her mobile phone signal was virtually non-existent the deeper into the woods she went, so if she did fall badly, she could be there for hours, if not days, before someone found her.

Unlike her daredevil friend, Abi wasn't a fan of going through the woods, and had only been persuaded to change from her usual route along local roads when the two of them started running together. She could feel her heart pounding in her chest and knew that it wasn't only because she had been running faster than normal to try and catch up with Hannah. Abi was always fearful of someone lying in wait, ready to pounce on them in the half-light of the woods, but Hannah reassured her by saying the two of them were more than a match for some sad pervert. *Maybe that's why I'm feeling nervous*, Abi thought, *without Hannah I feel more vulnerable*. Despite knowing that she should keep her eyes trained on the uneven path, Abi risked the occasional glance ahead, hoping for a flash of her friend's bright running gear. But there was no sign of her.

Perhaps she didn't come out running after all. Maybe I should turn back, Abi thought, rounding a turn in the path. She managed to stifle a scream as she came abruptly to a halt. Off to the left of the path some fifty metres away, Abi could make out a shadowy figure. Her eyes had adjusted to the gloom and in the split second before she turned to run from whoever it was, her brain registered that it was too tall to be a person. Fearfully backing away while still peering at the outline, trying to make out what it was, she felt the blood in her veins turn to ice. It *was* a person, after all, but they were suspended in mid-air, hanging by the neck from the branch of a tree. Abi's heart began to thump against her ribcage as the full horror of what she was seeing became apparent. She recognised the navy-blue hoodie, grey tracksuit bottoms and lime-green running shoes that should have been pounding the paths through the woods with her that morning.

Abi's shrill scream pierced the silence, startling birds into taking flight and filling the air with the sound of their flapping wings. She turned and began to stumble back along the path towards the university, tears blinding her eyes, her legs threatening to give way beneath her. 'Help me!' she cried. 'Somebody please help! I think my friend has killed herself.'

CHAPTER ONE

The Day Before – 4.00 p.m. – Friday

DCI Rachel Hart was feeling a bit of a fraud. Although she had been back at work for a week, it was obvious to her that her second in command, DI Graham Wilson, was bearing the brunt of the workload and only passing minor things in her direction. She appreciated his kindness, but there wasn't enough to occupy her mind and stop her thoughts drifting to her twin sister, Ruth, and her possible whereabouts. For almost six weeks she had been missing from Mountview Hospital where she had been a resident in the psychiatric wing for the previous ten years after a failed suicide attempt. Ruth had never fully recovered from the horror of the kidnap and sexual abuse she had been subjected to as young child, and Rachel had never truly got past the guilt she felt as a result of the kidnapper abusing her sister but not laying a finger on her. Rachel had thought she was doing the right thing for Ruth, paying the extortionate monthly fees not only for her to be looked after, but also to protect her from herself. Her sister, it seemed, viewed things differently. There had been no communication from Ruth other than a text message the day after she had left, stating that she was finally free.

The message had completely devastated Rachel, who had repeatedly said to her boyfriend, Tim, 'Why didn't she tell me she was unhappy? We could have worked something out.'

The days following Ruth's disappearance had passed in a blur. She was wrapping up the final details on a triple murder case, while desperately trying to locate her sister. By the end of the week, after encouragement from Tim, Rachel had visited her GP, who said she was not in a fit state to work and signed her off with stress for a fortnight. The fortnight stretched to three weeks, then four, at which point Rachel insisted she needed to keep busy or she would lose her mind. Reluctantly, the GP had allowed her to return to work, but had made it clear that she believed Rachel was in a fragile state and might benefit from medication or at the very least some therapy. The doctor's advice was ignored.

Rachel picked her phone up to check for text messages, even though she knew she would have heard the alert or felt the vibration. It was a habit she had got into while she was off work, and now she was finding it very difficult to break. At first, she'd had several messages a day from her newsreader friend, Maddy, and the occasional 'how are you doing, Guv?' from her DI, but Maddy's life was busy and now that Rachel was back behind her desk there was no need for Graham to message her. More often than not, she found herself looking at a screen displaying the time in very large numbers. *As if I'm not already aware of how slowly time is moving*, she thought, returning her phone to the desk, screen down. Even Tim, who had texted her on the hour, every hour while she was off work, had obviously decided that she needed to regain some semblance of normality and restricted himself to once or twice a day. It didn't really matter. It wasn't any of them that she wanted to hear from. Rachel was hanging onto the faint hope that her sister would realise she had made a dreadful mistake and call her asking to return to Mountview. Each passing day with no word from Ruth made that less and less likely.

As Rachel struggled to refocus on her paperwork there was a knock at the door.

'Come in,' she called.

'I'm just getting myself a coffee, Guv. Do you fancy one?' Graham said.

Rachel glanced down at the barely touched coffee he had brought her an hour earlier. There was a film across the surface of the liquid and the brown line just above it served as an indication that she had allowed her drink to go cold before she'd had more than a sip of it.

'I think I'll pass, thanks, but come in and tell me what's going on. Any interesting cases on the go?'

'Nothing much, to be honest,' he replied, closing the door behind him and crossing the room to sit down opposite Rachel. 'I've sent a back-up team over to Egham at their request to help them evict some travellers off the big field by the Runnymede roundabout. They've been there a couple of weeks and were refusing to move on, but I think it's all in hand now. Apart from that it's just the usual: petty burglary and domestic violence, nothing to get our teeth into.'

'I don't suppose Missing Persons have come up with anything on Ruth?' Rachel could see the pity in Graham's eyes and hated herself for bringing her personal life into work. *But if I can't use my police contacts to try and find my sister, what's the point of it all?* she thought.

'No, sorry, Guv. We're still checking all the shelters in the area regularly and asking around and showing Ruth's photo, but nobody seems to have seen her at all. My gut feeling is that she left the area after sending you that text.'

There had been a moment of real hope when the techie boys had been able to trace Ruth's mobile phone to its last-known location, until it became apparent that it was somewhere in the shrubbery close to the entrance of Mountview. Rachel suspected that Ruth had watched her go into the hospital, sent her final communication and then deliberately discarded the phone for them to find. Even the television appeal instigated by her friend

Maddy on News 24/7, the channel she worked for, had drawn a blank. There had been several sightings of a woman fitting Ruth's description, but they had all turned out to be Rachel, unsurprising as they were virtually identical. 'Like two peas in a pod' had been a phrase bandied around throughout their schooldays, but their likeness didn't extend to their personalities. *I would never have put Ruth through all this anguish*, Rachel thought. *It's as though she has simply disappeared off the face of the earth.*

'I know it's a long shot, but please keep trying, Graham,' Rachel said, trying to control the wobble in her voice.

'Of course, Guv. I was wondering whether you've signed Eleanor Drake's application to train as a detective?' he asked, adeptly steering the conversation in a new direction.

'I've just done it. I can't see any reason why it wouldn't be approved, can you?'

'No. She's certainly at the top of my list for thoroughness and efficiency, although she could try and open up to her colleagues a bit more. She's not the most popular officer because she's clearly hell-bent on climbing the career ladder. I think a few of the others think she's using them as rungs.'

'I'll have a quiet word,' Rachel said, while thinking, *that's exactly what people used to say about me.* 'It's hard being young and ambitious without coming across as a cold fish,' she added, a knowing smile playing at the corners of her mouth.

'I couldn't possibly comment. I've only known you at the top of the ladder.'

'Hardly the top, but I take your point.'

'Are you sure I can't get you a coffee? Or maybe a tea?'

'No, honestly. I'll probably call it a day soon. I'm supposed to be cooking tonight and I've got nothing in.'

'Why put yourself through the hassle, Guv? Just do what I do when it's my turn to cook.'

'And what's that?'

'Get a takeaway,' Graham said, grinning broadly as he left her office.

As the door closed, a text message alert sounded on Rachel's phone. She grabbed for it, but such was her hurry that she sent the phone flying to the floor along with a pile of papers.

'For God's sake,' she muttered under her breath, dropping to her knees to retrieve the phone from under her desk. *Please let it be her, please let it be her*, she silently prayed, but once again her prayers went unanswered. It was Tim.

So sorry Rachel, but I'm not going to make it for dinner tonight. I've got a meeting with a prisoner who's due for release soon out in the sticks and I can't see me getting back much before midnight. I hope you hadn't gone to too much trouble buying stuff in for dinner. Maybe we could have it tomorrow instead of eating out? I'll try and call you later, Tim xxxx

Rachel suppressed a pang of disappointment. She had been looking forward to seeing Tim to take her mind off the looming weekend. Sunday had become the worst day of the week for her; it was the day she used to visit Ruth at Mountview. *How many times over the years did I wish for a Sunday to myself?* she reflected guiltily. *I guess it's a case of be careful what you wish for.* She tapped out a quick message in response and hit SEND, before gathering up the papers she had knocked to the floor in her haste. She stacked them neatly on the corner of her desk and checked the time. Although it was only 4.30 p.m., she decided to finish early and head home, despite the prospect of a solitary evening and a less than appetising supper of beans on toast.

CHAPTER TWO

6.45 p.m. – Friday

Tim Berwick sat at one side of the small grey table, drumming his fingers on the shiny surface and tapping the toe of his black brogues on the tiled floor. He hated coming to this place, with its overly bright lights, clanging doors and the constant sound of jangling keys. It was one of the reasons he had become a defence lawyer, to keep as many innocent people as he could out of prison. *Mind you*, he thought, watching a man who looked a lot older than his sixty-three years shuffle across the floor in his direction, *it would help if people didn't break the law in the first place.*

'How are you doing?' he asked, as the prisoner sat down opposite him on the uncomfortable wooden chair.

'Same as I'm always doing in this shithole,' the old man replied gruffly. 'The beds are hard, the showers are cold, the food is like eating puke and the screws are more corrupt than the inmates. Apart from that, everything is just fine. You said you'd got some news?'

'Yes. We've heard back from the parole board.'

There was a glimmer of interest in the old man's green eyes. 'And?'

'We should get the official notification first thing on Monday morning, but I wanted to come and give you the news myself. You've been granted conditional release. Well done, Jack.'

There was a sharp intake of breath before a slow smile spread across Jack's face. 'I'm the one that should be saying well done, boy. You knew all the right things to say to get me released. It's a shame I didn't have you as my lawyer earlier.'

*

Tim cast his mind back to their first meeting almost two years previously. Jack had seemed something of a lost cause, constantly in trouble for petty misdemeanours. He'd had parole denied on several occasions because the board didn't feel confident in his ability to integrate back into society without reoffending. Tim had gradually persuaded Jack that there was a way to regain his freedom if he changed his attitude. When a slot with the parole board had unexpectedly become free after one of Jack's fellow inmates had his hearing cancelled as a consequence of slashing another inmate with a razor, Tim had immediately driven out to the prison to tell Jack the good news.

'I know it doesn't give us much time to work on what you need to say if you want to have a chance of getting out of this place early,' he had said, 'but it was too good an opportunity to miss. Do you think you can be ready?'

'I know what to say, you've told me often enough,' Jack had said. '"I'm sorry. I've learned the error of my ways and I promise to be a model citizen if you release me".'

'That won't cut it because they won't believe you. I've told you before, you have to think of specific things that have helped change you while you've been in prison.'

'Like what?'

His tone needs working on too, Tim had thought. It had always been brusque and confrontational, right from the very beginning. 'Well, give examples of some of the ways you've interacted with other prisoners over the years, so that the board will be confident in your ability to integrate back into society.'

'I don't think some of those do-gooding old dears on the parole board would take kindly to hearing about my interactions with other prisoners, if you get my drift,' he had cackled.

Tim had fought back the urge to be sick. *Had Jack learned nothing over his thirty years of incarceration?* But he had promised to get him released when he had first taken him on as a client, and that's what he intended to do; failure wasn't an option. The problem was it had become increasingly apparent to Tim that despite his early optimism that he could influence him to be a better person, Jack was not a reformed character and he had no intention of changing his ways.

'Don't look like that, boy,' Jack had growled. 'I'm not a piece of dog shit on the sole of your expensive shoes. I was just having a little joke, all right?'

'In pretty poor taste, if I'm honest with you,' Tim had replied. 'If you really want me to help you get out of here, you're going to have to do as I say.'

'Don't you worry about me, I'll be good. I've learned my lines and I'll come up with some believable examples of how prison has made me a better person. I've waited a long time for this.'

'You wouldn't have been in here so long if you'd behaved better in the early days of your sentence,' Tim had said, thinking *and if you hadn't committed such disgusting crimes.* 'With good behaviour, you'd have been out years ago.'

'But I didn't know that until you became my lawyer.'

'Well, you know now, so don't do anything to screw it up.'

*

To his credit, Tim thought, looking at Jack's smiling face across the table, *he had given a very impressive performance at the hearing.* And now, six months later, he had finally been granted his partial freedom.

'Is everything ready for me on the outside?'

'Almost. Look, I've another appointment I need to get to, so I have to go,' Tim lied.

'At this time on a Friday night? Are you sure about that, or is it just that you can't stand being around me?'

Is it that obvious? Tim thought. His visits with Jack always made him question his own integrity. 'I didn't say it was a work appointment, did I?'

Jack sniggered. 'A lady friend, eh? Young, is she, and pretty? Or maybe it's a bloke,' he said, misunderstanding Tim's look of revulsion. 'I've often wondered if you bat for the other side.'

Tim stayed silent, choosing not to dignify the comment with a response.

'You've turned into a good-looking young man, and smart with it. I shouldn't imagine you'd have much trouble, whatever your preference,' Jack added. 'Who'd have thought it, from such unpromising beginnings.'

Tim pushed his chair back from the table and stood up. *I need to get out of here*, he thought. 'I'll see you first thing Monday morning. In the meantime, keep your nose clean.'

'I will, don't you worry. I'm not as stupid as "Slasher". Mind you, I suppose I owe him one. If he hadn't gone at Tony with a razor blade, I wouldn't be getting out of here. He deserved it, by the way, the dirty little snitch.'

Jack always had to have the final word.

Back outside in the fresh air, Tim glanced at his watch. It was only a little after 6.00 p.m. *If the traffic's light, I could be back in Reading by half past nine. That's not too late to call in on Rachel*, he thought. Part of him wished he hadn't texted her earlier to cancel their evening plans; he could have done with her company after a stressful week. He considered ringing her and suggesting dropping in with a late supper, but decided against it. Rachel had been quite fragile since Ruth's disappearance and if the traffic was bad, as it was likely to be on a Friday night, and he arrived much later than expected, it could result in another petty argument, exactly what Tim didn't want. *No, it's best to leave things and see her tomorrow as agreed.*

He climbed into his car and switched the engine on, selecting 'home' on his satnav and Classic FM on the radio. *I'll be glad when this business with Jack is over,* he thought, reversing his car out of the parking space and heading towards the prison security gate.

CHAPTER THREE

8.00 p.m. – Friday

The cat's eye was perfect. Hannah had learned the technique from watching her mum, Miranda, get ready night after night for the numerous events that filled her social calendar. She would rest the elbow of the hand holding the eyeliner brush on her glass-topped dressing table while the fingers of the other hand gently pulled the skin near the corner of the eye upwards. Miranda maintained it gave a smoother surface and a more lifted look to the flick. *She's right*, Hannah thought, leaning back from the mirror to examine her handiwork, *but then she would be*.

Miranda had been taught by the best throughout her short-lived modelling career, which had followed her crowning as 'Miss Martinique'. Everyone had heralded her as the next supermodel, but she had other ideas. After a whirlwind romance, she had chosen instead to marry Rupert Longcross, one of the judges from the beauty pageant. If Miranda ever regretted her decision, she never mentioned it, and she'd done very well financially out of her recent divorce settlement, allowing her lavish lifestyle to continue.

Hannah pressed her lips together to evenly distribute bright pink lipstick before adding a wet-look lip gloss. The mirror reflected back an image of a very beautiful girl wearing far too much make-up, but that was what the punters at the club seemed to like, and tonight was a working night.

When her friend Abi had first suggested becoming a shot girl as a way to raise money for her Everest expedition, Hannah had rejected the idea, particularly as they had both been critical of their friend Chloe when she started at Velvet nightclub a few weeks before Christmas to earn some extra cash. In previous years, Chloe had always asked to borrow money from the other girls, which she rarely paid back, and she had never before bought any of them a Christmas present. But on the morning they all went their separate ways for the Christmas holidays, they had each been surprised to receive a small package from Chloe, containing a gold necklace with an initial charm suspended from it. 'I'm telling you, Hannah,' Abi had said a few days after Hannah had made her unexpected announcement about the Everest expedition, 'she earns a small fortune. She showed me a backpack under her bed stuffed with notes of all denominations, and she's only been doing it a few months. Not only that, but I'll bet there's no way that she pays tax on the cash because there can't be an accurate record of how much she's earning. Really, you should consider it.'

Hannah had considered it. Chloe was all right looking with a decent figure, if a little on the curvy side. *If she's earning enough money to splash out on expensive gifts, it shouldn't take me too long to make what I need*, Hannah had thought. It was just the idea of it she hated: dressing in a fishnet body suit with skimpy satin shorts over the top and having drunken idiots pawing you, thinking their ten or twenty pounds was buying them more than alcohol... it filled her with revulsion. Hannah liked to be in control in all areas of her life, and her encounters with members of the opposite sex were no different. But Abi was right: it would be easy money and Hannah needed it in a hurry. That was when she had turned on the waterworks. 'I don't really want to do it, Abs, but I'm miles off my target. I've been working so hard on my fitness, and now it looks like I'm not going to be able to go after all. I might do it if you'll do it with me,' she had snivelled. Reluctantly Abi had agreed, although she'd begged Hannah to be vague about the actual job they were going to be doing at Velvet as she was pretty sure her boyfriend wouldn't approve. Hannah had shrugged and said, 'That's your call, Abs. I'll be telling Jamie what I'm doing and why I'm doing it even though I don't expect he'll be overly keen either. Relationships are built on trust and understanding. Without that, you've got nothing.'

Hannah slipped her feet into her stiletto-heeled ankle boots and zipped them up before reaching into the back of the wardrobe for her work backpack that contained her shot belt. All the girls had to purchase their own, which meant quite an outlay up front, so Hannah had swallowed her pride and allowed her mum to treat her. *Not that Mum really knew what she was buying me*, Hannah thought, a smile twitching at the corners of her mouth.

Miranda had been in a taxi on the way back from the airport after yet another trip to the Caribbean when Hannah had rung to ask her if she could borrow some money to buy a belt she needed for her new job.

'Did you say job, darling? I can't hear you very well, it's a terrible signal. Why are you getting a job? Hasn't Daddy paid you your allowance this month?' Miranda had asked.

'Yes, of course he has, but I just wanted to feel a bit more independent and earn some money of my own.'

'Very commendable. What sort of job is it?'

Hannah had taken a deep breath. 'You're not going to approve, Mum, but I'm going to do it anyway. Me and Abi are going to be shot girls.'

'I don't have a problem with that if it's a decent establishment, although I don't expect they'll pay much, and you'll be on your feet a lot of the time. Still, if that's what you want, it's fine by me. How much do you need for your belt?'

'They're a hundred pounds each. Can I borrow the money for Abi's, too? She's a bit short. Don't worry, we'll pay you back.'

A few weeks later, when it had come out that the girls were working as 'shot' girls rather than 'shop' girls, which was what Miranda had heard, Hannah had asked, 'Didn't you think that was a bit pricey for a belt, Mum?'

Miranda had replied, 'I just assumed it must be some very upmarket boutique which required their staff to wear a fancy uniform.'

Hannah could remember her friends howling with laughter when she told them the story, although Miranda had been less than amused when she realised what her daughter's job actually entailed. 'I'm not sure I like the idea of you wandering around a nightclub in skimpy clothing trying to persuade people to buy alcohol,' she had said. 'Does your father know about it?' Miranda always referred to Rupert as 'your father' when she wanted him to sound like a more authoritarian figure than he actually was.

'No, and I don't suppose he'll care. He's far too busy trying to keep up with Tamara to bother about anything I might be doing.'

Mentioning her dad's latest girlfriend, who was only three years older than Hannah, had the desired effect in closing the subject, just as she had known it would.

Hannah was just reaching for her car keys when her phone pinged to alert her to a text message. It was from Abi.

> *Sorry, Hannah, but I'm not going to make Velvet tonight. I'm still at the hospital with Phil and by the time I get home, changed and get my slap on it'll be too late. Can you explain to Max for me? See you first thing for our run. Xx*

Hannah's jaw clenched. She'd had a feeling when she'd spoken to Abi earlier that Phil would do his utmost to stop her from working that night. He hated her job and blamed Hannah for getting her into it. Phil and Abi had had a massive argument when it eventually came to light what she did at Velvet. Abi had been economical with the truth, implying that she was working as a cloakroom attendant, but one of his rugby-playing teammates had put him straight.

'Why did you lie to me?' Phil had shouted at her in the street after waiting for Abi and Hannah to come out of the club.

'Because I knew you'd react like this,' she'd replied.

'Really? Or is it because you know that what you're doing is cheap and sluttish?'

Abi had burst into tears and finished with him on the spot, but he'd managed to win her back with an apology and several bunches of flowers. Hannah knew that Abi choosing to work alongside her at Velvet, despite her boyfriend's obvious disapproval, spoke volumes for her best friend's loyalty. She experienced a brief pang of guilt before writing her reply.

No worries, it'll just mean more tips for me. I might even be able to buy my climbing boots next week – exciting! I hope Phil feels better soon. I think he and Jamie would have a photo finish for most jealous boyfriend xx

CHAPTER FOUR

8.35 p.m. – Friday

'What did she say?' Phil asked. 'Was she mad?'

'Not really,' Abi replied, slipping her phone back into her handbag before Phil asked to see the message. She thought she detected a note of victory in his voice. 'She said she hopes you feel better soon.'

'I'll bet she did.'

'I don't know why you've got such a problem with Hannah. You two always seemed to get on okay before we started working at Velvet. You should remember that if it wasn't for the extra money I've been earning, we wouldn't be staying in a luxury apartment in Portugal for our summer holiday. We'd be in a caravan in Skegness with your parents and their farting Jack Russell, like we were last year.'

'Thanks for pointing that out and making me feel like a totally inadequate boyfriend,' Phil said.

'You're being ridiculous – that was supposed to be funny. My point is that the shot girl stint is a means to an end so Hannah can achieve her dream of climbing Mount Everest.'

Abi could clearly remember the late-January morning when Hannah had dropped her bombshell. She was eating breakfast with Lucie and Chloe at the dining table in the kitchen of their halls of residence when Hannah had bounced in, full of energy, holding a letter in her hand.

'I've got something to tell you,' she'd said, unable to control her excitement. 'I'm going to climb Mount Everest.'

The reaction had been mixed. Lucie sprayed milk across the wooden tabletop as she choked on her cereal, while Chloe shook her head and rolled her eyes, an expression of mild exasperation on her face.

'Of course you are,' Abi had said. 'We're out of milk, by the way. It was your turn to buy some, so we didn't feel too bad finishing it.'

'No, I really am,' Hannah had continued, taking two slices of bread out of the plastic wrapper and dropping them into the toaster. 'I want to be the youngest British woman to achieve it, and they've accepted my application providing I can raise the money and pass the fitness tests.'

Abi had lowered her Coco Pops–laden spoon from her mouth back to her bowl. 'Oh my God, you're actually serious.'

'Completely,' Hannah had replied.

'She's just attention-seeking as usual,' Chloe had said dismissively. 'There's no way she'd be seen dead in mountain-climbing boots and she's always moaning about being cold.' She'd turned to face Hannah. 'Are you forgetting you wouldn't even go to the top of the Shard because you said you had no head for heights?'

'If everybody stuck to their comfort zone nobody would ever achieve anything,' Hannah had replied pointedly.

Although the four girls were friends, Chloe and Hannah had never really got on. They were from completely different backgrounds, and neither made any attempt to try and accept their differences. The four of them had shared a house throughout their second year at university, but had decided to move back into halls for their final year in the hope that there would be fewer arguments. It hadn't had the desired effect, and things had really come to a head when Chloe had called Hannah 'a rich bitch with no understanding of how real people have to struggle to make ends meet', to which Hannah had responded, 'Just because you're poor it doesn't mean you have to live like a slob.' The two hadn't spoken for weeks until Lucie and Abi, unable to bear the tense atmosphere any longer, had made them apologise to each other and call a truce. A fragile peace ensued, but all of them were only too aware that things could kick off again with the tiniest provocation. To avoid an argument that morning, breakfast had continued in near silence until Chloe and Lucie headed off for lectures.

'Why Everest?' Abi had asked.

'I want to leave my mark on the world,' Hannah had replied.

'Don't we all? But I can think of other less extreme and less dangerous ways of doing it. People die on that mountain, Hannah, lots of people.'

'Well, it won't beat me. I won't let it.'

Hannah's jaw was set in a way that Abi recognised. She'd known there was no point in trying to change her friend's mind. 'So, when are you planning on attempting this madness?'

'Next spring, if I'm going to beat the current record holder, Bonita Norris. She was twenty-two when she did it and I won't turn twenty-two until June next year. I'll only get one shot at it, though, so I'll need to get super-fit.'

At the time, Abi had seriously doubted whether her friend could go from couch potato to super-fit in a little over twelve months, but she had to admit Hannah was proving her wrong. And the job at Velvet wasn't as bad as they had both feared.

'Hannah just needed a bit of moral support, and the side benefit is that we get to go on a fabulous holiday on our own. From where I'm sitting it's a win-win situation,' Abi said, reaching for Phil's hand.

'I suppose you're right,' he said, returning the squeeze she had given him, 'but it's not as though you're not supporting her in other ways. You're up at the crack of dawn to go running with her in all weathers and working out as her gym buddy three nights a week. I hardly ever see you,' he moaned. 'Couldn't Hannah just have done the Velvet job with Chloe? She was already working there, wasn't she?'

'You know they don't see eye to eye, and it's even worse now because Chloe's tips have more than halved since Hannah started working there. Once we're done with uni, I don't think those two will bother to stay in touch.'

'Will you?'

'What?'

'Stay in touch with Chloe?'

'Probably not. She's got a bit of a nasty streak in her. If she hadn't been Lucie's friend from school, I think it would have been a threesome rather than a foursome.'

'Now there's a thought,' Phil said, a lascivious look in his eye.

'Don't be disgusting,' Abi said, letting go of his hand. 'I think your dirty mind is the problem with me being a shot girl, not what actually goes on. You're obviously feeling a bit better.'

'Looks like I'm about to find out,' he said, indicating the approaching doctor.

'Good news, Mr Carter, all the scans are completely clear. You're free to go home once we've completed the paperwork.'

'Great, thanks,' Phil responded.

Abi glanced at her watch. It was only 8.45 p.m. *If they get the paperwork done quickly, I could call an Uber and potentially make it to Velvet by 10 p.m., still early for the club on a Friday night,* she thought. She looked up to see that Phil was watching her.

'Don't go, Abs,' he said with a whine in his voice that was intended to be more appealing than it actually sounded. 'Hannah's not expecting you now, and we could get a takeaway and a few beers to have at mine.'

Abi hesitated for a moment. It had been tiring sitting in the stuffy hospital all afternoon. *Can I really be bothered to get all glammed up and go to work?*

'Please?' Phil urged. 'We don't often get the chance to have a Friday night in together, and when we do, I can't usually drink because there's a match the next day.'

'All right. You win, but only if it's a nice bottle of wine rather than a few beers, you know they make me feel bloated. And if Hannah asks, we didn't get out of here until midnight.'

'Yes, boss,' Phil said, unable to keep a smile of victory from his lips.

'I won't be staying over, though. We're running at 6.30 a.m. and then I've got a meeting about the Leavers' Ball at 9.30 a.m.'

'That's okay. Despite lying around in bed all day, I'm knackered. I didn't sleep a wink last night with his snoring,' Phil said, indicating the man in the next bed, 'and his coughing,' he added, nodding his head towards the man in the bed opposite. 'I'll probably fall asleep on the sofa.'

'That sounds like a fun evening! I'm joking,' Abi added, seeing the expression on Phil's face. 'Lighten up. I don't know what's happened to your sense of humour lately.'

'Exams, and the uncertainty of getting a job once I'm out in the big wide world.'

'It's the same for all of us, Phil. There's no point in worrying about the future, it will just make you miserable. There are plenty of jobs as long as you're prepared to do them and not expect the perfect career opportunity to land at your feet immediately.'

'Jobs like being a shot girl?'

'You couldn't resist having another little dig, could you? It's only for another few weeks and then I'm done. My shot belt will go on eBay the very next day. Satisfied?'

Phil grunted.

'I'm going to see if I can hurry the nurse up with the paperwork,' Abi said, sliding off the bed where she had been sitting. 'Get your things together, then we can make a quick escape,' she added over her shoulder.

Sometimes she struggled to remember what she had found so irresistibly attractive about Phil… apart from the fact that he had chosen her over Hannah when they had first met in one of the university bars. As usual on a night out, Hannah had been the centre of attention, the majority of male students hovering around her like moths attracted to a flame, when Phil had pushed his way into their group and made a deliberate show of offering to buy Abi a drink. As he'd handed her a gin and tonic, he'd chinked glasses with her and said, his voice barely above a whisper, 'Gentlemen prefer blondes.' They'd been an item ever since, although lately there had been times when Abi questioned whether Phil was really her Mr Right.

CHAPTER FIVE

12.25 a.m. – Saturday

The beat of the music was pulsating in time with the pounding in Hannah's head as she stepped behind the bar to replenish her belt with clean shot glasses. Velvet was packed to the rafters, and although she'd visited the VIP area a couple of times to cover Abi's absence, there was more money to be made in the main areas of the club, where the queues at all of the bars were four or five people deep. Max, the manager, hadn't been best pleased when Hannah had arrived earlier in the evening and told him that Abi wouldn't be in. He had turned on his heel and marched off towards his office, muttering under his breath about people being unreliable. Now, as she emerged from behind the bar, she could see him pushing through the crowds on the dance floor towards her.

'So, what happened?' Max asked, raising his voice to be heard. 'Did he trip over his own ego?'

Hannah laughed, partly in relief that her boss was now speaking to her again but mostly because what he said was a pretty accurate assessment of Phil's character. 'No, his head collided with someone's knee while he was playing rugby and it knocked him out. Abi says it was a mild concussion, but they wanted to keep him in for observation.'

'Hopefully it's knocked some sense into him. He's such an arrogant little prick. I can't imagine what someone as nice as Abi sees in him… unless he *isn't* a little prick, if you get my drift,' Max said, winking.

Hannah blushed. 'I wouldn't know,' she replied, pretending to adjust her shot belt to avoid eye contact with him.

'Really? I thought you girls talked about that sort of stuff all the time. You know, comparing notes.'

'Maybe some girls do, but Abs and I have more important things to talk about.'

'Like how you're going to spend all the cash you earn here.'

'You already know how I'm going to be spending mine,' Hannah said, 'I told you when I took the job.'

'Oh yes, I remember. You're planning to conquer the highest mountain in the world,' Max said, a hint of scepticism in his voice. 'How's all that going?'

'Really well, actually. I've already been able to pay the deposit for all the travel and accommodation, and I'm hoping to get my climbing boots next week so I can start to do some training in them.'

'Why didn't you just go for corporate sponsorship? Yours is quite a unique story, and companies would get good publicity out of sponsoring you.'

'I want to pay all the costs myself,' Hannah said, her jaw jutting forward slightly as it always did when she was determined to do something. 'It will feel like more of a personal achievement then. I've got some corporate sponsors and I'm looking for more, but I want their money to go to the various different mental health charities I'm doing this for. I'm aiming to donate half a million pounds.'

Max whistled. 'Good luck with that. Money is pretty tight at the moment, and all the charities are really struggling.'

'That's exactly why I'm doing it.' Hannah paused, and then added with a twinkle in her eye, 'And to get my face on the front page of all the national newspapers, of course.'

'Well, I hope you manage it, Hannah, it will be a hell of a feat if you pull it off,' Max said as she walked off towards a group of people, her hips swinging in time to the music.

Unlike most of the shot girls, who always made a beeline for the men in the club, hoping their feminine charm and skimpy outfits would persuade the punters to purchase a few shots, Hannah had a different modus operandi. She had worked out that by being friendly and chatty with groups of girls or the woman in a couple, they wouldn't feel threatened by her. She always opened with the line, 'My boyfriend doesn't really like me doing this, but we're trying for a baby, so we need the money'. Usually the groups of girls were onside immediately and would buy shots to help her out. The woman in a couple would relax, safe in the knowledge that Hannah wasn't trying to hit on her boyfriend. She would then go on to do Hannah's job for her, persuading the boyfriend to dip his hand in his pocket to buy some shots. It was a hugely successful technique that had turned Hannah into the top earner among the shot girls within a fortnight of starting at Velvet.

On busy nights she would sell through both the bottles of liqueur she had slung in the holsters on either side of her shot belt. The girls weren't allowed to bring their own bottles in; they had to purchase them from the bar at a slightly inflated price, which was where the club made their money. Hannah had sussed that the most popular and profitable shots were pink sambuca, which had a sweet raspberry flavour, and the bright green Sourz apple liqueur. Because she always sold so many shots, Hannah never had to resort to watering the bottles down, as Chloe and some of the other girls had suggested she should.

After another circuit of the ground floor of Velvet, once again replenishing her shot glasses while noting that she had taken a second bottle of apple Sourz to be paid for at the end of the night, Hannah headed up to the VIP area again for a bit of a breather before the final push for business in the run-up to closing time. Numbers were always restricted to fewer than a hundred in the VIP section to keep it special. As she let herself in, unfastening the large gold clip attached to the padded red velvet rope that marked the entrance for the select few, she noticed a group of girls collected around what she assumed must be a minor celebrity. *Maybe it's a soap star*, she thought, *or someone from reality TV*. She smiled. Although she knew there was absolutely nothing real about those programmes from the obvious things, like the blindingly white teeth and huge boobs, to the scenarios the 'stars' found themselves in – delivering stilted, scripted dialogue – she certainly wouldn't say no if she was offered a part in one.

'Who has honoured us with their presence tonight?' she said, flashing a smile at Dave, one of the bouncers she had made a point of becoming friendly with. 'Reality star or actually famous?'

'I wouldn't exactly say famous, unless you're into boxing, that is. It's Lloyd Tennant, the former bantamweight world champion. I used to be a fan of his, so it's disappointing to find out he's a bit big time, flashing his cash around.'

'Just how I like them,' Hannah said. 'Please tell me he's a bit tipsy, too. I've got a fresh bottle of apple Sourz to sell, and if he treats all that lot to a couple of shots each, I might be able to get rid of the whole thing tonight.'

'Always thinking about business, eh? For one horrible moment, I thought you meant that's how you like your men.'

'You know me better than that, Dave, and besides, I've got a boyfriend,' Hannah said, heading in the direction of the group.

'More's the pity,' Dave muttered under his breath.

'Evening, ladies,' Hannah said, noticing some familiar faces in the group surrounding the former boxer. The priority for some girls on an evening out was to get off with someone famous. 'Is anybody thirsty?'

'You're all right, thanks, babes, we're on the champagne,' Lloyd said, waving the bottle around, 'but you're welcome to join us,' he added, undressing her with his eyes.

Hannah was always very polite with her rejection of advances of this sort.

'Maybe another time,' she said, turning away, 'I'm working, and I've got a whole bottle of apple Sourz to sell before closing time.'

Lloyd grabbed her arm with his free hand and pulled her back round to face him. Hannah immediately made eye contact with Dave, who was watching from the entrance to the VIP area.

'How much do you want for the whole bottle, babes? Money's no object for me,' Lloyd said, releasing her arm and pulling a roll of fifty-pound notes from his pocket. 'A hundred, two hundred, name your price.'

It wasn't the first time Hannah had experienced this kind of behaviour. Tempting as it was to accept his money, and it would certainly boost the Everest fund, she knew that he would expect something in return for his generosity.

'That's very kind of you, but I'm only allowed to sell individual shots, not the whole bottle. I could get in trouble with the management,' she said, starting to back away. 'I could even lose my job. I'm sure you wouldn't want that.'

'Who fancies a shot?' Lloyd said, not taking his eyes off Hannah's.

The girls clamoured in acceptance.

'We'll have a round of shots, please,' he said, placing huge emphasis on the word *please*. 'How much is that?'

'They're usually five pounds each, but I can do you three for ten pounds, making it thirty for the round,' she suggested after counting eight girls in the group.

'You don't need to do me any favours,' he replied. 'I'll pay full whack. Like I said, I've got plenty of money and I'm used to paying for what I want.'

There was an edge to his voice that Hannah didn't like, but she pulled the bottle from the holster anyway and started to pour the shots.

'That's forty-five pounds then, please,' she said as she handed him his glass.

Lloyd peeled off one of the fifty-pound notes. 'Keep the change, babes,' he said, leaning towards Hannah as he handed it over. He was close enough for her to smell the alcohol on his breath and feel the heat of it against her cheek. 'You might pour the shots,' he slurred, 'but I call them. I always get what I want,' he added, knocking the emerald-green liquid back in one. 'Another round, girls?'

'Is everything all right here, Hannah?' Dave had moved from his position by the velvet rope and was standing behind her.

'Hannah. That's a pretty name. Everything's fine, isn't it, Hannah? We're just doing a couple of rounds of shots.'

'It's okay, Dave. I'll just do this second round and then I'll head back out into the club.'

'You're sure?'

'She said so, didn't she?' Lloyd said, glaring at the man-mountain standing protectively at her shoulder.

The two men locked eyes momentarily, like a pair of rutting stags locking antlers in their attempt to gain supremacy.

'Thanks,' Hannah said, taking the second fifty-pound note from the former boxer and stuffing it in her already bulging bumbag, which was slung loosely beneath her shot belt.

'You're welcome, babes, and if you change your mind about joining the party, you know where to find us at closing time.'

'Jerk,' Dave said, as Hannah approached him back at the entrance to the VIP area. 'You just let me know if he gives you any more trouble. He might be a former boxing world champion, but I reckon I could handle him.'

'You're such a sweetheart, Dave, always looking out for me. You're like the big brother I never had,' Hannah said, giving him a peck on the cheek before disappearing into the milling throng of clubbers, oblivious to his lingering look.

*

Hannah gave the VIP area a wide berth for the rest of the evening, which was better for business, but tougher on her feet. She had worn strappy sandals on her first night as a shot girl, but quickly learned that boots were a better option. The busier the club was, and the drunker people became, the more likely she was to get trodden on. It was always a relief when the lights went on to signal the end of the night, and tonight especially so. She headed straight for the cloakroom and the small curtained-off area at the back of it that was reserved for staff members to take their breaks. Unzipping her boots, she kicked them off and sank down onto the floor to tot up her takings.

Allowing for the money she owed Velvet for the three bottles of liqueur she had sold, Hannah had made a profit of £340. *It was a good night for tips*, Hannah thought. *That boxer wasn't the only one who told me to keep the change.* After taking Velvet's cut from her money, she bundled the rest of the cash back into her bumbag, which she fastened diagonally across her chest before slipping her hoodie over her head. She felt safer with the money close to her body, disguised by her baggy top. She shoved her shot belt and boots into her generously proportioned backpack to replace the trainers and jogging bottoms which she always wore on her way home from work. Most people were too drunk to realise how much they had spent buying shots, but there was the occasional one who would pick on a shot girl outside the safety of the club. Hannah wasn't taking any chances. In her joggers and trainers and with her hood up, no one would recognise the beauty who had been egging them on to buy drinks all evening.

She stopped by the bar to hand over what she owed before they finished cashing up and headed to the club entrance.

'Do you want me to walk you to your car?' Dave offered.

Hannah sometimes took Dave up on it if there was still a crowd of people hanging around outside. Through the glass doors she could see there were only a few couples lingering, probably waiting for taxis home.

'It's all right, Dave. I managed to get a parking space near the stairwell in the multistorey, I'll be fine.'

'It's no bother. The club emptied out pretty quickly tonight, including that idiot boxer and his entourage. I thought he was going to be trouble, but he turned out all right in the end. He even tipped Lynsey in the cloakroom for taking care of his designer backpack. I ask you, who brings a backpack to a nightclub?'

'Me?' Hannah replied, laughing and turning to show Dave the navy-blue nylon backpack she was wearing.

'That's different,' he replied. 'You've been working. I could walk you to the bottom of the steps. You've had a busy night, and I'd rather be safe than sorry.'

By 'busy night', Hannah knew that Dave was referring to the fact that she was carrying a lot of cash. Her boyfriend, Jamie, was always warning her to keep Dave at arm's length. 'Don't you realise he's got a major crush on you?' he'd said on more than one occasion. 'It's not fair to encourage him.'

'You're just jealous,' she always responded, 'and I definitely don't encourage him, as you put it. We're just friends. He's a nice guy.'

With Jamie's words in her mind, she flashed Dave a dazzling smile and said, 'Okay, if you insist, although I don't know what all the other girls will make of the preferential treatment you give me.'

'Neither do I, but quite frankly I couldn't care less,' he said, holding the door open for Hannah and slipping into step at her side.

She had to admit that she felt safer with six feet six inches of beefcake at her side, even though the car park was only two hundred metres away and the street was policed by CCTV. As they approached the pedestrian entrance to the car park, she resisted the urge to tell Dave to smile for the camera, although she gave it a little wave as he held the door open for her before they both disappeared into the foot of the stairwell.

CHAPTER SIX

8.30 a.m. – Saturday

A slight breeze rustled the leaves of the silver birch tree that towered over Rachel's back garden, creating the shade in which she sat sipping her second cup of coffee of the day. After a restless night, filled with dreams of Ruth reaching out to her and then slowly sinking into murky water, her skin deathly white and eyes unseeing, Rachel had got up out of bed as soon as it was light, realising that there was very little chance of further sleep.

In an attempt to distract her mind from worrying about her sister's whereabouts, she decided to clean her small terraced house from top to bottom, despite the fact that it was already spotless thanks to her cleaner, Marta. Rachel got out various bottles of cleaning fluid and lined them up on the kitchen counter with the intention of immersing herself in physical activity. While the mug of black coffee she had made was cooling sufficiently for her to drink without scalding her mouth, she stripped the sheets off her bed and loaded them into the washing machine. She carried her hot drink over to the sofa and started flicking through the free local magazine that had been lying on her doormat when she had got home from work the previous evening. It was mostly filled with adverts for local tradespeople, everything from bespoke kitchen fitters to odd-job men, but there were also a couple of articles about interesting local people.

Rachel skipped over the piece about a 1980s pop star whose band had re-formed and begun touring again. The last thing she needed was any reminders of the 1980s. She and Ruth had been born early in the decade, but 1989 was the year that their lives had changed irrevocably after they were lured into the home of their next-door neighbour and Ruth had been repeatedly sexually assaulted by him. The consequences for both of them had been far-reaching. Ruth had only ever had one relationship and had reacted so badly to it that she had tried to take her own life, resulting in her being admitted to Mountview Hospital where she could be permanently supervised.

Rachel's reaction to the abduction was very different. She had developed a massive fear of rejection, a feeling that she wasn't good enough. It had presented its own problems, with her total inability to commit to any of the men she dated, until she had met Tim. He seemed to understand her fear of rejection, because he too had experienced something similar as a child. He had needed to be patient and show perseverance, but gradually he was breaking down Rachel's barriers. She took a sip of her scalding coffee and reflected on how her life had changed since Tim had come into it. It felt good to have someone to share life's ups and downs with, and there was no denying the tremendous support he had shown her since Ruth's disappearance. *I can't have been easy to be around these past few weeks*, she thought, turning the magazine pages.

An article caught her eye and she began to read about a twenty-year-old local girl who was in training to climb Mount Everest. Rachel was interested to find out what had inspired the girl to embark on such a challenge. The next thing she knew, she was roused by the melodic tune her washing machine played when the wash cycle was finished. Glancing at her half-drunk cup of coffee and the magazine that had slid off her knee onto the floor, she realised that her disturbed sleep the night before had caught up with her and she must have dozed off.

Let's start again, Rachel thought, carrying her mug through to the kitchen and tipping the cold liquid down the sink. She flicked the switch on the kettle, emptied the contents of the washing machine into the laundry basket and headed for the back door, leading on to what the estate agents had described as a compact back garden when she had bought her house eight years previously. *Compact is one way of describing it*, she thought, opening up the rotary dryer in the only part of the garden that had any sun at that time in the morning, *although small would be more accurate*. It didn't bother Rachel. A big garden required time to keep it looking nice, something Rachel had precious little of when she was working on a major case. As long as she had somewhere to sit with a cup of coffee and to breathe fresh air, she was happy.

The bedding made a flapping sound as a small gust of wind caught in the fitted bottom sheet and inflated it like a sail, rotating the airer in the process. *There's nothing quite like the smell of bedding that's been dried outdoors*, Rachel thought, blowing the top of her coffee before taking another small sip. As she blew, her phone started to ring. She snatched it up from the café-style table in the hope that it might be Ruth. A stab of disappointment ran through her when she saw DI Wilson's name. *Why is he ringing so early at the weekend?* she wondered.

'Morning, Guv, hope I didn't wake you?'

'Morning, Graham. No, you didn't wake me, I've been up a couple of hours already, but I assume you're not ringing to check up on me. What's happened?'

'Eleanor Drake just called me. She's working overtime this weekend,' he added by way of explanation. 'She was passed the details from a 999 call. One of the groundsmen from the university rang to report the discovery of a female who appears to have hanged herself in the adjacent woods.'

Rachel's mouth became dry. 'Is it Ruth?' she asked, her voice barely above a whisper. 'Is that why you're calling me?'

She heard a sharp intake of breath before Graham answered, 'I'm so sorry, Guv, I hadn't even considered that it might be Ruth.

I – I just thought you would want to head up the investigation. Drake's already on her way, and I said either you or I would meet her there.' He paused, waiting for a response, but when there was none he continued, 'Maybe it would be best if I go, Guv? We'll call in the forensic team and run a check to establish the identity of the victim and then I can let you know...' His voice tailed away.

'Let me know what, Graham?' Rachel snapped. 'Let me know if my missing sister has turned up dead?'

Neither spoke for a few moments. Rachel's heart was pounding. She and her twin sister had always had a sixth sense when something was not right in each other's life. In the past they had often picked up the phone to speak to one another at exactly the same moment, but since Ruth had walked out of Mountview, Rachel hadn't felt the same connection and it had both frightened her and left her feeling bereft. *Maybe the horrid dream I had last night was Ruth reaching out to me before she killed herself*, she thought. Ruth had attempted suicide previously, but that had been after the specific trigger of trying and failing to have a relationship with a man. *What could possibly have happened for her to try to take her own life again?* Rachel wondered. She was trying to employ the breathing technique she had been taught as a young child to calm herself in times of severe stress, but it wasn't proving particularly effective.

'We could both meet Drake there, Guv,' Graham suggested tentatively.

'Yes. That's a good idea. Where did you arrange to meet?'

'In the university car park nearest to the sports fields. I can be there in thirty minutes.'

'I'll be there,' Rachel said before ending the call and rushing inside to hurriedly dress.

There was already a small crowd gathering in the car park at the side of the university playing fields as Rachel brought her Audi to a halt. She could see Graham had arrived before her and was talking to PC Eleanor Drake. She locked her car and made her way towards them.

'Morning, Guv,' Eleanor said as she approached.

'What have we got, Eleanor?' Rachel said, nodding her greeting to Graham.

'Nothing much so far. That's the girl who thought she saw a body hanging in the woods. Her name's Abi Wyett,' she said, indicating a young blonde woman in fitness gear being comforted by a burly looking man and another man in a suit. 'She was out running when she came across it. It must have been terrifying.'

'No doubt,' Rachel said. 'Who's with her?'

'The one in the green polo shirt is Dennis Kirby, the grounds-man who made the 999 call. She ran headlong into him when she was fleeing the woods.'

'And the other man?'

'He's the university doctor. He was already attending to Abi when I arrived, so I haven't been able to ask her any questions apart from her name and the approximate location of the body. She's so distressed that she's not even a hundred per cent sure that she actually saw a body. The doctor's given her something to calm her down and is taking her to the "San" to monitor her.'

'Obviously we need to speak to her as soon as she's up to it, but in the meantime we'd better go and find out if the body is real or imagined,' Rachel said, catching Graham's eye and angling her head towards the path leading into the woods.

'Do you need me to come, Guv, or should I start questioning some of the other students?' Eleanor asked, glancing over at a small group gathering in the car park.

'DI Wilson and I can manage, Eleanor. Once we've ascertained whether or not there is a body, we'll have a better idea of how to progress. In the meantime, just make sure nobody goes into the woods. The last thing we need is people destroying potential evidence. And maybe speak to the groundsman to find out exactly what Abi said when she ran into him,' Rachel added, heading towards the path.

'On it, Guv.'

The two police officers walked silently, both filled with trepidation. They had a close working relationship, and Rachel knew that her earlier remarks on the phone had been unfair and unprofessional. She was the one who had raised the possibility that the body might be Ruth, if in fact there was a body. Rachel tried to put herself in Abi's position. Running through the dimly lit woods with strange shadows cast by what little light permeated the thick overhead foliage would be enough to make anyone nervous. Add to that the break and crack of the dried twigs littering the path with each footfall and she could imagine how the girl might have overreacted and thought she had seen something that wasn't really there.

Rachel was just starting to believe that it might all be a figment of Abi's imagination when Graham, who was slightly ahead of her, stopped abruptly and raised his hand.

'Over there, Guv,' he said, pointing to the left. 'I think the girl was right. It looks like a body to me.'

Rachel swallowed hard. There was no mistaking what they were both looking at, although from that distance it was impossible to determine whether the body was male or female.

'Should we take a closer look, or call for the forensic team?' Graham continued.

Rachel knew the correct procedure would be to keep their distance so that they wouldn't destroy any potential evidence, but she had to know if it was Ruth. She started to move in the direction of the body.

Graham stayed rooted to the spot. 'Guv?' he said, a note of anxiety in his voice. 'We might make things trickier for forensics.'

'Let's be certain of what we have before dragging the team out here on a Saturday morning. It could be a dummy strung up in the tree to give passers-by a fright, for all we know. This close to the university, it might be a student's idea of a sick joke,' Rachel said, anxious to justify her unorthodox actions.

Reluctantly, Graham followed his senior officer towards the tree, trying to tread as closely as possible in her footsteps. As he reached her, she turned to face him, her expression a mixture of shock and relief.

'It's not her. It's not Ruth. This woman is quite young, around twenty I'd say, and she's mixed-race.'

CHAPTER SEVEN

11.30 a.m. – Saturday

'Do you ever get used to it, Guv?' PC Eleanor Drake asked.

DCI Rachel Hart turned off the Audi's engine after arriving outside a generously proportioned detached house in the Berkshire village of White Wittering and cast a sideways glance at the young constable. Her face was pale, and she looked a million miles away from her comfort zone.

'Do you mean finding a dead body or telling the parents?'

'They're both awful, but I meant telling the parents. I can't imagine anything much worse than opening the door to see two police officers who you haven't summoned standing there with serious expressions on their faces. I mean, you're always going to fear the worst if you know you've done nothing to break the law.'

Eleanor was a methodical and hard-working officer who showed a lot of promise, but she had never previously been confronted by the utter devastation of a victim's parents. It was never easy, but Rachel knew there was a particular poignancy when telling parents that their child had died, whatever the age of the child. When she had first joined the police force, Rachel's mother had confessed to her that she still suffered nightmares in which she opened the door to the police to be told that her twin girls had been found murdered. 'It's something that will never leave me,' she had said, 'the guilt that my girls could have ended up dead because I left them on their own for a few minutes. I thank God in my prayers every night that I was at least spared that.' Her mother's anguish had stayed with Rachel, making her particularly sensitive when delivering news that no mother should ever have to hear.

'I'm not going to lie, Eleanor, it's traumatic for everyone concerned, but it's our job to be as calm and supportive as possible and not to divulge any information other than the bare facts. I wanted to be with you for your first one because unfortunately it probably won't be your last, and you'll remember this day for a long time.'

Eleanor stood beside her senior officer on the doorstep, the expression in her eyes midway between pity and apprehension.

'Ready?' Rachel asked, her finger poised over the doorbell. Eleanor nodded. 'Then let's do this.'

Moments later the door opened to reveal a tall, immaculately dressed woman. Her jet-black hair was pulled away from her face in a high ponytail, accentuating her chiselled cheekbones, chocolate-brown eyes and full lips enhanced with a deep-plum lipstick; she was strikingly beautiful. The smile froze on her face as she registered Eleanor's police uniform.

'Mrs Longcross?' Rachel asked. 'Mrs Miranda Longcross?' The first rule was always to establish that you had the correct person.

'Well, Miss Dubois, technically. I've reverted to my maiden name since the divorce, but yes, I was Mrs Longcross. What's wrong? Has something happened to Rupert? Not that it's any concern of mine any more.'

'This isn't about your ex-husband,' Rachel said, watching Miranda's eyes widen as fear crept into them. 'I'm DCI Hart and this is PC Drake. Would it be possible to step inside a moment?'

'If this isn't about Rupert, then what is it about?' Miranda demanded, looking from one woman to the other. 'Is it Portia? Has my daughter been arrested or something?'

The two policewomen exchanged a look. Their information was that Miranda Longcross only had one child and her name was

Hannah. *If that was the case, who was Portia?* Rachel wondered. She reached into her handbag for her mobile phone. They had to be sure they had the right person before delivering such devastating news.

Earlier, when Rachel had been unable to detect a pulse, confirming that the young woman they had found was dead, she had noticed a small tattoo of a feather on the inside of her wrist. She had taken a photograph of it on her mobile phone, thinking that it could potentially help with identification. Once the forensic team had arrived and begun their painstaking investigation of the area, she and Graham had returned to the car park where Eleanor Drake was talking to the groundsman, Dennis Kirby.

'Guv, you need to hear this,' Eleanor had said.

Dennis had told them that before Abi broke down completely, she had said she recognised the clothing that the person hanging from the tree was wearing, particularly the bright green trainers. She'd identified them as belonging to her friend, Hannah Longcross. He'd also told them that Abi had repeatedly said that it was all her fault that Hannah was dead, something Rachel was keen to follow up on once the doctor had given them permission to talk to her. While they had waited for forensics to provide them with something more concrete to identify the young woman, Rachel showed some of the students who were gathered in the car park the photograph she had taken of the tattoo. Several of them had said it looked exactly like the one Hannah Longcross had on her wrist, so when Sam from the forensic team rang to say they had found the victim's purse with Hannah's student card in it, there seemed little doubt about the victim's identity. Nevertheless, Rachel needed to be sure.

'Do you recognise this tattoo, Mrs Longcross?' Rachel asked, showing Miranda her phone.

The woman glanced down at the screen and then back up at the detective. *There it is: the moment of realisation that something is terribly wrong*, Rachel thought, watching the panic building in Miranda's eyes.

'Portia has one just like it,' she said, steadying herself by reaching out for the door frame.

Rachel was reasonably confident they had the right person, but she needed to be sure. 'We were under the impression that this young woman's name is Hannah,' she probed gently.

'Hannah is her middle name. She thought Portia sounded too posh and didn't want to alienate the other students, so she started using her middle name when she went to university. Rupert went along with calling her Hannah, and her uni friends only know her by that name, but she'll always be Portia to me. Are you going to tell me what this is all about?'

'Would it be possible to continue this inside, Mrs Longcross?'

Miranda leaned back against the door to allow Rachel and Eleanor to enter the hallway, before closing the door and leading them into a sitting room that looked as though it belonged in the pages of a high-end interior design magazine. She perched on the edge of a chair and indicated for them to sit on the sofa opposite.

'What's happened? Has Portia been involved in an accident? She is going to be all right, isn't she?' she added, gripping the arms of the chair until her knuckles turned white.

Miranda's question struck a chord deep in Rachel's heart. They were exactly the same words her own mother had used to the ambulance crew after the discovery of her twin daughters in the basement of their next-door neighbour's house over thirty years previously. Wrapped in a blanket and huddled in a corner of the ambulance as it rushed the two girls and their parents to hospital, Rachel could clearly remember the doubt in her mother's voice as she sat with tears streaming down her cheeks, waiting for reassurance from the ambulance crew. Her mother's eyes had never left Ruth's pale face as she lay semi-conscious on the gurney. 'She's safe now,' had been the measured response. That memory, that exact moment in time, was one of the reasons why Rachel had no desire to have children of her own. It was too awful to contemplate that a child of hers would ever be the victim of the abuse she and Ruth had suffered. Looking over at Miranda Longcross, Rachel fervently wished that she could have uttered the same response. She took a deep breath, fully aware of the life-shattering blow she was about to inflict.

'I'm so sorry, I'm afraid there's no easy way to tell you this. We believe your daughter's body was discovered in woodland earlier this morning,' she said, watching the blood drain from Miranda's face, leaving the warm honey tone of her skin with an ashy greyness as the words every mother dreads began to sink in.

After a few moments of shaking her head from side to side, a bemused expression on her face, Miranda said, 'No, there must be a mistake. I'm her mother, I'd know if something had happened to Portia, I know I would. There must be hundreds of girls with feathers tattooed on the inside of their wrist.'

Denial of the facts was a fairly common reaction to receiving traumatic news, in Rachel's experience. 'It isn't only the tattoo, I'm afraid. One of her friends identified the victim's clothing as being Portia's,' Rachel said, careful to use Hannah's birth name, 'and a backpack containing her purse with her bank card and student ID were found at the scene.'

Miranda continued to shake her head but remained silent.

'I'm sorry to have to ask you this,' Rachel continued, 'but can you think of any reason why your daughter might take her own life?'

'What are you talking about?' Miranda said, the question provoking an animated response. 'Of course Portia wouldn't do that. She has everything to live for. She's one of the brightest, most self-assured young women you could imagine. Why would you even suggest she might kill herself? Now I know it's not her.'

It was Rachel's turn to shake her head. 'All our evidence so far points to it being your daughter.'

'Well, I don't believe you,' Miranda said, the volume of her voice rising and her tone becoming more insistent. 'It must be a case of mistaken identity. You should check the facts more carefully before you come into people's homes saying such dreadful things. Rupert will have something to say when he hears about this. He plays golf with the Police Commissioner. He'll have you both suspended for this,' she continued, glaring across at Rachel and Eleanor. 'I'll fetch my phone from the kitchen and call her, then we'll see who's right.' She tried to rise from her chair, but fell back as her legs buckled beneath her. The anger from moments before appeared to have drained away and she slumped forward in the chair, her body convulsed by huge, racking sobs.

'Can you make some tea, please, Eleanor,' Rachel instructed, crossing the room to place a comforting hand on Miranda's arm. 'It needs to be strong with plenty of sugar. And you'd better make one for yourself,' she added, reacting to the young PC's shocked expression. Rachel's fifteen years in the police force had prepared her for every type of response after delivering dreadful news. An angry outburst after the disbelief that followed the initial shock usually gave way to an uncontrolled outpouring of grief. 'Is there anyone you'd like us to call, Miranda?'

With a huge effort, Miranda tried to regain control of her emotions. She breathed in deeply, held her breath for a few seconds before releasing it, then repeated the process. Wiping the tears from her cheeks, she straightened her back and brushed Rachel's hand from her arm.

'I think the first person to try should be Portia. You could have made a mistake. It's best to double-check, don't you think?'

'There's no harm in that,' Rachel responded. 'I'll fetch your phone. I think you said it was in the kitchen?'

'Yes. It's on the central island next to the magazine I was reading.'

Moments later, the two policewomen re-entered the room, Eleanor carrying two mugs of tea and Rachel with Miranda's phone.

Putting it on speaker so that they would all be able to hear any conversation, Miranda pressed Portia's name to dial the number.

It rang four times before the voice message kicked in. A female voice, full of life and energy, filled the room:

Hi, this is Hannah, I can't talk now but leave me a message after the beep and I'll get back to you if you sound interesting, so don't hold your breath, the message said, followed by laughter and then the beep.

'Portia, it's Mummy,' Miranda said, her voice cracking, 'I need to speak to you quite urgently, darling, so call me straight back when you get this message.'

Miranda pressed the button to end the call and positioned her phone within easy reach on the coffee table, raising her gaze to Rachel's as she did so. 'It doesn't mean anything,' Miranda said, defiantly. 'Portia rarely picks up. She'll ring straight back when she gets my message.'

The three women sat in uncomfortable silence, all eyes trained on Miranda's mobile phone, the only sound the ticking of the grandfather clock in the hallway.

'Would you like me to pass you your tea?' Eleanor asked, breaking the silence.

Miranda shook her head.

'Perhaps there is someone else you could call?' Rachel ventured. 'Your ex-husband, maybe?'

'Why would I want to speak to Rupert? If you're thinking Portia might be at his place, think again. She hasn't spoken to him since Easter, when he dropped the bombshell that he and his girlfriend Tamara are expecting a baby. Imagine that – Tamara is only three years older than Portia. She hasn't even told any of her friends she's going to have a baby brother because it's too embarrassing.'

As Miranda finished speaking, her mobile phone began to ring and she snatched it up from the table. 'Portia?' she asked, her voice filled with hope.

There was a short pause before a male voice with a hint of irritation in it said, 'Hi Miranda. It's Jamie. I was ringing to see if Hannah's with you, but I'm guessing not. I've been trying to get hold of her but she's not answering her phone.'

Rachel saw the spark of hope in Miranda's eyes once again replaced by fear.

'We were supposed to be meeting at Costa for coffee after her run this morning,' Jamie continued, 'but she's a no-show, so I wondered if she'd forgotten and driven over to see you?'

Miranda's hand started to shake violently. 'Oh God,' she whispered as the phone fell from her grasp and clattered to the polished oak floor.

'Miranda?' Jamie said, his irritation from moments earlier turning to concern. 'Are you all right? What's going on?'

When Miranda made no attempt to retrieve the phone, Rachel stooped to pick it up.

'Jamie, this is DCI Hart from the Reading police department. Would it be possible for us to ask you some questions regarding Hannah?'

'Is she in some kind of trouble?'

Rachel didn't want to give anything away over the phone. She wanted to be able to look into Jamie's eyes when she told him that his girlfriend was dead. Although Hannah's death looked like suicide, they couldn't be sure until they had the forensic report, and a lot could be gained by observing someone's first reaction to news of that kind.

'That's what we're trying to establish, Jamie. Which Costa are you at? The one in the town centre? I can be there in twenty-five minutes and we can have a chat over a coffee. Or you could come to the police station if you'd rather?'

There was a small pause before Jamie said, 'I'll wait for you here, but you'd better have some bloody answers for me.'

And hopefully you'll have some for me, Rachel thought as she terminated the call. 'Miranda, I'm going to leave Eleanor here with you for the time being. If you've got a close friend you could call, I'd suggest asking them to come over. You shouldn't be on your own at a time like this. Eleanor, a moment please,' she said, indicating for the PC to follow her back out into the hallway. She pulled the door closed and lowered her voice. 'I know it's hard, because Miranda will start to ask questions, but don't say anything specific about where or how Hannah was found. You weren't actually present, so stick to the fact that you were questioning students and university staff after responding to the 999 call.'

'Yes, Guv.'

'Contact the station once Miranda has someone here with her and they'll send a car to pick you up. Are you okay?' Rachel asked.

Eleanor nodded.

'The first time is always the worst,' Rachel said, pulling the front door closed behind her. 'But it never gets any easier,' she added under her breath.

CHAPTER EIGHT

11.45 a.m. – Saturday

Tim yawned and stretched, trying to release the tension in his neck after a morning spent painting the walls of one of the upstairs bedrooms in the terraced house on Grove Street. Manual labour was not something he was used to and not something he particularly enjoyed, but at last the house was almost finished. The end was in sight, thanks to 6.00 a.m. starts on the days he wasn't staying over at Rachel's and she wasn't staying with him. He had been able to squeeze in a couple of hours before his workday began, and that had made all the difference. It was usually easier at weekends, but today he was bone-crushingly tired after his late finish and lack of sleep.

He checked his phone before beginning the onerous job of cleaning the paint roller and brushes and was mildly surprised that there was nothing from his girlfriend. Rachel normally texted or called at the weekend once she'd finished her breakfast to arrange what time they would be meeting up later in the day. *Maybe she had a lie-in*, he thought, pushing up the sleeves of his hoodie and wriggling his fingers into surgical gloves before plunging his hands into the bucket of cold water. *In fairness, it's only her first week back at work, so she's probably feeling pretty shattered.*

Tim ran his hands up and down the pile of the roller to release the majority of the paint, turning the water from clear to a pale silvery grey. He shuddered. It was reminiscent of the colour of

Jack's skin, fairly common in long-term prisoners. *Why does he have to be such an arsehole?* Tim thought, attacking the roller with more vigour than was necessary. *I'll be so glad when this is all over.* He tipped the paint-stained water down the sink and refilled the bucket, his thoughts returning to Rachel. *I hope she's not starting to have second thoughts about me after all this hard work. Maybe I'll suggest going out to see a film tonight rather than just staying home – more of a date night to make her feel special,* he thought, wringing the roller out as best he could and standing it on end in the paint reservoir section of the roller tray to drain.

Tim racked his brains trying to think of some of the new film releases he'd heard advertised on the radio that might appeal to her. It wasn't easy. Rachel didn't like thrillers, saying watching them was too much like a busman's holiday and that she had enough drama in her everyday work life. She wasn't a fan of sci-fi or horror, and neither of them liked predictable romantic comedies. *Maybe a trip up to London to see a West End theatre show would be a better bet, if I can get last-minute tickets.* He remembered someone in his office raving about *Tina, The Musical* after they had been to see it recently and Rachel had seemed quite interested when he'd mentioned it in conversation. He propped the brushes up behind the taps and peeled off his gloves before going onto a ticket website on his phone to check availability. To his surprise, there were some seats for the evening performance. His finger hovered over the 'book now' button. Instead of pressing it, he went into his contacts and selected Rachel's name, deciding it would be better to check that she was up for going out before wasting his money on tickets that might not get used. It went straight to voicemail, but he didn't leave a message, assuming she would call him back.

After making sure the lids were firmly on the paint pots, and stuffing the food wrapping and paper coffee cups into a black bin liner, Tim checked that the back door and the door down to the cellar were locked before letting himself out and double-locking the front door. He had managed to get a parking space directly opposite the house and as he looked back at it, he gave himself a virtual pat on the back. Not only for the enormous amount of work he had already completed to get the house back into a habitable condition, but also for spotting the 'For Sale by Auction' sign just over a year ago.

He had been driving along Grove Street, part of his daily route to his office on the outskirts of Reading, when he had noticed the red-and-yellow sign. The house had stood empty for years and was in a terrible state, with metal grilles over the windows and doors to prevent squatters moving in. They'd been decorated by a graffiti artist with far less flair and imagination than Banksy. That was one of the reasons there had been little interest from other buyers on the day of the auction: that, and the house's grim history. It hadn't reached its reserve price, but undeterred, Tim had gone to the auctioneer at the end of the day and offered £5,000 under the guide price. The next morning, his offer was accepted.

Unbeknown to Tim, there were three golden rules for buying property at auction. The first was to view the property internally, the second was to have a survey done and the third was to read the legal pack thoroughly. He had followed none of them, so he only set foot in the property when he became the legal owner. Although it was clear from the outside that the house was in a run-down state, it had still come as a bit of a shock when the metal grille over the front door was removed and he had stepped inside. It was immediately obvious that the grilles had been a case of shutting the stable door after the horse had bolted. The whole place had been vandalised. All the removable fixtures and fittings, such as curtain poles, light fittings and even the electric shower from the bathroom were missing, leaving bare wires and holes in the plaster of the walls. The place stank of damp and urine and not a single pane of glass was intact behind the metal covers. Tim was unfazed, knowing he could take his time. Recent events had put him under a little more pressure, but now the renovation was almost done and the house looked amazing.

Getting the basement finished as a self-contained flat had been his priority, before gradually working upwards through the house, using tradespeople for the things he couldn't do himself like plumbing and electrics. Earlier in the week he'd had a state-of-the-art alarm system installed covering both the inside and the outside of the property, which he was yet to try out. The gardeners had also been in on the same day to clear the overgrown jungle that was the back garden. It looked very different now, laid mostly to lawn with a shrub border and only the apple tree surviving the chainsaw.

Tim checked his phone again. It was past midday and there was still no word from Rachel. He began to wonder if maybe he had misread her reaction to him cancelling their date the previous day. Perhaps she had been really cross and was deliberately not contacting him to punish him. He smiled. *I know how to fix that*, he thought. *I'll nip home for a shower and then call round at hers with lunch from her favourite deli. That should get me back in her good books.*

CHAPTER NINE

12.05 p.m. – Saturday

The smell of freshly brewed coffee greeted Rachel as she pushed open the door of the crowded coffee shop and glanced around, looking for a lone man. She'd realised on the drive over that she had no idea what Hannah's boyfriend looked like. She needn't have worried. She was barely through the door when she noticed a tall and muscly young man pushing his way through the busy tables towards her. *He's older than I imagined*, she thought, realising she had been expecting a student of a similar age to Hannah.

'So, are you going to tell me what the hell's going on?' the man demanded.

Rachel was aware of the glances of the other customers. Keeping her voice low and calm, she said, 'You must be Jamie. It's a bit noisy in here, shall we try and find somewhere quieter to talk?'

'Fine by me. I've been here since half past ten waiting for Hannah, and I've been nursing the same latte since I spoke to you on the phone. The guy wiping the tables was hovering around me waiting to pounce on my cup and saucer the minute I took the last sip, 'cos they need the table. Don't worry,' he said, pushing past Rachel towards the door, 'I've paid.'

What an angry young man, Rachel thought, falling into step behind him and catching the door that he hadn't bothered to hold open for her. *Odd that he's angry rather than concerned over his girlfriend's whereabouts.* She quickened her pace to catch up with him.

'How long is this going to take? I'm supposed to be going to the match this afternoon. It's the last home game of the season and I don't want to miss it. Hannah hates football, which is why I arranged to meet her for coffee before she spends her afternoon shopping. What is it with women and shopping? How come you lot enjoy it so much? Why can't you just buy online, like us blokes do?'

'I'm with you on that, Jamie. I hate shopping, even for food. And to answer your question, it should only be ten or fifteen minutes once we find somewhere quiet. Any ideas?'

'The park's probably our best bet. All the pubs will be full to bursting now until people start making their way out to the Madejski. You okay with that?'

'Of course,' Rachel said, noticing that his tone had become slightly less aggressive.

She fell into step at his side as they threaded their way through milling crowds of people trying to decide which delicacy to treat themselves to from the food stalls along the bank of the River Kennet. The aromas of rich chocolate waffles, beefy quarter-pounders and spicy tortilla wraps were all competing for attention, reminding Rachel that the only breakfast she'd had was half a cup of black coffee about four hours previously. She was starting to wish they had stayed in the coffee shop, where she could at least have treated herself to a coffee and a Danish pastry. Suddenly, Jamie ducked down an alleyway that led to the side entrance of a small park with a children's play area at one end. It wasn't picturesque, but it was quite empty and there was a free bench that he was making a beeline for.

'Quiet enough?' he asked as she sat down.

'Perfect. Jamie, I need to know when you last saw Hannah.'

'Yesterday lunchtime. We got a sandwich from the Munchbox on the university campus and ate it outside because the sun was shining. Why?'

'So you didn't see your girlfriend on a Friday night? Do you mind if I ask why?'

'I never see her Friday evenings since she started working at that bloody club. Apparently it's the busiest night of the week, so she can make the most money to put towards her Everest fund. It's all about Everest with Hannah at the moment, she couldn't give a shit about anything else, including me,' he moaned, his tone of voice becoming aggressive again.

The moment Jamie mentioned Everest, Rachel realised what had been niggling at the back of her mind since she'd learned that the dead girl was Hannah Longcross. At the time she had thought the name sounded vaguely familiar and now Rachel knew why.

'Oh yes. Strangely enough, I was reading about Hannah's plans this morning in a local magazine. It seems quite an extreme thing to attempt. Is there a reason Hannah chose to climb Everest?'

'I have no idea. She didn't discuss it with me. She just told me she was going to do it because no British female of her age has ever achieved it. She's nuts! It's never gonna happen.'

He's right, Rachel thought, *sadly she isn't going to be breaking any records, but not for the reason he might think.*

'Look, are you going to tell me what this is all about?' he continued. 'Is Hannah in some kind of trouble?'

'All in good time, Jamie. There are a couple more questions I need you to answer first.'

'And if I refuse to cooperate until you tell me what's going on?'

'Then we can continue our conversation down at the police station. It's your call.' When Jamie didn't respond, Rachel took it as her cue to carry on. 'This club you mentioned. What's it called and what did Hannah do there?' Rachel asked, flipping open her notebook.

'Velvet. It's a decent enough club, but I can't go there any more now that all my mates know my girlfriend is one of the club's slutty shot girls,' he said, anger creeping into his voice.

Rachel was taken aback. 'That's not a very nice way to describe your girlfriend.'

'It's not a very nice job,' he countered. 'Dressing like a tramp and flirting with blokes who are already half-drunk to get them to buy shots to make them even drunker. We had a massive argument about it when she first started, in fact we almost split up over it, but for all her faults I can't stand the thought of not being with her. We've agreed not to mention it now, and she's only got a few more weeks of it until she finishes uni, so I guess she's trying to milk it for all it's worth.' Jamie paused, a look of realisation dawning on his face. 'Shit, is that what this is about? Is she in trouble for not paying tax?'

'No, Jamie, nothing like that,' Rachel said, looking up from her notebook.

'Then what? Come on, I've answered all your questions.'

Rachel took a deep breath. 'I'm sorry to have to tell you that Hannah was found dead this morning. At the moment, it appears to be suicide, but we'll know more when we have a full autopsy report.' If there was such a thing as the blood draining from someone's face, Rachel was watching it happen.

'No. You've made a mistake. I'm not having that.'

'There's no mistake, Jamie,' she said gently. 'Her friend Abi identified Hannah from the clothing she was wearing, and this photo is of the feather tattoo on the dead girl's wrist,' Rachel said, holding out her phone for Jamie to examine. 'We also found her bag in the vicinity with her personal belongings in it.'

Jamie curled forward, his arms hugging his torso. Rachel couldn't be sure, but she thought he might be crying. She waited a few moments before continuing with her questions. 'Do you have any idea why Hannah would want to end her life?'

There was no response from Jamie.

'Was something troubling her, do you know? Her exams, maybe?'

Jamie raised his head. Rachel had been right about the crying.

'You don't know her. When Hannah sets her mind to something, she does it. This time two years ago she failed her exams and was thinking of quitting uni because she didn't like the course she had chosen. All it took to get her back on track was for her dad to say, "You can't win at everything". It was like a red rag to a bull. She's had straight As ever since. Trust me, Hannah will have achieved a first-class honours degree – she simply can't tolerate the idea of being second best at anything.'

Rachel found his use of the present tense overwhelmingly sad. She had witnessed the young woman's body being cut down from the tree, her eyes bulging and lifeless, livid purple marks around her neck visible from beneath the rope. Although they didn't yet know if the cause of death was asphyxiation or whether the rope biting into her neck had broken it, there was no question that she should be referred to in the past tense. For whatever reason, Hannah Longcross's life was over. To Rachel it seemed such a futile waste. She was reminded of her sister attempting to take her own life but failing, and she found herself wondering if it had only been a temporary setback for Ruth, and if she had now succeeded. Rachel shook her head to clear it from thoughts of her sister. She needed to concentrate; she owed it to Hannah.

'How has Hannah's training been going? It's just a thought, but if it hasn't been going too well, maybe she couldn't face the thought of failing so publicly.'

'Like I said, when Hannah sets her mind to something, she succeeds. I devised a gym programme for her and she's been out running with her friend Abi every morning. She's in the best shape of her life and there's still ten months to go before she sets off for the attempt. I know I said earlier that it's never gonna happen, but knowing Hannah, she'll probably smash it, just like she always does.' He stopped abruptly, realising what he had said. 'I can't believe she's fucking dead, I just can't,' he said, resting his elbows on his knees and forcing the heels of his hands into his eyes to try and prevent himself from crying again.

Jamie is either an amazing actor or he really cared deeply about Hannah, Rachel thought as she retrieved a tissue from her bag and handed it to him. He took it silently.

'I need to get back to the station to coordinate the investigation. We may need to speak to you again on a more official basis, but I think that's all for now. Is there somewhere I can drop you?'

'I think I'll just stay here for a while,' Jamie said in a muffled voice without raising his head.

'Okay, if you're sure,' Rachel replied, getting up from the bench and squeezing his shoulder. She headed back across the grass towards the gate through which they had entered the park and only looked back once. Jamie was still hunched over, his broad shoulders heaving up and down. A shiver ran through Rachel. From that distance, it was impossible to tell if he was laughing or crying.

CHAPTER TEN

1.30 p.m. – Saturday

There was a knock at her office door as Rachel Hart popped the final piece of her chicken wrap into her mouth and tossed the screwed-up cellophane wrapper in the bin. She had stopped off at her favourite deli on the way back to the police station and had been surprised to learn that her boyfriend had been in there buying exactly the same lunch twenty minutes earlier, according to Anya behind the counter. Rachel hadn't realised they were such regulars that the girl would recognise them separately, but the fact that she was on first-name terms with Anya should have been a clue.

Tim wasn't a big fan of wraps, preferring a 'proper sandwich', as he called it, so she realised that he must have been buying it for her. Sure enough, when she checked her phone, which she had put on silent before knocking on Miranda Longcross's front door, there were two missed calls from him and a voice message:

Hi Rachel, are you angry with me for cancelling last night? It was unavoidable I'm afraid. I'm on your front step with your favourite lunch. Are you going to let me in or am I going to be forced to eat this tasteless cold pancake myself?

Rachel had immediately called Tim's number, but it too had gone to voicemail.

Hi Tim, sorry I wasn't in when you came round. I was called out on a case first thing this morning. Look, instead of playing phone tag all afternoon, shall we just say seven at mine and we can decide then on a takeaway or dinner out? I hope you enjoyed the cold pancake, she had added, laughing.

He had responded with a text message of an emoji face spewing green gunk and the words *see you at 7.*

'Come in,' Rachel mumbled in the direction of her office door through a mouthful of lettuce and mayonnaise. 'Apologies,' she said, indicating her mouth and swallowing the remnants of the wrap, 'but that's the first thing I've had to eat all day and I was starting to feel a bit faint.'

'No problem, Guv, we're all entitled to a lunch break even if it is a working one,' DI Graham Wilson replied.

'Is PC Drake back yet?'

'Yes, just now. She's popped to the toilet and then she's joining us in here.'

'Good. I can fill you both in on Hannah Longcross's boyfriend at the same time. It will save me repeating myself. How did you get on with Rupert Longcross?'

There was a tap at the door, which Graham had left ajar, and PC Eleanor Drake's face appeared round it.

'Come in and sit down,' Rachel said, indicating the chair opposite. 'DI Wilson was about to tell me how he got on with Hannah's father.'

'I haven't actually told him about Hannah being dead. He and his girlfriend Tamara left for Devon at seven this morning to visit her parents, and I didn't think it was the sort of thing he should hear while he was driving. I asked for him to call me when they stopped at the motorway services, but he demanded to know why.

I said there was a problem with Hannah and he immediately said they would come back to Reading. I suggested he drop Tamara at home and then come here on his own. To be honest, it was almost as though he was grateful for an excuse not to visit Tamara's folks.'

Rachel raised her eyebrows. She didn't have any such problems in her relationship. Tim's mother had abandoned her family when he was only a toddler, so he had no knowledge of her whereabouts or any inclination to find her, and he was also estranged from his father who had been unable to cope alone.

'Do you have an ETA for him?'

'He said it should be before 2.00 p.m., so any time at all really. Anyway, because I didn't have to go and meet up with Rupert, it gave me a chance to put a bit of pressure on the university doctor to allow me a few minutes with Hannah's friend, Abi. He wasn't best pleased, but permitted it as long as he was able to stay in the room.'

'Did you tell her she wasn't imagining things and that it was Hannah?'

'Yes, Guv. I didn't think it would be helpful to lie to her.'

'How did she react?'

'Pretty much as you'd expect. She got quite upset, despite the medication, saying, "it's all my fault, I should have been with her last night", before breaking down completely.'

'That phrase again, "it's all my fault". She obviously feels very guilty that she wasn't with Hannah last night. Did you ask her to elaborate?'

'I didn't get the chance. The doctor ushered me out when she started to get upset and said no more questioning until she's allowed to leave the San. He wanted to contact her parents so they could be with her, but she told him they were camping in Wales. I guess we'll have to wait until later to find out where the two of them should have been together last night.'

'According to Hannah's boyfriend, Jamie, she was working at a nightclub in Reading called Velvet,' Rachel said. 'I'll tell you more about my meeting with him in a minute. Did Miranda Longcross have much to say to you after I'd left, Eleanor?' she asked, turning her attention to the young constable.

'Not really, Guv. She called a friend of hers, Anoushka Parsons,' Eleanor said, checking her notebook to make sure she had the name right, 'and asked her to come round. She lives in the same village, so she was there within ten minutes. At first I thought she was going to be a big help in calming Mrs Longcross, but when Miranda told her that we think Hannah took her own life, Anoushka started crying as well. Then she said, and I'm quoting here, Guv, "it would never have happened if Rupert had been able to keep his dick in his pants".'

'Hmmm, so maybe Hannah was more affected by the divorce than everyone realised. But would someone with so much zest for life commit suicide because her parents couldn't make a go of their marriage? It doesn't seem likely. Half of marriages today end up in the divorce courts and it's not as though she was a young child and was going to have to make a choice about which parent to live with.'

'Actually, I wondered if Anoushka meant something else entirely, Guv,' Eleanor said.

'Go on.'

'I'm probably way off the mark here, but you don't think Rupert Longcross had been sexually abusing his daughter and that's what led to the marriage breaking down?'

Rachel could feel her flesh crawling and she was aware of Graham flinching. The thought that a father could do that to his own daughter filled her with revulsion, but it wouldn't be the first case of its kind.

'How did Miranda react to the comment?'

'She just said she didn't think it was helpful to hurl accusations around without any proof. Again, I'm quoting here,' Eleanor said, referencing her notebook, '"Rupert was a good dad to Portia, he

loved her more than anything in the world, you know he did".
And then Miranda started to sob uncontrollably.'

Rachel rubbed her fingers over her lips thoughtfully. 'What do
you think, Graham?'

'I think it seems a bit improbable, but I can certainly bear it in
mind when I'm questioning Mr Longcross. After all, it wouldn't
be the first time a loving father has behaved in this way.'

'Did Miranda say anything else?'

'No, she was too upset. Anoushka suggested calling her doctor
for something to calm her down. He was just arriving as I was
leaving.'

'It sounds as though we may have to rely on Rupert Longcross
to visually ID Hannah. I doubt Miranda would be able to cope
with it.'

'But she'll want to see her daughter one last time, surely?'
Eleanor said.

Rachel wasn't so sure. She hadn't wanted to see either of her
parents after their deaths, preferring to remember them as they were
in life. They had both died fairly peacefully, but not so Hannah.
Even the most talented of post-mortem make-up artists would
have their work cut out to cover up the lurid marks on her neck.
Seeing her beautiful, vibrant daughter lying pale and lifeless would
be an image that would haunt Miranda forever.

'It really is down to the individual if, as in this case, we have
more than one person who could confirm identification. Obviously,
the final decision will be hers. So, moving on to my conversation
with Hannah's boyfriend. Exactly like Miranda, he refused to
believe that Hannah was dead, particularly when I mentioned
that it looked like suicide. He seems quite a volatile young man,
especially with regard to Hannah's job at Velvet nightclub which
he obviously hated her doing.' In response to Graham's questioning look, Rachel continued, 'Hannah was a shot girl – you know,
dressing in a skimpy outfit in order to persuade men to buy shots.'

'Really?' Eleanor said. 'Why would she be doing a job like that? It seems a bit out of character to me. It's not as though she needed the money, judging by her mum's house.'

'You're assuming she could simply ask her parents for anything and they would give it to her?'

'Well, yes, if you put it like that.'

'We need to be careful not to assume anything in police work, Eleanor.'

'Yes, Guv,' Eleanor said, colour creeping up her cheeks as she accepted the reprimand.

'Apparently, Hannah was in training to be the youngest British woman to climb to the summit of Mount Everest. She had big corporate sponsorship, but wanted all of that money to go to charity. She was determined to fund the trip herself rather than ask for help from her parents. As I understand it, selling shots in a nightclub can be very lucrative. You have to hand it to her, she was working damn hard in a job she probably didn't enjoy to prove that she could stand on her own two feet. You know,' Rachel said thoughtfully, tapping the end of her pen on her notepad, 'the more we learn about Hannah, the more I'm inclined to agree with the people closest to her that she doesn't seem the type to give up on anything, including life.'

'Is there a type, Guv?' Graham asked.

'I suppose I don't really mean a type as such, but people who don't have a clear goal to work towards. Hannah doesn't fit into that category. She knew what she wanted and was prepared to put in the effort to get it. Have we had anything from the lab yet?'

Before Graham could answer, there was a knock at the door and PC Harman stuck his head round it.

'Sorry to interrupt, Guv, but Rupert Longcross is here to see DI Wilson and he seems pretty agitated.'

'You go, Graham, we're pretty much up to speed with everything so far.'

'Right, Guv,' Graham said, getting to his feet, 'although I'm not looking forward to this. I can't imagine what it must be like to be told that your child is dead,' he added, closing the door behind him.

'Is DI Wilson all right, Guv? I could talk to Mr Longcross if he's uncomfortable with it.'

'I think I've chosen the right person for the job, PC Drake,' Rachel said, observing the young policewoman with a steady gaze which clearly flustered her.

'Yes, Guv, of course, I just meant—'

Rachel raised her hand to stop her in mid flow and said, 'Besides, I need you to start gathering information on the people Hannah worked with at Velvet nightclub. If that's where she spent her final few hours, I want to know what frame of mind she was in throughout the evening, and if maybe something happened that caused her to take such a drastic course of action.'

'On it, Guv,' Eleanor said, scraping her chair backwards and heading towards the door, her cheeks still flaming. As she closed it, Rachel's desk phone began to ring.

'DCI Hart,' she said, answering the call.

'Ah, just the person I wanted to talk to.'

Rachel recognised the senior pathologist's voice. *Who did Toby think would be answering my personal line?* Rachel thought, shaking her head slightly.

'It's Toby Morrison here. We've just removed the rope from Hannah Longcross's neck and there's something you need to see. It seems we might have jumped to conclusions when we assumed it was suicide.'

'I'm on my way,' Rachel said, grabbing her bag and jacket. *What did I say to Eleanor less than ten minutes ago about not assuming anything in police work?* she thought. *Maybe I should start taking my own advice.*

CHAPTER ELEVEN

'Thanks for coming in, Mr Longcross,' DI Wilson said, extending his hand to shake that of the tall, thickset man standing opposite him.

Rupert Longcross kept his hands firmly in his pockets. 'Are you going to tell me what the hell is going on?' he demanded. 'I've been worried sick the whole of the drive back. Not exactly the right atmosphere for my girlfriend in her condition. I've dropped her off at home as you suggested I should. Whatever trouble Hannah has got herself into, I don't think it's fair to worry Tamara with it, she's not past the point of possible miscarriage yet.'

'Of course,' Graham said, indicating the seat opposite. 'My intention wasn't to worry you, but I didn't think you should receive this sort of news while you were driving. I'm sorry if it's ruined your plans for the weekend.'

'Tamara's plans. I was quite glad of the excuse to get out of it, although she's still talking about driving down to Okehampton later. Apparently her mum and dad have organised a Sunday brunch get-together to introduce me to some of their friends. I can't wait,' he said, rolling his eyes. 'But back to the point: what's going on with Hannah? We're not exactly on speaking terms at the moment, you see.'

'Yes, we gathered as much from your ex-wife.'

'You've been speaking to Miranda as well? God, this must be serious. Spit it out, man.'

'Can I just ask when you last saw or spoke to your daughter, Mr Longcross?'

'Easter Sunday. We'd invited her and her boyfriend for lunch, but Jamie couldn't make it, or more likely didn't want to come. I've no idea what she sees in that bloke. Rude and sullen with no interpersonal skills whatsoever. That's what comes of spending half your life looking at your phone and the other half pumping iron in the gym. Not only that, he's got a short fuse. A good-looking girl like Hannah could do so much better for herself,' Rupert said, 'but you can't tell them how to live their lives. Are you a father?'

Graham nodded.

'Then you'll know what I'm talking about.'

'Not really, my boys are only young. I've got all that to look forward to.'

'That's what we're having – a boy,' Rupert said, unable to disguise the flicker of excitement in his eyes. 'I thought Hannah might be pleased that she was finally going to have a sibling, but I was wrong. When I told her we were expecting, she stormed out and we haven't spoken since. I suppose she'll come round eventually, maybe after I help get her out of whatever scrape she's got herself into. I play golf with the Police Commissioner, if you know what I mean,' Rupert said, tapping the side of his nose and winking.

'I'm afraid the Police Commissioner isn't going to be able to help with this, Mr Longcross,' Graham said, clearing his throat in preparation for the devastating news he was about to impart. 'I'm so sorry to have to inform you that your daughter's body was found in woodland adjacent to the university earlier this morning.' Graham watched Rupert's confident manner from moments earlier disintegrate, his face appearing to crumple before the DI's eyes.

'No. Not my Hannah. Not my little girl. There must be some mistake.'

'Well, we will need visual confirmation from either you or Mrs Longcross, but everything so far leads us to believe it is your daughter. I really am very sorry. This must come as a huge shock.'

'How? How did she die?'

Graham shuffled his feet awkwardly. 'She… we believe she may have taken her own life.'

'No. Not possible,' Rupert said, dismissing the suggestion immediately. 'Hannah saw suicide as weakness, the coward's way out. If there was ever anything on the television news, she would be scathing about the people who ended their own lives, saying how selfish they were for not considering those they were leaving behind. Whatever it may look like, I can absolutely assure you Hannah would not take her own life. You people need to start doing the job you are paid for and investigate this properly.'

'I can understand your reaction,' Graham said, his voice calm and even. 'I'm sure I would feel the same way in your position, but I did say we *believe* it to be suicide. Of course, we'll be keeping all lines of enquiry open until we have more information on the cause of death. We're hoping to get the preliminary findings from the pathologist this afternoon.' Graham felt his phone vibrate in his pocket. On glancing down, he could see it was his DCI. 'Excuse me a moment,' he said, moving towards the door, 'I need to take this. Guv?'

'Are you still with Rupert Longcross?'

'Yes, Guv.'

'Be very careful what you say to him. I'm at the lab now and there's evidence to suggest that this is not an open-and-shut suicide case as we initially thought.'

'What evidence?'

'I take it Longcross is out of earshot?'

'Yes. I'm outside the interview room.'

'When Toby removed the rope from around Hannah's neck, he found bruising along the line where the rope had cut in, as he would expect in the case of hanging. However, he also found two marks on either side of the windpipe, consistent with human thumbs, suggesting she had been strangled before being strung up. At this stage, Toby isn't sure if the pressure applied to Hannah's neck before the noose was put around it is what actually killed her, but what is clear is that the perpetrator wanted to make it look as though she hanged herself.'

'Are you thinking premeditated murder or an accidental killing? Maybe an argument that got out of hand? Shit, Guv, you don't think it could have been Jamie, do you? Maybe he finally snapped over her working as a shot girl.'

'We shouldn't jump to conclusions, but I think we need to get him down to the station and ask him to confirm his whereabouts last night during and directly after the times his girlfriend was working. You should also ask Longcross about his movements.'

'You're not seriously suggesting that he killed his own daughter, are you?' Graham said, lowering his voice.

'Everyone's a suspect when you're dealing with murder, Graham, you know that.'

'Yes, I do,' Graham said, carefully checking over his shoulder to make sure he couldn't be overheard, 'but if Longcross did kill Hannah and try to make it look like suicide, why would he have been so adamant just now that his daughter would never take her own life?'

'Double bluff? Jamie was exactly the same, but we can't rule either of them out. Somebody killed Hannah and the motive wasn't robbery. She was wearing a cash-stuffed bumbag under her sweatshirt that would have been obvious to the killer and easy to remove. I'm on my way back now. Get everyone together for a meeting at 3.00 p.m. and we'll go from there.'

'Yes Guv,' Graham said, ending the call. He took a deep breath before turning to go back into the interview room. The thought of quizzing a grieving father on his whereabouts at the time his daughter was killed didn't sit well with Graham, but he was well aware that it was a necessity now that the circumstances of Hannah's death had changed.

'I'm sorry about the interruption,' he said to Rupert Longcross. 'That was my DCI. Some new information has come to light regarding Hannah's case.' For a split second Graham was sure he saw a flash of hope in Longcross's eyes. It would have been cruel to prolong it by not divulging what the new information was. 'It seems we were premature in assuming Hannah took her own life. Her case will now be investigated as an unlawful killing.'

The flicker of hope Graham had witnessed was extinguished. Tears started to roll down Rupert Longcross's face. 'I thought you were going to tell me it was all a misunderstanding, a case of mistaken identity,' he said, pulling a large white handkerchief out of his pocket and mopping his eyes with it.

'I'm sorry it wasn't what you wanted to hear, but at least you were right when you said Hannah wouldn't have taken her own life.'

'I knew Hannah wouldn't have done that. She would never deliberately have put me and her mother through that pain.'

Graham allowed a few moments to pass before asking the question he didn't want to, but knew he had to. 'Can you tell me where you were between 2.45 a.m. and 6.45 a.m. this morning?'

Rupert looked shocked. 'I can't believe you're asking me that. Surely you don't think I had anything to do with Hannah's death?'

'I wouldn't be doing my job if I didn't ask the question,' Graham said, almost apologetically. 'All I need to do is eliminate you from our enquiries.'

'I was at home in bed with my girlfriend.'

'And she'll be able to verify that when we ask her?' Graham persisted.

Rupert was tight-lipped when he spoke, as though struggling to contain his anger at being asked such an impertinent question. 'We were both sleeping. You're talking about the middle of the night – what else would we be doing?'

'You said on the phone earlier that you left for Devon around seven. What time did you wake up, and did you both get up together?'

'That's it! I'm not answering any more questions,' Rupert exploded, banging the flat of his hand down on the table. 'How dare you insinuate that I had something to do with my daughter's death? I would never have hurt a hair on my beautiful girl's head. I loved her, do you hear me?' he shouted. 'More than I loved Miranda, or Tamara for that matter, in fact more than any other living being. I always have. And now she's gone. I can't believe it.' He slumped forward across the table, huge, noisy sobs racking his body.

Graham wanted to believe that the distraught man in front of him had nothing to do with his daughter's death, but his DCI's words about everyone being a suspect were ringing in his ears. *Maybe this is a fake display of emotion so that we won't suspect him of committing this awful crime*, he thought. *Or, Hannah's death could be the accidental result of an argument between the two of them and this is a genuine outpouring of grief; a realisation that he'll never see his daughter again.* Graham hoped that neither scenario was true. He couldn't imagine a worse crime than killing your own flesh and blood.

CHAPTER TWELVE

3.00 p.m. – Saturday

Rachel could hear the low hum of chatter as she paused outside the incident room, taking a moment to gather her thoughts. It had already been a challenging morning, discovering Hannah's body and having to break the tragic news of her death to both her mother and her boyfriend, neither of whom had been willing to accept that Hannah would take her own life. *They were right*, Rachel conceded, pushing the door open, *but is their refusal to accept that she committed suicide reached from a position of innocence or guilt?* By the time she had walked across the room and taken her place in front of the whiteboard, the room had fallen silent.

'For those who don't already know, the body of a young woman, Hannah Longcross, was found hanging from a tree in woodland adjacent to the university early this morning,' Rachel said, turning to write Hannah's name on the whiteboard. 'Early indications were that it was suicide. However it has now become clear, following a primary forensic investigation, that we have a case of unlawful killing. Hannah was strangled prior to being strung up in the tree,' she added, pausing to allow the information to sink in. 'As yet, we don't know if she was already dead before the noose was placed around her neck, but it's fairly obvious that it was done to make it look like suicide. We don't have an exact time of death yet, but it would have been after she left Velvet nightclub, where she worked, and before 6.40 a.m., when her body was discovered by her best friend, Abi Wyett,' Rachel said, adding her name to the whiteboard. 'They were supposed to go running together this morning, but Hannah didn't respond when Abi knocked on her door shortly after 6.30 a.m. A 999 call was made to the emergency services by one of the university groundsmen, Dennis Kirby, at around 6.50 after Abi had calmed down sufficiently to tell him what she thought she had seen. Unfortunately, she has been proved right. DI Wilson, I want you and PC Leverette to go back to the university to interview Abi, once she has been given the all-clear by the doctor, and any other close friends of Hannah's, after this meeting.'

'Yes, Guv.'

'Beneath the hoodie and tracksuit trousers that Hannah was wearing when she was found, was the clothing she wore for her job as a shot girl at Velvet, an establishment I'm sure some of you will be familiar with,' Rachel said, casting her eyes around the room and acknowledging that only she, DI Graham Wilson and DS Errol Green were over the age of thirty. The mumbling which followed her comment ceased as Rachel continued, 'This indicates that she was attacked after leaving the club and never made it home. We need to know the exact time she left and whether she left alone. PC Drake, I want you to pick up this part of the investigation.'

'Yes, Guv.'

'Start by contacting the club for their CCTV footage and a list of employees who were working last night. I don't suppose any record is kept of customers, but there will have been a lot of credit and debit card transactions which will help to identify some of them. PC Harman can help you with that. I also want you to view CCTV from the surrounding area. There is a possibility that Hannah was followed by a disgruntled customer who had spent more on shots than they intended and got into an argument about it with our victim, which could be a motive,' Rachel said, writing *motive* on the board in capital letters with a big question mark after it. 'It's early days to be certain of the motive, but one thing we can rule out is robbery. A bag containing a considerable amount of cash was on Hannah's body when she was found. There is also no evidence of sexual assault,' she added, and was fairly certain that she heard a collective exhaling of breath from the female officers in the room.

Rachel had taken the call confirming that Hannah had not been raped on her way back to the police station. She had felt strangely relieved. Although Hannah must have been terrified as the pressure on her neck increased, squeezing the life out of her, at least she hadn't suffered the ultimate violation.

'Which brings us to opportunity. If Hannah left the club on her own, there was plenty of opportunity for either a customer or someone who knew her movements to attack her. Due to the position of the thumbprints on her neck, Hannah would have been face to face with her assailant, which begs the question, did she know them?' Again, Rachel turned to the board and wrote the question as a heading. 'We need to compile a list of possible suspects from people she knew, including but not exclusively friends and family. I hope you didn't have plans for this evening, DS Green.'

'Guv?'

'You and I will be going clubbing.' A few people sniggered, while others dropped their heads and pretended to look at their notebooks to hide their smiles. 'I'm glad you all find it so amusing,' Rachel said, happy to have broken the tension in the room if only for a few moments, 'but hard as it may be to believe, I was young once upon a time. That aside, what I actually meant is that DS Green and I will be going to Velvet to talk to all the members of staff who knew Hannah, especially the ones who were working last night. I'm sorry if you had other arrangements, Errol,' she said, making eye contact with her sergeant, 'but I'm afraid you will have to cancel them.' *As will I*, Rachel realised, thinking of the text message she had sent Tim arranging to meet at her house at 7.00 p.m.

'No problem, Guv,' Errol replied, grinning from ear to ear. 'I wasn't looking forward to the soppy film my wife had planned for us to watch after the kids had gone to bed, so you've done me a favour.'

Rachel shook her head. Errol Green was six foot four inches of muscle and yet he was afraid to tell his wife that he didn't want to watch the film she had selected. *I hope Tim and I can be more honest with each other*, she thought. *It's annoying that I'm going to miss out on seeing him for a second night running, but it comes with the territory of both our jobs.*

'Is Rupert Longcross still here, Graham?'

'I believe so, Guv. He was in a bit of a state when I finished talking to him, so I organised a cup of tea and told him to take as long as he needed. Did you want to speak to him?'

'Yes. Just a few questions to get a feel for the man, particularly after the comment made by Miranda Longcross's friend,' she said, writing his name at the top of the list under the heading DID HANNAH KNOW HER KILLER? 'Have you had a chance to check his alibi with his girlfriend?'

'Not yet, Guv, I came straight into the meeting after my interview with him. It's top of my to-do list.'

'Let me know as soon as you've had it confirmed. I also want to speak to Hannah's boyfriend again,' she said, writing the name *Jamie* on the whiteboard, 'and preferably here at the station.'

'Right, Guv, although didn't you mention that he was going to the match this afternoon?' Graham asked.

'Would you still go to a football game after finding out your girlfriend is dead?'

'No, Guv.'

'Nor me. I think it will say a lot about his character if he went ahead with his original plans after receiving such awful news. I've got his mobile number in my office. You can try and make contact with him while I speak to Mr Longcross. Yes, Eleanor?' Rachel said in response to the police constable's raised hand.

'Should we let Mrs Longcross know that her daughter didn't commit suicide? She seemed very distressed at the thought.'

'Not until I've spoken with her ex-husband. Leave that with me for now. Does anyone else have any questions?' Rachel said, surveying the gathered officers. No one responded. 'Good, then let's make a start on finding out who did this and why.'

CHAPTER THIRTEEN

3.25 p.m. – Saturday

After handing over Jamie's number to DI Wilson, Rachel made her way to the interview room, having been told that Rupert Longcross was still incapacitated. She knocked lightly on the door before pushing it open to reveal a middle-aged man, dressed in a striped polo shirt and navy-blue chinos, hunched forward over the table clasping a barely touched mug of tea between his hands.

'Mr Longcross? I'm DCI Rachel Hart. I'm heading up the inquiry into your daughter's death.'

He flinched, as though hearing the word *death* in the same sentence as *your daughter* was too painful. Without raising his head, he said, 'I told the other officer it wasn't suicide. I knew my Hannah would never do that.'

'I'm so sorry to have to ask you questions at a time like this, but I'm sure you'll understand the need for accuracy in order to conduct our investigations fully.'

'What sort of questions?' Rupert asked, raising his head to reveal red-rimmed eyes and a tear-streaked face. 'I've already told your colleague that I was in bed with Tamara around the time that Hannah was…' His voice trailed off.

'I know, and DI Wilson is in the process of verifying that with your girlfriend.'

'Then what else do you want to know? Hannah and I haven't been in touch recently. Oh God,' he said, dropping his head into his hands, 'what have I done? This is all my fault.'

Rachel considered Rupert's comment as she crossed the room and pulled a chair up opposite him. Graham had quickly briefed her on their conversation prior to the 3.00 p.m. meeting, and she had thought Hannah's reaction to finding out that she was going to have a baby brother pretty extreme. It made her wonder if there was anything to Eleanor Drake's interpretation of Anoushka Parsons's comment. *What if Rupert Longcross did abuse his daughter when she was younger?* Rachel thought. *Hannah could have viewed his starting a relationship with someone of a similar age to her as a rejection and the pregnancy as the final act of betrayal.* Rachel knew all about the irrational thoughts that rejection could bring on.

'I know this must be incredibly difficult for you, but do you have any explanation as to why your daughter cut all contact with you after finding out your girlfriend was pregnant?'

'No. She wouldn't talk to me about it. For about a week after she walked out on us at Easter, I tried to call her several times a day, but she never picked up. If only I'd just driven to the university and confronted her with that very question,' Rupert said. 'Why didn't I just do that?'

The policewoman in Rachel couldn't help wondering if that's exactly what he had done last night if he had wanted to clear the air with his daughter and get her back on side before the trip to Okehampton to meet his girlfriend's parents. *If Hannah pushed him away, both metaphorically and physically*, she thought, *it's possible that he lost his temper with his daughter and unintentionally hurt her.*

'If we needed to verify your story, would you be happy for us to have a look at your recent phone records?'

Rachel was watching Rupert carefully. She knew they would be granted access to his phone records as part of a murder investigation, but his reaction to her request was what she wanted to see. *If he refuses, it could suggest he has something to hide.*

'You're barking up the wrong tree if you think I had anything to do with Hannah's death. For God's sake, she was my daughter. What kind of a monster do you think I am?'

'So, you wouldn't mind us reviewing your phone activity over the past few weeks?' Rachel asked, deliberately ignoring his question.

'You're some piece of work. I take it you don't have children.'

Rachel flinched.

'I thought as much. My little girl has been murdered, and the tone of your voice seems to suggest you think I'm responsible. I've got nothing to hide, but I'll be damned if I'm going to let your lot trawl through my phone without some kind of warrant or whatever it is you need,' Rupert said, the volume of his voice increasing with every angry word. 'I hope you and your DI are not on any kind of fast-track promotion scheme, because it will come to an abrupt halt when the Police Commissioner hears how badly you've both treated me. I'm not answering any more questions. Should you even be asking them without a neutral third party present?' he demanded, towering over her as he got to his feet.

Rachel also stood, refusing to allow him to intimidate her. She wasn't sure how the situation had escalated so quickly when she was only doing her job.

'I'm going home now to break the news to my girlfriend and grieve for my daughter,' he said, storming towards the door. 'I hope you're proud of the way you've dealt with the victim's father.'

As the door slammed behind Rupert Longcross, Rachel wondered if she could have handled things differently. *Was I too hard on him?* she thought. Her own dad had always said that the police who handled the case when she and Ruth were abducted were kind and compassionate. It was what had given them hope in their darkest hours. *I joined the force intending to be that kind of police officer*, Rachel recalled. *Have I changed? Has the reality of modern policing turned me into someone cruel and uncaring?* Her legs felt like jelly as she sank back down onto the chair. *Maybe I wasn't ready to come back to work after all*, she thought, pressing her fingertips against her forehead.

'Guv? Are you all right?'

Rachel looked up to see PC Drake in the doorway. 'Fine thanks, Eleanor, just a bit of a headache. I probably haven't drunk enough water today,' she said, recovering her composure.

'DI Wilson has just left for the university to speak to Abi Wyett, but he wanted me to let you know that he's been in contact with Rupert Longcross's girlfriend.'

'And?'

'She confirmed that she and Rupert went to bed early, around ten o'clock, apparently, because they wanted to be on the road to Okehampton by seven this morning to avoid the worst of the traffic. Assuming she's telling the truth, Rupert Longcross couldn't have killed his daughter.'

'You know my view on assuming anything, Eleanor. It seems unlikely that he's our killer, but we wouldn't be doing our jobs properly if we just took his girlfriend's word for it. I want you to check the CCTV cameras and see if his car was in the vicinity of Velvet nightclub last night, and we need to see his phone records, too. Even if it shows no activity away from his house, it won't be conclusive because he and his phone could have parted company, but it will make his involvement in Hannah's death less likely. How's the list of Velvet employees coming along?'

'That's the other reason I was looking for you. I rang the club on the off-chance, not expecting anyone to pick up until much later, but the manager is already in as he had to sign for a delivery today. His name is Max Sullivan,' she said, consulting her notepad.

'I asked if it would be all right for you to go down to the club now for a chat, and he said it would suit him better than when the club is open as Saturday nights are very busy. I didn't tell him what it was about, just that you needed to ask him some questions about one of his employees.'

'Good work, Eleanor. Did you ask him for their CCTV footage from last night?'

'I did, and he's fine for us to have a look at it. He said he'll send it over as soon as one of his security staff gets in, as they're the only ones with the access codes. Shall I ask DS Green to meet you downstairs in the car park?'

'Perfect. Oh, and Eleanor?'

'Yes, Guv?'

'You can contact Miranda Longcross now and tell her that her daughter's death wasn't suicide. It's only fair that she knows as much as her husband does. Perhaps just check that her friend is still with her, and if not, it might mean you need to go back out to her house. It's not the sort of news she should hear alone.'

'That's not a problem, Guv.'

Five minutes later, DS Errol Green climbed into the driving seat of the police vehicle and handed his DCI a bottle of water.

'What's this?'

'It's from PC Drake. She said you need to keep hydrated.'

Rachel couldn't resist a smile as she twisted the top and took a swig. *If anyone is on a fast-track programme*, she thought, remembering Rupert Longcross's harsh words, *it's Eleanor, and she's not the type to let anything stand in her way.*

CHAPTER FOURTEEN

4.00 p.m. – Saturday

DI Graham Wilson exchanged a look with PC Leverette, his hand suspended in mid-air as he prepared to knock on the door of number 27 Bowater House. There were raised voices inside; clearly someone was having an argument.

'Can you make out what they're saying?' Graham asked in a hushed voice.

'No, Guv, but it sounds like a man and a woman and they both seem pretty irate.'

Deciding it was better to intervene rather than risk the war of words turning more physical, Graham knocked loudly on the door. The shouting stopped. Moments later a male voice asked, 'Who is it? Abi's a bit busy at the moment.'

'It's the police,' Graham replied, offering no further explanation as to why they were there.

The door was opened by a man who appeared to be in his early twenties, wearing a T-shirt and jeans. Over the man's shoulder, Graham could see Abi. *She looks as though she's been crying*, he thought, *but I guess that's understandable in the circumstances. She's most likely still in a state of shock.*

'Is everything all right here? We heard raised voices.'

The man looked puzzled. 'Is that why you're here? Did someone report us?'

'No,' Graham replied, 'although in my experience it's usually better to settle your differences without getting into a shouting match. It's surprising how quickly a silly disagreement can escalate from words into domestic violence. Sadly, we see it all the time in our job.'

'Well, you don't have to worry about that with us. I would never hit a woman, isn't that right, Abs?' he said, putting his arm around her as she moved to his side.

'Don't I recognise you from this morning?' Abi asked.

'Yes, I'm DI Wilson and this is PC Leverette. My DCI and I found Hannah after your 999 call. How are you feeling now?'

'Is that why you're here, to talk about Hannah? I – I still can't believe she's dead. It just doesn't seem possible. Why would she do something like that when she has everything to live for?'

'Would we be able to have a few words with you in private?' Graham asked, glancing briefly at the young man before returning his gaze to Abi. 'Things have moved on a bit with our investigation, and I need to ask you a few questions.'

'What sort of questions?' Abi asked, her eyes widening.

'Nothing to worry about,' PC Leverette said reassuringly. 'You know, when you last saw or spoke to Hannah, a list of her other friends, that sort of thing.'

'Would you rather I was with you, Abs?'

'No, Phil, I'll be fine. You should probably get some rest anyway. The hospital said to take it easy for forty-eight hours.'

'If you're sure,' he said, dropping a kiss on the top of her head. 'I am feeling a bit knackered, if I'm honest. Just call me if you need me, okay?' he added, squeezing past the police officers as he headed for the stairs.

'You'd better come in,' Abi said, standing to one side to let them past. 'Can I get you anything? Tea, coffee, a cold drink, maybe?'

'We're fine, thanks. This shouldn't take too long,' Graham said, sitting on the chair by Abi's desk while PC Leverette perched on the end of the bed and took out her notebook.

'Sorry, it's a bit of a tight squeeze. These rooms aren't exactly made for group gatherings.'

'No worries. Like I said, it shouldn't take too long. Is your boyfriend all right?' In response to Abi's puzzled expression, he continued, 'I heard you mention the hospital.'

'Oh, that. Phil got knocked out playing rugby on Thursday, so they took him in as a precaution, but he's absolutely fine. That's actually what we were arguing about. If I hadn't been at the hospital with him, I would have been at Velvet with Hannah last night, and maybe I could have prevented her from doing this awful thing. Phil took it the wrong way. He thought I was somehow blaming him.'

'Actually, Abi, we have some new information. It seems Hannah didn't commit suicide.'

'I don't understand. She was hanging from the tree; you saw her yourself.'

'Whoever killed Hannah tried to make it look like she had taken her own life, but forensic evidence shows that she had already been strangled.'

Abi gasped, the full implication of the police officer's words seeming to dawn on her. 'Oh my God, then it *is* all my fault. We always came back together from working at Velvet. If I'd been with her, she wouldn't have been attacked. She'd still be alive,' she said, bursting into tears.

'You mustn't blame yourself, Abi,' PC Leverette said, trying to comfort her. 'There's no way you could have known something like this was going to happen. It's just an unfortunate set of circumstances,' she added, handing her a tissue.

Graham waited for a few moments until Abi's sobs had died down before he continued. 'Did you let Hannah know that you wouldn't be going to work last night?'

Abi nodded. 'Yes. I texted from the hospital,' she sniffed. 'She was a bit pissed off that I'd chosen to stay with Phil rather than go to work with her. They don't really like each other much, especially since Hannah roped me into the job at Velvet. Both Phil and Jamie, Hannah's boyfriend, seem to have the wrong impression of what the job of being a shot girl entails and neither of them approves of us doing it.' Abi stopped, something akin to fear evident in her eyes. 'Does Jamie know?' she whispered.

'He knows that Hannah was found dead this morning, but we've been unable to contact him this afternoon,' Graham said. He was struggling to believe that Jamie would have gone to the football match as planned after finding out his girlfriend was dead, and was hoping he had gone home and turned his phone off instead in order to grieve without interruption.

'He'll never forgive me,' Abi said, her face as white as a sheet.

Graham was taken aback. It appeared as though Abi was frightened of Jamie. 'What makes you think he would blame you?'

'It was my idea to get a job at Velvet in the first place. Hannah needed to raise quite a bit of money for her Everest expedition and I told her how much Chloe was making.'

'Chloe?' PC Leverette asked, writing the name down in her notebook.

'She's another friend of ours, along with Lucie. We all shared a house last year but moved back into halls for our final year because we thought there would be fewer arguments.'

Graham noticed PC Leverette nodding her head as though she completely understood the comment. *Why can't women be more like us blokes when it comes to house sharing,* he thought? *Six of us lived together for two years with never a cross word.*

'And was that the case?' PC Leverette asked.

'Not really. It turns out Chloe and Hannah were just too different to ever really get on without sniping at each other. I think that's why Hannah wanted me to work with her at Velvet, even though I really didn't want to and didn't actually need the money. When Hannah made such a success of it, Chloe was livid. She was always saying her earnings halved from the moment Hannah started working there. That's why she stopped working on the same nights. She said it was a waste of time putting her make-up on.'

'So, Chloe wasn't working last night either?' Graham asked.

'Not as far as I know, unless they persuaded her to go in to cover for me. We could ask her – her room is three doors along, number 30.'

'We'll give her a knock when we've finished here. Did Lucie work at Velvet, too?'

'Absolutely not. She had a very strict religious upbringing. She doesn't wear make-up and doesn't approve of alcohol. Don't get me wrong, we all really like Lucie, she's just a bit different from most girls of our age.'

For some reason, Eleanor Drake's image filled Graham's mind. Now he came to think of it, he'd never seen her with an alcoholic drink in her hand even on the rare occasions when she had socialised with the rest of her colleagues. *Each to their own*, he thought, finding it hard to imagine relaxing on a Friday night with a takeaway curry and no bottles of Cobra beer to wash it down.

'We're almost done, Abi, just a couple more things,' Graham said, checking his watch. If Jamie had been at the football it was almost time for the final whistle, and DCI Hart was keen to interview him now that they knew Hannah had not killed herself. 'Can you think of anyone who disliked Hannah sufficiently to want to hurt her? Anyone she has argued with recently either here at uni or at Velvet?'

'No. She was really popular. It probably sounds a bit weird, but I felt kind of honoured to be her friend. She could have palled up with anyone during Freshers' Week, but she chose me, and we've been best friends ever since. I still have no idea why, although it could have been because she didn't view me as competition,' Abi said, giving a nervous little laugh.

'Hardly,' PC Leverette replied.

Graham cleared his throat and fixed his younger colleague with a stare. Jackie Leverette was about the same age as Abi but couldn't be more different in appearance. Where Abi had thick, golden hair almost down to her waist, Jackie had her wiry, dark hair cut close to her head, presumably in an attempt to keep it under control. And where Abi had beautiful clear skin and defined cheekbones, Jackie's round face was in a constant battle with acne and had crater-like scars from previous outbreaks. *Either Abi is fishing for compliments or she sees someone else when she looks in the mirror*, Graham thought, *a bit like anorexia nervosa sufferers seeing themselves as fat.*

'Sorry, Guv,' PC Leverette muttered.

'One final thing. You mentioned Hannah's boyfriend, Jamie. How well do you know him?'

'What do you mean?' Abi asked, flushing slightly.

'Well, I know you said Hannah and Phil weren't too keen on each other, but I was wondering if you ever socialised together as a foursome?'

'Never just the four of us. Sometimes in a bigger group, but not often.'

For some reason that Graham couldn't quite put his finger on, he thought that was odd. Two girls who had been best friends for the past three years but didn't socialise with their boyfriends. *Something doesn't seem right here*, he thought. 'All right, Abi, I think that's all for now. You've been most helpful.'

'You will find whoever did this to Hannah, won't you?'

'I'm sure we will. Criminals think they're so clever and have everything covered, but they almost always make one critical mistake, which is a good thing from our point of view. Did you say Lucie's in this building too?'

'I didn't, but she is. Number 4 on the ground floor. Will you let me know if there are any developments?' Abi asked, leading the way to the door.

'We will, and thanks again for your help.'

*

After the door had closed, Jackie Leverette said, 'Do you think she'll be all right, Guv? She seems to be so on edge, nervous almost.'

'I know what you mean, but I'd have said frightened rather than nervous. The question is, who is she frightened of?'

CHAPTER FIFTEEN

4.45 p.m. – Saturday

Rachel stood at the edge of the large circular dance floor and looked up. The unimpressive entrance to Velvet nightclub certainly belied the interior. It was cavernous, extending upwards over three storeys with a sweeping staircase along the walls leading to the different levels.

'I'm sure it looks better at night-time,' Errol commented, 'with the proper lighting and the music playing.'

'It would need to,' Rachel responded, 'or I'm pretty sure they wouldn't be able to attract many customers. One thing's for sure, we're going to have our work cut out trying to trace everyone who was in here last night if it was full.'

'Virtually impossible, I'd say, Guv, even with the help of the club's CCTV cameras and the appeal for witnesses going out on tonight's local news.'

'You could be right,' Rachel agreed, watching the club's manager Max Sullivan striding towards them across the dance floor, 'but hopefully tracking down all the staff won't be such an issue.'

'I'm sorry about that,' Max said, a frazzled expression on his face. 'I don't know what's the matter with everyone at the moment. One of my shot girls let me down last night, and now Chloe has texted to say she can't make it tonight because she's had to go home to Sheffield to nurse her sick mum. It wouldn't be so bad if I could get hold of my best girl to cover, but she's not answering her bloody phone. Still, that's my problem, not yours. How can I help? The officer I spoke to on the phone didn't say much, just that you wanted to talk to me about one of my staff. If any of them have been breaking the law, I don't want them working here,' he said, looking from one to the other of the police officers. 'You've got to be able to trust your employees, particularly the ones who are handling money.'

'Actually, Mr Sullivan—'

'Please, call me Max,' he interrupted. 'Mr Sullivan sounds so formal. It makes me feel like I'm the one who has done something wrong, which I haven't,' he added quickly.

'Max it is, then,' Rachel conceded. 'I think PC Drake mentioned that we need your help with a list of people who were working here last night. Everyone,' she emphasised. 'Bar staff, security, cloakroom attendants, even the DJ.'

'I've already made a start on it, but can I ask why?'

Rachel knew the story was about to break in the media, so didn't see any harm informing Max Sullivan in person.

'Would I be correct in thinking that Hannah Longcross worked here as a shot girl?'

'Yes. She's the one I was referring to as my best shot girl a few moments ago. She's only been here a few months, but she's got the job down to an art form. She's not in trouble, is she?' Max asked, frowning. 'Hold on, did you say "worked here", as in past tense? Has something happened to her?'

Rachel got the feeling that Max's concern for Hannah was genuine, even if it was only because she was his best shot girl. 'I'm sorry to have to inform you that Hannah is dead,' she said, watching his jaw drop as the awful news sank in.

'Oh my God! What happened? Was she in a car accident or something? She hadn't been drinking, if that's what you're thinking. She never drank alcohol when she was working. If the customers offered her a drink, she would always take the money as a tip instead. God, I can't believe it, we were only having a bit of banter, virtually on this spot, a few hours ago.'

When she had briefly spoken to Graham on the phone prior to entering Velvet, he had passed on Abi's remark that everybody loved Hannah. Max Sullivan's stricken face certainly backed that up on a personal level, but the girl was dead, so it couldn't have been quite as universal as Abi thought.

'It wasn't a car accident,' Rachel said, making a mental note that they needed to locate Hannah's car as a top priority. If she had driven to work as Max Sullivan was suggesting, then its whereabouts could be key to discovering where the actual crime had taken place. 'Her body was found in woodland this morning. She was still wearing her work clothes underneath a hoodie and a pair of tracksuit bottoms, which suggests she never made it home. I don't suppose you saw her leave?'

Max shook his head. 'Like I said, we had a chat during the evening, but I didn't see her after that. Poor kid, she was so full of life. Why would anyone want to hurt her?'

Rachel examined Max's face. 'I didn't actually say anyone had. Hannah could have taken her own life.' *In fact, we were initially under the impression she had*, she thought.

'You wouldn't say that if you knew Hannah. She was one of the most positive people I've ever had working for me. I don't suppose she liked her job much, but you would never know it. She told me when she started here that she would only stay for as long as it took her to raise enough money for her Everest trip expenses, and judging by what she said last night she wasn't far off.'

'So she would have been leaving soon, anyway. Were you hoping that you could persuade her to stay?'

'I understand what you're getting at, but trust me when I say I know it would have been pointless trying. Once she'd made her mind up about something, or someone, there was no changing it. You're looking at the wrong person if you're after a suspect.'

'Everyone's a suspect until we find the killer, Mr Sullivan,' Rachel said, deliberately using his full name. 'I'm sure you appreciate that we're simply trying to get to the truth.'

'Of course, you're only doing your job. Is there anything else I can help you with?'

'Actually, there is. You mentioned Hannah didn't drink when she was working. Is that because she drove to work?'

'Yes. She used to give her friend a lift too, but Abi couldn't work last night, so I presume Hannah was on her own. Do you think that's when she was attacked? Someone from here might have followed her back to her car?'

'It's possible. I don't suppose you know where she parked, do you?'

'We all use the multistorey car park at the end of the street. I negotiated a concessionary rate for our staff because it's all double yellow lines around here and a few of us got parking tickets. Mine are all paid,' he added hastily.

'Does that mean you've got a note of everyone's registration numbers, including Hannah's?'

'Yes, it's pinned on the noticeboard in the office. I'll fetch it for you,' he said, heading back in the direction of his office.

'He's a helpful chap,' Errol remarked.

'So it would seem,' Rachel replied. She'd come across his sort before. Keen to help in order to avoid any close scrutiny of themselves. *I'll reserve judgement on Max Sullivan for now*, she thought. 'We can check out the multistorey when we get out of here. You never know, Hannah's car might still be there,' she added as Max Sullivan hurried towards them with a scrap of paper in his hand.

'There you go,' he said, handing the paper over. 'It's a silver-grey Mercedes, if I remember rightly.'

Rachel raised her eyebrows.

'A present from her rich parents. I never really got my head around why she didn't just ask them for the money for her Everest expedition. I suppose she must have had her reasons.'

'Maybe if you've always had everything handed to you on a plate, there comes a point where you need to prove your self-worth,' Rachel suggested.

'That sounds about right. I'll finish writing the list of staff who were working last night and email it over to you ASAP. One of them might have seen Hannah talking to someone, or even seen her leave.'

'Are any of them in tonight?'

'Most of them. The shot girls are the only ones who work on a rota system, which reminds me, I still need to get cover for Chloe.'

Rachel checked her watch; it was ten past five. 'What time do the staff start to arrive?'

'It depends. The bar managers are due in an hour before we open to get the bars ready, but it's usually quiet for the first hour, so the rest of the bar staff get here to start serving at 10.00 p.m. The DJ, bouncers and cloakroom girl start at 9.00 p.m. when the doors open and the shot girls arrive around the same time to prep their belts, although their hours are more relaxed as we don't pay them a wage. They earn a percentage of what they sell,' he explained.

'There's no point in us waiting here until then,' Rachel said, glancing at Errol. 'We'll come back at 8.00 p.m. so we can stagger the interviews and cause as little disruption as possible. If you could allocate a few minutes for us to speak with each of them, it would be much appreciated.'

'No problem,' Max said. 'I'll do it once I've made the list.'

'What about the CCTV footage, Guv?' Errol asked.

'That will have to wait until my security guys start to arrive, I'm afraid,' Max replied. 'I don't have the access codes needed, but Big Dave is usually in early, so I'll get him on it straight away. He'll be devastated when he hears about Hannah.'

'Oh?' Rachel said.

'He was very protective of her. He treated her like a little sister. We were always teasing him about it. He's going to take it very hard. For a tough guy, he has a very soft centre. I don't want to rush you, but if we're done for the moment, I really need to press on trying to get another shot girl for tonight. If the queues at the bars are too long, the customers start to get a bit aggressive with each other, if you get my drift, and we try to avoid trouble of that sort.'

'Of course. Just one last thing,' Rachel said. 'We may need to access your tills for details of credit and debit card transactions.'

'You can speak to my senior bar manager, Justin, when he gets in. He'll be able to assist you with that. Are you all right to let yourselves out? Press down on the bar and it will lock behind you.'

It was a relief to get out of the gloom of the nightclub and back into the late-afternoon sunshine.

'What's the plan, Guv?' Errol asked, falling into step alongside his senior officer as they headed for the multistorey car park. 'We've got a couple of hours to kill.'

Rachel raised her eyebrows at her sergeant's insensitive choice of words.

'Sorry, Guv,' he muttered, realising what he had said.

'We'll check to see if Hannah's car is still in the car park, and then you can head home for a couple of hours after dropping me back at the police station. I'm sure your wife will be pleased to have you home for dinner with the family, although unfortunately there won't be time to watch any films,' Rachel said, a smile playing at the corners of her mouth.

'I owe you, Guv,' Errol said, holding one of the double doors open for Rachel to pass into the bottom of the stairwell.

Their senses were immediately assaulted with the stench of urine and cigarettes. *Some people really are disgusting*, Rachel thought, putting her hand over her mouth and pinching her nostrils together, while reading the sign on the wall that showed the layout of the car park. Access to the parking levels from the stairwell was on alternate even-numbered floors, so for the odd-numbered levels pedestrians had to use the concrete steps built into the side of the vehicle ramps. Ahead of them was a door leading to ground-floor parking, and through its window Rachel could see cars queuing to exit through the barriers.

'You check this level and the next, I'll take two and three, and so on, alternating until we get to the top level.'

'Yes, Guv,' Errol said, pushing the heavy blue door open. They were immediately met by a wall of sound that had been muffled with the door closed.

'Call me if you find anything,' Rachel said to her sergeant's disappearing back.

There was no sign of the silver-grey Mercedes on level two, so Rachel took the steps at the side of the ramp up to level three and began walking back in the direction of the stairwell. She was about to head up the next ramp towards the pedestrian exit on level four when she realised there were a couple of parking spaces beyond the ramp that were partially obscured by a concrete wall. Rachel caught her breath. One space was occupied by a red Mini, and parked at the side of it was a silver-grey Mercedes. Rachel checked the registration number against the number Max had scribbled on a piece of paper; it was Hannah's car. *She didn't even make it to her car*, Rachel thought, pressing Errol's number on her phone.

'I found it.'

'Where?'

'On level three, to the right of the ramp.'

'I didn't realise there were any spaces to the right of the ramps.'

'Neither did I. They're pretty hidden away, and as far as I can see,' Rachel said, looking around, 'there are no cameras covering this area, which won't help our investigation.'

'Shall I get a tow truck organised?'

'Yes, and I'll get the forensic team down here,' Rachel said, wondering if they would be quite as amenable to having their Saturday-evening plans changed as Errol had been.

CHAPTER SIXTEEN

5.55 p.m. – Saturday

Once the forensic team had arrived, DCI Hart and DS Green were free to head back to the police station. On the way, Rachel decided to ring Tim. She had tried to speak to him to cancel their date before leaving for Velvet, but he hadn't answered so she had been forced to leave a voicemail. He hadn't responded to it, which was unusual, and she wondered if maybe he hadn't played it. He picked up on the fourth ring.

'Hello?'

Rachel thought his voice sounded groggy. 'Hi,' she said, 'it's me. Did you get my voicemail earlier?'

'Voicemail? No, sorry. I must have dozed off out on the balcony. I was shattered after my long drive yesterday. Was it anything important? Did you want to change our meet-up time tonight? I can do later if it suits you better.'

'Actually Tim, this new case has taken an unexpected turn and it means I've got to work late tonight.'

'Oh.' She could hear the disappointment in his voice from that one word. 'I was really looking forward to seeing you, particularly after I cancelled last night. When you say late, how late? I was going to bring stuff round to yours to cook, but we could get a takeaway of some sort instead if you fancy it.'

Rachel hesitated. They should be done interviewing all the staff at Velvet by 10.00 p.m., meaning she could be home by 10.30. *If I ring Tim when I'm leaving, he could order the takeaway and I could pick it up on my way back. It would be good to see him*, she thought, imagining herself snuggled up on the sofa with him, her head resting against his chest. Things hadn't been quite such plain sailing with him since Ruth's disappearance. She knew she had been difficult to be around at times, but if it had bothered Tim, he hadn't let it show and he had been incredibly supportive and sensitive to her feelings. She could feel herself wavering.

'You've got to eat,' he said persuasively, 'particularly if all you had for lunch was a chicken wrap.'

'How did you like yours?' she asked.

'It was disgusting. Most of it went in the bin. I don't know how you can eat that pretentious muck. Give me a good, honest cheese and pickle sandwich every day of the week,' he laughed. 'Anyway, stop trying to change the subject. Just say no if you don't want to see me.'

'You know that's not true, but we'd be eating very late and I have to be back in at eight in the morning. This has turned into a much bigger investigation than I initially thought,' she said, glancing at Errol in the rear-view mirror, careful not to give away anything that could be considered classified information.

'Look, it's your call. We can leave it and catch up tomorrow evening if that works better for you.'

Rachel had no idea whether that was going to work better for her. There were no rules when she was working on a big case. The only thing she was sure of was that she had a two-hour break before she needed to be back at Velvet. She was about to suggest that she call in at Tim's flat with a peace offering of fish and chips when her phone rang on another line.

'Hang on a minute, Tim, I've got another call. Talk to me, Graham,' she said, her voice switching into work mode.

'Hi, Guv. The good news is that I eventually got hold of Jamie Bolten and he's on his way here. He didn't go to the football, he said he was out walking, trying to get his head around what had happened to Hannah.'

'And the bad news?'

'Did I say there was bad news, Guv?'

'Not exactly, but I'm presuming there is as you started the call by talking about good news.'

'Well, it's not exactly bad news, but I thought you should know that I still haven't been able to get hold of either of the other girls in the group of friends, although I was about to try the mobile phone numbers Abi gave us again. Like I mentioned when we spoke earlier, neither of them answered their door when we knocked after leaving Abi's. I was particularly interested to see if Chloe had covered for Abi at Velvet last night.'

'Hold on a minute,' Rachel said, 'did you say Chloe?'

'Yes. The other two girls in Hannah's group of friends are Chloe Basset and Lucie Immingham. I thought I mentioned them. Is it important?'

'I'm putting two and two together here a bit, but if it's the same girl, Chloe has gone home to Sheffield to care for her sick mother. Try them both again, and if you still can't reach either of them, call Abi to find out if Chloe is from Sheffield and then we'll know for certain.'

'Okay Guv, I'm on it. Are you on your way back to the station?'

'We're pulling into the car park now. I'll see you in a couple of minutes,' Rachel replied, ending the call. 'Just drop me here, Errol, and I'll meet you back at Velvet at eight,' she said, flicking back to her call with Tim. 'I'm sorry, Tim, I think I'm going to have to give tonight a miss.'

'Don't worry about it, the chilli con carne ingredients will still be fine for tomorrow.'

'Thanks for understanding,' Rachel said, ending the call. As she got out of the car, the text message alert pinged on her phone; it was a row of heart emojis from Tim. Rachel smiled. She slid her phone back into her handbag. *How on earth did I get so lucky to meet someone like Tim?*

CHAPTER SEVENTEEN

5.55 p.m. – Saturday

After the police had left, Abi locked her door and put the chain across before getting into the shower. She had allowed the hot water to drench her thick mane of golden hair and pour over her face, washing away both the sweat from her earlier aborted run and the saltiness of her tears. The effects of the calming medication she had been given had started to wear off and the enormity of the situation, now she knew Hannah had not killed herself, was sinking in. *When I'm done in here, I'll see if Chloe and Lucie are around*, she had thought; *I can't bear the idea of being on my own all evening.*

Fifteen minutes later, after washing and conditioning her hair and vigorously exfoliating her body, Abi had wrapped towels around both and reached for her phone. Neither of her friends picked up, so she had left them voice messages and got on with drying her hair. Despite the warmth of the late-spring evening, Abi had felt shivery, so after trying both Chloe and Lucie again and still getting no response, she climbed into bed and pulled the covers around her. When her phone did eventually ring, she reached for it sleepily, realising she must have fallen asleep.

'Hello. Is that you, Lucie?'

She was surprised to hear a man's voice.

'Abi? I'm sorry to disturb you. It's DI Graham Wilson. Are you all right to talk for a moment?'

Abi wriggled herself into an upright position and hugged her knees into her chest.

'Yes, but I thought I answered all your questions earlier.'

'You did. I just wanted to ask you something about Chloe,' Graham said, the lie tripping easily off his tongue. He had just concluded a short phone conversation with Lucie and she'd confirmed Chloe's home town as Sheffield, but she'd also said something else that Graham wanted to run by Abi. He wanted it to seem like an afterthought though, rather than his main purpose for ringing.

'Wasn't she in when you knocked earlier?' Abi asked.

'No, neither of your friends were. It seems there's a possibility that Chloe might have gone home because her mum's sick. Do you know where her home is, by any chance?'

'Not the actual address. Like I said, we're not really that close, but she and Lucie are both from Sheffield. Has Lucie gone with her then?' Abi asked, wondering if maybe that was the reason neither of them had replied to her voice messages.

'No. I just got off the phone from talking to Lucie. She's only just got back from spending the day in Bath. Understandably, she was shocked when I told her about Hannah, and asked if you were okay. From what she said, it sounded as though she was planning on stopping by yours to make sure you're all right.'

'That sounds like Lucie, she's always looking out for other people. It'll be good to have some company, actually. I wasn't looking forward to spending the evening on my own.'

'Actually,' Graham said, trying to sound nonchalant, 'she did mention something that I wanted to ask you about. You seemed to be a little nervous earlier when I mentioned Hannah's boyfriend.'

Abi licked her lips; she had an idea what might be coming next.

'I asked Lucie what she thought of Jamie and she was a bit cagey, too. She said that Hannah would sometimes have unexplained bruises on her wrists and upper arms when she had been out on a date with him. As her best friend, you must have noticed them. I just wondered why you didn't tell me about them?'

Abi could feel her heart thudding against her ribcage. 'I – I didn't want to get Jamie into trouble. Hannah always had an explanation for the bruises.'

'And you believed her?'

'Well, not exactly, but when I plucked up the courage to ask her about it, she told me to mind my own business, so I did.'

'Even though you suspected that your best friend's boyfriend might be physically abusing her?'

'I don't know what I thought, but Hannah made it clear that she didn't want me interfering. She said she was perfectly capable of looking after herself.'

'You're sure that's the reason you didn't report it to anyone?' Graham asked.

'Yes, what else would it be?'

'I thought you might be afraid of him if he has a tendency to be violent. Has he ever hurt you?'

'No, of course not. I'm not afraid of him, I just find him a bit intimidating, which is probably to do with his size and his line of work.'

'Which is?'

'He's a bodyguard. I've seen him manhandle groupies who get too close to the bands he works with. I know he's only doing his job, but he seems to enjoy that side of it a bit too much for my liking.'

'Interesting.'

'Look, I'm probably giving the wrong impression of Jamie. I'm sure he wouldn't hurt Hannah – he adored her.'

There was a knock at her door.

'If that's all, I need to go, there's someone at my door,' Abi said, climbing out of bed and padding across the room.

'That's fine. You've been most helpful, Abi. We'll be in touch.'

As Abi pressed the red button to end the call, her hands were shaking.

There was another light knock at her door, followed by the words, 'Abs, are you in there?' She flung the door open and threw her arms around her friend, Lucie.

'Hey, hey, calm down,' Lucie said, inching into the room and closing the door behind her. 'It's okay, I'm here now.'

'Where have you been, Lucie? I called and called earlier, but you didn't pick up,' Abi said, clinging onto her friend as though her life depended on it.

'I was on a spa day in Bath with Beth from the choir. It was her birthday treat, I told you all about it weeks ago. We didn't take our phones because we didn't want to risk leaving them in the lockers.'

'Oh, yes, I remember now,' Abi said, still clinging onto Lucie.

'I'd only just got back and turned my phone on when the policeman rang, so I hadn't even played your messages. I can't believe this could happen to Hannah. It must have been awful for you, finding her like that,' Lucie said, her concern for Abi evident on her pale face.

'I'm so scared, Lucie. Why did you tell the police about the bruises? If they say anything to Jamie about it, he'll know it must have come from us. He's going to be so angry.'

'Listen. We don't really know him that well. What if he did hurt Hannah, even unintentionally? We owe it to our friend to help the police find her killer. We don't owe Jamie anything.'

'I can't believe this is happening. I want it to be yesterday and for me to go to Velvet with Hannah like usual on a Friday. If I had, she'd still be alive,' Abi said, climbing back into bed and rocking herself backwards and forwards, hugging her knees into her chest.

'Stop blaming yourself, this isn't your fault. You were always there for Hannah. You were a better friend to her than she ever was to you.'

'What do you mean?'

'Nothing, really. It's just that you viewed Hannah through rose-tinted spectacles, and she wasn't always so perfect.'

'That's not a very charitable thing to say. What's Chloe been telling you about her to taint your opinion? She's always been jealous of Hannah, you know that.'

'Forget I said anything. None of us is perfect, and you're right, I shouldn't speak ill of the dead. Will you be okay on your own for a little while? I need to let the rest of the choir know that I can't make practice tonight, and then I'll get us a takeaway. I'll bet you haven't eaten all day.'

Abi shook her head. 'I'm not really hungry.'

'I know, but you've got to eat something. Do you think Chloe will want to join us? She's meant to be working at Velvet tonight, but I'm pretty sure she won't feel like going after what's happened. Shall I give her a knock and she can sit with you while I'm out?'

'Chloe's not here. Didn't the policeman tell you? She's gone home. He said her mum's sick.'

'No, he didn't mention it to me,' Lucie said, frowning, 'and neither did Chloe, for that matter. Well, it's just the two of us then. I'll be back as soon as I can.'

As Lucie let herself out, Abi recalled her earlier words, 'You were a better friend to her than she ever was to you'. *What exactly did she mean?* Abi wondered.

CHAPTER EIGHTEEN

6.00 p.m. – Saturday

Graham was on the phone as Rachel walked through the incident room and into her office, signalling for PC Eleanor Drake to join her.

'Did Max Sullivan send the list over yet?' she asked as the young constable entered the room.

'About half an hour ago, Guv, and I've already run some preliminary checks for criminal records and the like.'

'Has anything interesting flagged up?' Rachel asked, checking the messages that had been left on her desk for her attention. Most of her officers had finished work for the day, but unsurprisingly Eleanor Drake had offered to work late.

'Nothing much so far. One of the barmaids has some unpaid parking fines and a bar manager has six points on his driving licence, all of them for speeding, but nothing else is showing at the moment. There is something you may find interesting, though. When I rang Miranda Longcross to tell her Hannah didn't commit suicide, she said she already knew because her ex-husband was with her. Apparently, Rupert showed up five minutes before my call.'

'I suppose it's not altogether surprising, after all they are Hannah's parents, and it's obviously very distressing for both of them, but he did say he was going home to his girlfriend. I wonder why he changed his mind?' Rachel said, rubbing her forefinger over her lips thoughtfully.

'You don't think it could be anything to do with her friend's comment, do you?' Eleanor asked. 'Maybe Rupert wanted to make sure Miranda didn't say anything that might cast suspicion on him.'

'It's possible, although the alibi his girlfriend gave him for the time of Hannah's death and the fact that his phone signal suggests he didn't leave home means he's no longer an obvious suspect. That said,' Rachel added thoughtfully, 'I'd still like you to check CCTV for the area around Velvet and the Bath Street car park for any sightings of Rupert and his car. You could also ask the traffic division if they picked up his vehicle on any of the roads close to where Hannah's body was found.'

'I've already checked with traffic and they've got nothing, but we haven't received any CCTV footage yet.'

Rachel suppressed a smile. *Eleanor's so on the ball... if only some of the others showed the same level of initiative it would make my job so much easier.* 'Did Miranda mention whether Anoushka was still with her?'

'She didn't say.'

'I know you're busy with the background checks on the Velvet staff, but it might be prudent to call in on Miranda Longcross to try and gauge her mood after her ex-husband's impromptu visit, and if Anoushka isn't there, perhaps call in on her too, briefly, to have her explain her earlier remark about Rupert.'

'Jackie Leverette's also working late. Maybe she could help me with the background checks before you leave for the club and start going through the CCTV footage when it comes in, while I head out to Miranda's. Mr Longcross should be long gone by then, so I'd be able to get a better sense of her mood.'

So many things about Eleanor Drake reminded Rachel of herself and her eagerness to please as she rose through the ranks. She knew what her own motivation was, after what had happened to her and Ruth as children, but she couldn't help wondering if it was only ambition that drove Eleanor Drake to go the extra mile.

'That's an excellent idea, Eleanor, and thank you for volunteering, especially as you've been here since eight o'clock this morning. I wouldn't send you alone, though, so DI Wilson will go with you once we've finished interviewing Jamie Bolten. Is that all right with you, Graham?' Rachel asked, transferring her gaze to her DI, who was now standing in the doorway of her office.

'Absolutely fine, Guv.'

'Good, that's settled,' Rachel said, noting the look of mild disappointment on Eleanor Drake's face. 'When you're done at Anoushka's, I want you both to go home and get some sleep after you've brought the night team up to speed on any developments, so that you're fresh for the morning. Please email me everything you find on the Velvet staff before you and DI Wilson head off, Eleanor.'

'Yes, Guv.'

'She's certainly keen,' Graham said, as Eleanor closed the door on her way out.

'She is,' Rachel agreed, 'but she needs to realise that she can't do everything herself. Working with others and delegating where feasible are important parts of a more senior officer's job. What's that look supposed to mean?'

'Nothing, Guv,' Graham said, smiling. 'I came to tell you Jamie Bolten is here. He's in interview room one waiting for us.'

His slight emphasis on the word *us* didn't go unnoticed by Rachel. *Should I have let him conduct this interview with a junior officer?* she wondered, following her second in command out of the room.

The interview with Jamie Bolten was inconclusive. When questioned on his whereabouts the previous evening, he said he had been at home alone watching *Friday Night Football* on the TV, taking advantage of the fact that Hannah was working as she wasn't a fan. His initial reaction to finding out that there was evidence that proved his girlfriend had been unlawfully killed was bullish.

'I told you so. I knew Hannah would never take her own life. She saw suicide as weakness, and in her world only the strong survive.'

'Obviously you knew your girlfriend very well,' Rachel said. 'How long had you two been an item?'

'We met at a Maguires gig last summer when I was heading up the security team. She was dancing near the stage,' he said, clearly reliving the moment he had first laid eyes on Hannah. 'To be honest, she looked so stunning, I think there were more people watching her than watching the band. I offered her backstage VIP passes as a way to get talking to her and the rest, as they say, is history.'

'And there have never been any problems within your relationship?' Rachel asked.

Jamie frowned. 'It depends what you mean by problems. We had the odd disagreement, like most couples, but nothing we couldn't sort out.'

'And in these "disagreements", as you put it, were you ever violent towards her?' Rachel persisted, flicking her eyes towards Graham.

'No, of course not. I loved Hannah.'

'So how would you explain the bruises she sometimes had on her wrists and upper arms?' Graham asked.

Shock registered in Jamie's eyes as the two police officers watched him, waiting for his explanation.

'I think I know where you're going with this, but trust me when I say you are way off base. It's not what you think.'

'Then perhaps you'd like to correct our thinking,' Rachel said.

Jamie concentrated on his hands. 'Who told you about the bruises?'

'We're not at liberty to say, as I'm sure you must understand.'

He nodded, still not raising his eyes to make contact with either of the police officers. 'This isn't easy,' he said, 'especially now that

Hannah is dead, but she liked to be quite… inventive in bed.' Neither officer spoke. 'In the early days of our relationship, she used to ask me to tie her wrists and ankles to the bed when we made love. I didn't like it, but it turned her on. After a while, that wasn't enough of a thrill for her, so she bought some handcuffs and leather straps.' He raised his head to look at Graham, studiously avoiding looking at Rachel. 'I was horrified when I saw the bruising on her wrists caused by the handcuffs. I said I didn't want to be part of something that was obviously hurting her, but she said she would find somebody who would give her what she wanted if I refused. I – I didn't want to lose her,' Jamie said, shaking his head and dropping his gaze back to his hands.

'Thank you for being honest with us,' Rachel said. 'I realise it can't have been easy for you to share that sort of personal information. I think we're done for the moment,' she said, checking her watch, 'but it might be necessary to question you again.'

'Whatever it takes to catch whoever did this to Hannah,' he said, pushing back his chair and getting to his feet. 'You do believe me, don't you, when I say I would never willingly have hurt her?'

'Thanks for your time,' Graham said, ushering Jamie towards the door and pointing him in the direction of the staircase leading down to the front desk. 'We'll be in touch.'

'Do you believe him, Graham?' Rachel asked her DI as he returned to the interview room.

'It's a perfectly reasonable explanation,' he replied.

'I agree, but I think it raises a question. If Hannah liked that type of masochistic physicality during sex, did she also push Jamie into applying pressure to her throat? What if her death is the result of a sex game that went wrong? We know she didn't leave the car park in her own vehicle. She might have arranged to meet Jamie after work and the two of them went back to his place for sex.'

'But Toby Morrison said that she hadn't had sex, and she was fully clothed when her body was found.'

'True, but it could have been an accident during foreplay. I think we urgently need the CCTV from the car park to see if Jamie's car was parked there.'

'I'll chase it up in the morning. If it was an accident, Guv, I don't understand why Jamie would lie,' Graham said.

'For the same reason he would he string her body up in a tree to try and make it look like suicide?'

'Because we would only have his word for it.'

'Precisely,' Rachel said. 'We also only have Jamie's word that Hannah was the one instigating the rough play. I think we need to keep a very close eye on Mr Bolten, we don't want him doing a runner.'

'As in physically following him, or putting a trace on his phone?'

'I think tracking his movements via his phone GPS signal will suffice for now. Can you organise that before you and Eleanor head out to Miranda's house, please? I'm going to grab myself a quick bite to eat before I meet Errol at Velvet.'

'On it, Guv,' Graham said to Rachel's back as she hurried out of the room. 'And I'll remind Eleanor to email you with the results of the background checks.'

'No need, she already has,' Rachel said, waving her phone in the air as she headed down the stairs. It was only half past six, and Rachel suddenly had an overwhelming desire to see Tim, even though she was tight for time. He picked up on the second ring.

'Well, this is a nice surprise,' he said.

'I'm on my way to the chip shop,' she said. 'Do you fancy sharing cod and chips?'

'Your place or mine?'

'Yours,' she said, her heart doing a dance at the thought of seeing him, albeit briefly.

CHAPTER NINETEEN

7.20 p.m. – Saturday

Despite tying the handles of the plastic bag as tightly as she could, the aroma of fish and chips had escaped its confines and Rachel knew she would be living with it in her car for the next few days. *It's worth it*, she thought, reaching for the bag from the footwell, *to have a reason to come and see Tim, although thanks to the queue in the chippy we'll only have twenty minutes together at the most.*

The interview with Jamie, during which he had expressed his wholehearted adoration of Hannah, had made her desperate to see her own boyfriend. It was as though she needed reassuring that Tim loved her as much as Jamie said he had loved Hannah. She took the lift up to the top floor and on stepping out, she could see that the door to Tim's apartment was ajar. She knocked instead of going in.

'Deliveroo,' she called out.

'I hope it's the same girl that brought me my last takeaway,' Tim said, opening the door wider. 'Oh good, it is,' he said, taking the bag from Rachel with one hand and pulling her into an embrace with the other. 'I've missed you,' he said, leaning down to gently plant a kiss on her lips. 'I need to order a takeaway more often.'

Rachel returned the kiss, then dropped her head to his chest, her arms reaching around him and holding him very tightly for a few moments.

'Hey! Are you okay?' Tim asked, wriggling free and lifting her chin so that he could look into her eyes.

'Yes. It's just been a pretty rough day and I needed to see a friendly face. You didn't mind changing your plans at the last minute, did you?'

'Don't talk rubbish. We'd arranged to meet up before work got in the way, and I'd much rather see you for even a short period of time than not at all. Speaking of which, we'd better get stuck in or you'll be going hungry. Do you want plates and cutlery, or are you happy to eat with your fingers straight from the box?'

'Let's save on the washing-up,' she said, following him over to the sofa.

Tim undid the knotted handles of the plastic bag and reached in for the two polystyrene boxes. 'It's not like the old days, when our fish-and-chip supper used to be wrapped in newspaper,' he said, opening one of the boxes and handing it to Rachel.

'That's because everyone reads the news online these days or watches it on television,' Rachel replied, thinking that the news about Hannah would have broken in the past hour. 'They probably don't print enough papers these days to deal with the demand,' she added, reaching for a chunky golden chip and sinking her teeth into it, savouring the waxiness of the potato.

'Just the right amount of salt and vinegar, too,' Tim said, using the two-pronged wooden fork provided to open up the crispy batter and get to the white flaky flesh of the cod beneath. 'I'm not a bad cook, but fish never tastes this succulent when I make it.'

'I'm saying nothing. The only fish I ever cook is the frozen boil-in-the-bag stuff with sauce. I guess it comes of living alone,' Rachel added. 'I can't be bothered to cook for one.'

Tim raised his eyebrows. 'That's an excuse, and you know it. And anyway, you might not be eating alone for much longer if you play your cards right.'

Rachel kept her head down, pretending to attack her cod, choosing to ignore Tim's comment. The two of them had been spending more and more of their free time together and it was inevitable that Tim might start thinking along the lines of them living as a couple. Part of her wanted exactly that, but the other part of her was still stubbornly holding onto the feeling that no man could be trusted after what had happened to her and Ruth as young girls. She decided to move the conversation away from their potential future together.

'I asked for extra scraps,' she said.

'Scraps?'

'You know, the fried batter bits that have come off the fish. They were always Ruth's and my favourites. We didn't have fish and chips that often when we were at home, but on holiday we made up for it. We'd call in at the chippy on the way back to our self-catering bungalow from the beach and then eat our supper sitting on the sea wall, listening to the waves crash beneath us.'

'The only thing missing is the seagulls,' Tim said, laughing.

'And Ruth.' Rachel sighed. 'I miss her so much. I wish I knew where she was.'

'She'll come back in her own good time, Rachel. Try not to worry about her.'

'I do try,' she said, closing the lid on her half-eaten supper, having lost her appetite. 'I just worry about how she's coping without her medication. She's been on antidepressant drugs for years. Who knows what state she might get into without their support.'

'You never know, it might be a blessing in disguise. If Ruth's been able to survive this long without her medication, she may be able to stay off the drugs for good. She could even integrate into the community instead of living in the protected environment of the hospital. Her walking out of Mountview might be the start of the next phase of her life.'

Rachel wanted to feel as positive as Tim did, but he had only met Ruth once and didn't know the dark places she retreated to when she was having a particularly bad time. She glanced at her watch; it was twenty to eight. 'I'm going to have to go, Tim. I have to meet my sergeant at eight.'

'I'm glad you came,' he said, standing up with her and walking over to the door.

'So am I,' she said, offering her lips for a kiss goodbye.

'Until tomorrow,' Tim said, watching her walk to the lift, a smile on his face.

CHAPTER TWENTY

8.15 p.m. – Saturday

Waking with a start, Abi was disorientated, her heart thumping in her chest. The surrounding darkness felt thick, as though there was choking smoke in the air. For a brief moment she wondered if the building was on fire until she realised there was no acrid burning smell in her nostrils. Her hands flew up to her throat and she took shallow gasps of air, struggling to gain full consciousness. A small whimpering sound escaped her lips and tears leaked from the corners of her eyes. She knew what had caused the nightmare from which she had just awoken.

Abi had been dreaming about Hannah. They were out running together, Abi falling into step behind her friend on the narrow woodland path as she always did, but when Hannah had turned to face her, her mouth was open and her lips moving, as though she was trying to say something. No words came, and Hannah's desperate, pleading eyes suddenly took on a blank, lifeless appearance, and her image floated off into the distance. Abi had tried to reach out to stop her friend from drifting away, but she couldn't move. It had felt as though she was pinned to the bed by a heavy weight.

What was Hannah trying to tell me? Abi wondered, forcing herself to take slower, more even breaths. *Did she know the person who did this to her? Was she trying to warn me to be careful around them?*

Her thoughts were disturbed by a knock at the door. It startled her until she realised that maybe that was what had awoken her in the first place. She glanced at the time on her phone. *It must be Lucie with our takeaway supper*, she thought, pushing the covers back and hauling herself into an upright position. *Whatever the doctor gave me earlier must still be in my system if I was in such a deep sleep that I wasn't even aware of what woke me.*

'Coming,' she said, making her way across the room, the panic from moments earlier replaced by relief at the thought of having some company for at least a couple of hours. 'What did you get us?' she asked, unlocking the door. 'I didn't think I'd be able to eat anything, but I'm actually—' Abi stopped mid-sentence. It wasn't Lucie at her door.

'Can I come in?' Jamie asked, and without waiting for a response, he pushed past Abi into the room.

Abi could feel her heart beating against her ribs. Jamie sounded angry rather than upset, and she was pretty sure she knew why. She glanced down the corridor nervously but there was no sign of Lucie.

'Why are you here?' she asked, reluctantly closing the door behind her and leaning back against it.

'Why wouldn't I come and see if my murdered girlfriend's best friend is all right?' he said, his words caring, but his voice lacking compassion. 'It must have been a hell of a shock finding her like that this morning,'

'It was,' Abi replied. 'I still can't believe it really happened. If it wasn't for the police coming to interview me, I'd think it was some terrible nightmare that I can't wake up from.'

'Ah yes, the police. I wish you'd spoken to me about your concerns before involving them.'

Abi's heart was properly pounding now. *He thinks I told them about the bruises*, she realised. *Lucie was right earlier when she said we don't know Jamie very well and have no idea what he's capable of.* 'I don't know what you mean,' she lied.

'Don't act dumb, Abi, it doesn't suit you,' Jamie said through gritted teeth.

Stay calm, she thought, *don't let him see that you're scared.* 'Really, I don't know what you're talking about.'

'Well, let's put that right then, shall we?' he said, his voice low and menacing. 'Earlier this evening I was summoned to the police station. It seems *somebody* has been telling them about the bruises Hannah sometimes had on her wrists. I wonder who that *somebody* could be?' he said, his angry face inches from her frightened one.

'It wasn't me. I swear on my mother's life. You made me promise not to tell anyone about the bruises when I asked you about them and I kept my word. You said it was between you and Hannah. I respected that, even though I didn't like it. I told her as much.'

'And what did she say to that?' Jamie demanded.

'Nothing,' Abi said, feeling the bones of her spine rub against the wooden door as she pressed back into it attempting to create space between her and Jamie. 'Hannah told me to mind my own business, so I did. There haven't been so many lately, or at least not that I've noticed, so I guessed you two had worked out your differences.'

'I take back what I said earlier. Maybe you're not acting dumb, you are just genuinely stupid. Did you really think I deliberately caused Hannah's bruises? It broke my heart to see those black and blue marks on her arms, but she liked them. They were like some perverse badge of honour.'

'I don't understand.'

'No, you really don't, do you,' Jamie said, running his hands through his hair in frustration. 'Let me spell it out for you. Hannah had quite specific needs in the bedroom.' He closed his eyes momentarily before continuing, speaking slowly and clearly enunciating each word as though talking to a young child. 'She liked to be tied up or handcuffed to the bed during sex. She said it turned her on to feel as though she was being "taken" against her will – her words, not mine.'

The bitter taste of bile filled Abi's mouth. She thought she was going to be sick. 'I don't believe you,' she said, sounding braver than she felt. 'Hannah always liked to be the leader in any relationship. Why would she want to be subservient to you, or any man?'

'Don't you get it, Abi? She was still the leader. By forcing me to do something I didn't want to, she had control over me.'

'You could have said no. Phil would never do something to willingly hurt me even if I asked him to.'

'You're right. Eventually, a couple of months ago, I refused to be part of her games, despite her threats that she would get her kicks elsewhere.'

'But I remember seeing bruises on her arms a couple of weeks ago when we were at the gym. She'd put some make-up on them to cover them up, but it had sweated off.'

'She used to hide them from me too, at first, but then she stopped bothering,' Jamie said, his voice cracking. 'It was as though she wanted me to know that she had carried out her threat and was sleeping with someone else who didn't mind getting involved in her games.'

Abi could feel a trickle of sweat running down her spine. *Is Jamie telling me this story to back up some lie he's told the police because it was he who did this terrible thing to Hannah?* 'Why are you telling me this? You're supposed to have loved Hannah, and yet you're making up this horrible story about her.'

'I *did* love Hannah, with all my heart. In fact, I still do, and I probably always will. But she could be cruel, especially to those closest to her.'

'She was never cruel to me and we were best friends.'

'That's where you're wrong, Abi,' Jamie said, a softness in his voice for the first time since he had pushed his way into her room.

'We were,' she said adamantly. 'We'd do anything for each other and we shared everything.'

'Even things you would never have imagined in your wildest dreams,' Jamie said, his voice tinged with pity.

'What are you talking about?' Abi demanded.

Jamie took a deep breath. 'I would have told you eventually, anyway: you're better than the two of them put together. Phil and Hannah have been seeing each other behind our backs.'

Abi's eyes widened in disbelief. 'No. Now I know you're lying. They hated each other.'

'Maybe that was Phil's motivation. Knowing Hannah needed him probably gave him a sense of satisfaction. But you've got to ask yourself, what sort of a bloke would do that without considering how much it would hurt his girlfriend if the truth came out?'

Before Abi could respond, there was a sharp knock on the door and Lucie's voice called out, 'Room service. Hurry up, it's getting cold.'

In one deft movement, Abi twisted her body around and unlocked the door, stepping backwards into Jamie as she flung it open.

'Lucie, thank God you're here. Jamie forced his way into my room, and he's been telling me a pack of lies about Hannah and Phil.'

It wasn't a long pause; just long enough for Abi to recall what Lucie had said earlier in the day. The room started to move around her. *What if Jamie isn't lying?* she thought. Her legs turned to jelly and she started to sink towards the floor, but before she crumpled completely, two strong arms swept her up and carried her over to the bed. As though from the end of a long tunnel, she heard the door shut and Lucie's voice saying, 'For goodness' sake, Jamie, did you have to tell her right now? Hasn't she been through enough for one day?'

'I wouldn't have said anything if she hadn't blabbed about the bruises to the police. What was I supposed to do? They were talking to me like I was their chief suspect, and I haven't done anything wrong.'

'It wasn't Abi. I told them about Hannah's bruises,' Lucie said, placing the paper carrier bag with the Indian takeaway in it on Abi's desk and hurrying over to her bedside.

'Well, thanks a bunch. Talk about throwing me under the bus.'

'That wasn't my intention. I just thought I owed it to Hannah to give the police as much to go on as possible. If you've got nothing to hide, then there's nothing to be afraid of,' she said, taking one of Abi's hands in both of hers and rubbing it gently.

'You knew about Phil and Hannah and didn't tell me?' Abi asked, withdrawing her hand from Lucie's.

'Only what Chloe told me she'd seen a couple of weeks ago, so I wasn't sure if it was true.'

'What did she tell you?'

Lucie took a breath before saying, 'I'm not sure this is the right time—'

'Tell me, or I'll never speak to you again,' Abi said, hysteria creeping into her voice.

'Chloe said she'd seen them coming out of Hannah's room together while you were at a Leavers' Ball meeting,' Lucie said reluctantly. 'They appeared to be arguing at first, and then apparently Phil grabbed Hannah and kissed her hard on the lips.'

Abi felt her heart contract. 'When did Chloe tell you this?' she whispered.

'On Thursday night as she was getting ready for her shift at Velvet. She was moaning about Hannah's popularity, as per usual, and when I told her to stop bitching, the whole thing came out. It was a dreadful shock, I can tell you. I asked her if she was going to tell you and she said she was going to confront Phil first. I'm so sorry, Abi. I wish I'd told you instead of you hearing this from Jamie.'

'How could she do that to me? She was my best friend. I'd have done anything for her. Do you think Chloe could have mistaken what she saw?' Abi asked, desperation in her voice.

'There's no mistake,' Jamie said.

Abi curled herself into the foetal position and mumbled, 'How can you be so sure?' uncertain that she wanted to hear his response.

'Hannah told me because she knew she'd been seen. She claimed it had all been a big mistake with Phil but blamed me because I'd stopped giving in to her demands. She excused her behaviour by saying that it was better to screw someone who was already in a relationship so they wouldn't expect anything except sex from her. I was so mad with her for betraying both of us and not giving a thought to our feelings. When I asked what she thought you would do if it came out, she fixed me with that stare of hers and said, "But she won't find out, will she, Jamie? And what she doesn't know won't hurt her".'

Abi gulped, trying to hold back her tears.

'You have no idea how much I wanted to finish with her that night, but I couldn't. She's always been like a drug to me. I don't know what I'm going to do now she's gone.'

The smell of curry had started to seep out of the plastic takeaway boxes and permeate the room. Without warning, Abi got up and pushed past Lucie and Jamie, heading for her bathroom where the two of them could hear her violently retching.

CHAPTER TWENTY-ONE

9.15 p.m. – Saturday

Rachel was feeling decidedly old and overdressed as she nipped to the ladies' powder room in Velvet. The club was already starting to fill up, and as she stood washing her hands, she was aware of the glances of scantily clad girls applying shiny gloss to their pouting lips. The club had a policy of showing ID at the entrance, but Rachel was pretty certain that some of the girls preening themselves in the tinted mirrors were barely in their teens, and had either borrowed ID or bought a fake one. *What a shame everyone is in such a rush to grow up these days*, she thought, dipping her hands into the air-dryer.

It had been very different for her and Ruth. They had a ten o'clock curfew imposed on them until the age of sixteen, and their parents wanted to know exactly where they were at all times and who they would be with. Their protectiveness, while understandable, caused a huge amount of resentment at the time, making the girls outcasts within their peer group as they weren't able to stay to the end of social gatherings. Eventually they had stopped being invited.

Before making her way back out into the body of the club, Rachel asked the girls if any of them had been in Velvet the night before. A couple of them shook their heads dumbly, but the other one, clearly the self-appointed ringleader, said, 'What are you, the police or something?'

Rachel took a small amount of pleasure in flashing her ID card and watching the girls' eyes widen with panic.

'Don't worry,' she said, 'I'm not about to bust you for being underage, unless I see you drinking, of course. I just want to know if any of you were here last night and happened to speak to one of the shot girls.'

They all shook their heads.

'Fine. Don't stay out too late, and make sure you stick together going home.'

Rachel couldn't be sure, but she thought she heard laughter as the door closed behind her. *I'm pretty sure they wouldn't find it so funny if they knew my reason for being here*, she thought.

She and Errol Green had conducted ten-minute interviews with most of the bar staff and also the cloakroom girl, Lynsey, who had burst into tears when she heard what had happened to Hannah. 'She was my favourite,' she had wailed. 'She always stuck up for me if anyone was being abusive about having to wait for their coats. I can't believe it. Why would someone want to kill her?' Lynsey had said through her tears.

My question exactly, Rachel thought, heading back to Max Sullivan's office where they were questioning the staff.

'Everything all right, Guv?' DS Errol Green asked as she entered the room. 'You were gone so long, I thought maybe you'd stopped off for a boogie on your way back.'

Rachel gave him a withering look. 'Don't be ridiculous, Errol. I was asking a group of girls if they were in the club last night. In other words, I was doing my job.'

'Yes, Guv. Sorry, Guv.'

It was no surprise to Rachel that Errol Green hadn't risen above the rank of sergeant. He was a competent police officer, but he came out with some incredibly stupid remarks at times.

'Let's get back to the job in hand, shall we, and then we'll both be able to go home. Who's next on the list?'

Suitably reprimanded, Errol looked down at his list and said, 'David Etheridge. He's one of the bouncers, or should I say security team.'

'I think we're both familiar with the term bouncer. Can you ask him to come in, please, and when he sits down, stand behind him so that he is aware of your physical presence.'

Moments later the office door opened and what could only be described as a giant of a man entered the room.

'Please sit down, David,' Rachel said, indicating the plush velvet chair on the opposite side of Max Sullivan's desk. While he eased his considerable bulk into the chair, Rachel found herself wondering which had come first, the name Velvet, with the designer choosing the opulent fabric for the interior, or the decor sparking the idea for the name. Either way, it seemed to be a reasonably classy operation; it rarely attracted the attention of the police.

'Please call me Dave, or even Big Dave. No one calls me David. Not even my mum, God rest her soul.'

'Dave it is, then. I presume you know why we're here?'

He nodded. Rachel wasn't sure but he looked as though he might have been crying, which seemed incongruous in such a big brute of a man.

'I understand you were working here last night in the VIP area.'

'Mostly, although I did have a stint on the door at the beginning and end of the night,' he said, with a gruffness to his voice.

'We'll come back to that later. Was the VIP area busy?' Rachel asked, anxious to get on with her line of questioning.

'Fairly, although we try to limit the numbers to around a hundred to keep the experience special.'

'And was the area full to capacity, would you say?'

'Pretty much. The booths were all taken and there were several groups standing around.'

'Did you have any actual VIPs in the club last night?' Rachel asked, unable to keep the scepticism from her voice.

Dave rewarded her with a weak smile. 'I know what you mean,' he said. 'Everyone thinks they're famous these days, even if it's just because they once appeared on a dating show. Pathetic really, but whatever floats your boat. To answer your question, though,' he added, 'we had a former world champion boxer in, so more famous than most. Actually, I was going to mention him to you anyway. He was surrounded by a group of girls because he was flashing his cash around, and I had to go and check that Hannah was all right because he touched her. We don't like the punters touching our female staff.'

'Touched her inappropriately, do you mean?' Rachel asked, immediately interested.

'No. Just on the arm, but you have to nip that sort of thing in the bud or it can escalate out of control.'

Rachel nodded. 'Does this boxer have a name?'

'Lloyd Tennant. I used to be one of his biggest fans, but his behaviour put me right off him.'

Something was nagging at the back of Rachel's mind. She wasn't a boxing fan, but the name sounded familiar.

'How did Mr Tennant react when you approached?'

'He didn't, really. After he paid for a second round of shots, Hannah left him to it and went back out into the main part of the club. It was something and nothing, but in the light of what happened to Hannah,' he paused, his bottom lip quivering, 'I – I just thought you should know.'

'You're right. We need to know everything because even the most innocuous thing could lead us to Hannah's killer. Did you see much of her after that?'

'Not until the end of the night. I sometimes offer to walk the girls back to their cars if there are drunken punters hanging around outside, just to be on the safe side. Hannah was on her own last night, so I walked her to the multistorey where she was parked.'

Rachel gripped the arms of the chair. *He was almost certainly one of the last people to see Hannah alive.* 'What time was this?'

'I didn't check, but it would probably have been about 2.45 a.m. We have a late licence on a Thursday, Friday and Saturday, and then the girls have to settle their account with the bar before going home.'

There hadn't been a confirmed time of death as yet, but Hannah had been killed at some point between Dave walking her to her car and Abi seeing her body hanging in the woods shortly after 6.30 a.m. It was a fairly small window of opportunity.

'One last question, Dave. Did you actually see Hannah get into her car?'

His face crumpled. 'No. I just waited at the bottom of the stairwell until she'd gone through the door onto level two. She said there was no need to go up with her. I don't know if I'll ever be able to forgive myself. I should have escorted her to her car.'

As an experienced police officer, Rachel had seen plenty of people appear to break down after a tragic event. *Either Dave is telling the truth or that's an Oscar-winning performance*, she thought.

CHAPTER TWENTY-TWO

'You have to admire her work ethic,' DCI Rachel Hart said, indicating PC Eleanor Drake through the glass wall of her office. She was sat at her desk tapping away furiously at her computer keyboard, shoulders hunched forward in concentration. 'What time did you two call it a day last night?'

'It wasn't too bad, actually, Guv,' DI Graham Wilson said. 'Miranda didn't seem that pleased to see us and, if I'm honest, I'd say she'd been drinking quite heavily. She didn't like it when we started asking questions about her ex-husband dropping in on her unexpectedly. In fact, I would go so far as to say she couldn't wait to see the back of us. We were only with her for a maximum of ten minutes and she didn't enlighten us on the reason for Rupert's impromptu visit. We didn't spend long with Anoushka either. She was reading her kids a bedtime story before heading back to be with Miranda, and didn't appreciate the interruption. She said her comment referred to Rupert getting together with Tamara while he was still married to Miranda. I think Eleanor's instincts may have been off on this one.'

Rachel nodded in agreement.

'I don't know about her, but I was home and eating my dinner in front of the TV by half past eight, which I should imagine was a good deal earlier than you and DS Green.'

Graham was right. Rachel had finally got home the previous evening at around half past ten, having stopped to pick up a microwave macaroni cheese from the petrol station; she'd eaten less than half of her fish and chips at Tim's earlier in the evening and still felt hungry. Although she was used to ready meals, it had proved a poor choice. It had been cloying and unpalatable, so most of it had ended up in the bin. *Yesterday really wasn't a good day for food*, she thought, sipping her black coffee and nibbling on a breakfast bar, *I must try and do better today.* Her mind skipped ahead to her possible evening in with Tim and his home-made chilli con carne, one of her favourite dishes. *Let's hope the developments in this case allow that to happen*, she thought, nodding her head to grant access to Eleanor Drake, who had appeared in her office doorway, an excited expression on her face.

'What have you got for us, Eleanor?' she asked, exchanging a half-smile with her DI.

'I was just reading through the transcripts of your interviews at Velvet last night, and one of the names mentioned jumped out at me.'

'Oh?'

'Lloyd Tennant. As the bouncer said in his interview, he's a former world champion boxer, but that's not the reason I recognised his name.'

'Wasn't he done for GBH after attacking his girlfriend?' Graham asked. 'If I remember rightly, it ended his boxing career.'

'Of course,' Rachel said. 'I knew the name, but last night I couldn't remember why it rang a bell.'

'I remember the case because my dissertation at uni was about allegedly unprovoked attacks on women,' Eleanor said. 'But it was his method of attack that struck a particular chord with me. I've just double-checked my old notes to make sure I hadn't misremembered.'

So that was what the frenzied tapping at the computer keyboard was all about, Rachel thought. 'And?' she asked.

'His girlfriend, Saskia Wendlebury, was rushed to hospital after being found unconscious in her apartment on Park Lane. She had marks around her neck consistent with strangulation.'

Rachel's mind began racing. Big Dave had said that Tennant was overly friendly with Hannah, but she rebuffed his advances. Men like Tennant were used to getting what they wanted and might not take rejection well. *What if he followed her to the car park in order to try and push himself on her again, staying out of sight until she was alone, and then things got out of hand?*

'I think we need to speak to Mr Tennant as a matter of urgency,' Rachel said. 'Do we have a current address for him?'

'At the time of the incident he had a big house on the river in Marlow,' Graham said. 'I remember seeing photos of the press camped outside his gates.'

'He still owns that,' Eleanor confirmed, 'but he also has a penthouse flat in Docklands.'

'Right, let's start with the Marlow house as it's nearer,' Rachel said. 'Graham, I want you to take a male PC with you, which is no reflection on you, Eleanor,' she added, noticing the constable's disappointed expression. 'I can't spare you this end. Tennant may have nothing to do with Hannah's death. It doesn't make sense to have two of my most thorough officers going off on a potential wild goose chase.'

'I understand, Guv,' Eleanor said, her voice lacking conviction.

'Shall we get straight off or wait until after the meeting?' Graham asked. 'If we go now, we might catch him still in bed at this time on a Sunday.'

Rachel resisted the urge to pass comment on who Lloyd Tennant might be in bed with, if, as Big Dave had suggested, he was a bit of a player. It was the other reason she thought it would be better if Graham took a male colleague rather than Eleanor Drake.

'You head straight off. I can bring you up to speed with any new developments when you get back. We don't want Tennant giving us the slip if he has got something to do with Hannah's death.'

'On it, Guv.'

As Graham pulled the door closed, Rachel turned her attention to Eleanor. 'Did we get the footage from inside Velvet that Max Sullivan promised us?' she asked.

'Yes, Guv. Jackie Leverette started to go through it last night. I can pick up where she left off, if you like. Do you want me to try and find the altercation between Hannah and Tennant?'

'Yes. I think Big Dave had a major crush on our murder victim, so I'm wondering if he made more of the incident than it warranted.'

'Why would he do that?'

'Good question. Maybe he thought that by casting suspicion on someone else we wouldn't take a closer look at him.'

'You don't think Dave's the killer, do you?' Eleanor asked, a note of incredulity in her voice.

'Nobody's above suspicion. He came across as very protective of Hannah, but what if he crossed the line and tried it on with her, only to receive the same treatment she'd dealt out to Lloyd Tennant earlier in the evening? His motive could be unrequited love,' Rachel mused. 'And he certainly had the opportunity, as we believe he was the last person to see her alive apart from her killer. We definitely can't rule him out.'

'I'll make a start on that before the meeting,' Eleanor said, hurrying from the room.

CHAPTER TWENTY-THREE

'Come on Abi, open up, it's me,' Phil said, knocking on her door more insistently. He had been standing in the corridor outside Abi's room trying to gain her attention for the past ten minutes, but to no avail. 'Were you drinking after I left?' he asked. 'Probably not a good idea on top of the medication the doctor gave you. No wonder you can't wake up.' He put his ear against the door to listen for some sound of movement within.

Abi was sitting on the end of her bed, her arms wrapped around herself in a hug, rocking gently backwards and forwards in a comforting motion. Eventually she and Phil would have to talk, but at the moment everything was too raw after the revelations of the previous evening. She got to her feet and moved slowly towards the door.

'I know you're in there, Abs, I can hear you,' Phil said. 'Open the door and let me in.'

She rested her cheek against the cool painted plaster of the wall. 'Go away. I don't want to talk to you right now.'

Phil took a step back from the door, clearly surprised by Abi's response. 'What's going on, Abs? Have you got someone in there with you?'

'We're not all cheating scum like you,' she said, the volume of her voice rising. 'I know what you and Hannah were up to behind my back. You're disgusting, the pair of you.'

'I can explain, just let me in and I'll tell you how it all started. It wasn't my fault, honestly. I didn't even like her, you know that,' Phil said, panic evident in his voice.

'No. I only know what you told me. And stupidly, I believed you.'

'I think she drugged me, Abs. People always assume it's only girls that get raped, but she must have spiked my drink.'

'Oh, please. You can't seriously expect me to believe that pile of crap?'

'It's true, I swear.'

'So, you want me to believe it was one night of drug-induced sex?'

'Not exactly. Please open the door, Abs, and let me try to explain.'

'Explain what? You claim you were raped by Hannah, but then you carried on seeing her. Why would you do that if she was forcing herself on you? You're not making any sense, Phil.'

'I wanted to stop. That's what we were arguing about when Chloe saw us outside Hannah's room, but she said if I stopped having sex with her, she was going to tell you that I loved her and not you. I was trying to protect you, Abs.'

There was a pause before Abi said, 'How convenient that Hannah's dead so she can't tell her version of events. For all I know, it could have been the other way round and you killed Hannah to stop her from coming to me with the truth.'

'You can't really think that I'm capable of killing Hannah? Or anyone, come to that,' Phil replied.

'I don't know what to think any more. You were the two people I trusted the most and you've betrayed me.'

'I promise it all happened exactly like I said. The end of term couldn't come quickly enough for me, knowing that I'd never have to lay eyes on that psycho-bitch again. You've got to believe me!'

'I don't know what to believe,' Abi said, her voice shaking with emotion, 'but I do know I need some space to think. I want you to go away now and leave me alone.'

'Not like this, with you harbouring all those terrible thoughts about me. Let me in and we can talk about it calmly.'

'I'm not feeling very calm right now. I want you to go away or I'll call the police,' she said, the volume of her voice rising. 'Do you hear me?'

'Okay, okay, I'm going,' Phil said, backing further away from the door, his hands making a placating gesture. 'I'll come back later when you're in a better frame of mind to listen to me.'

'I wouldn't bother, if I were you. Abi just said she doesn't want to see you.'

Phil spun round to see Lucie standing in a doorway further along the corridor. 'How long have you been standing there eavesdropping?' he demanded.

'Long enough to have heard Abi tell you to leave her alone. Shouldn't you just respect her wishes and do as she says?'

'Oh, I get it now. It was you who told her about me and Hannah, you sanctimonious little bitch,' Phil said, approaching Lucie and pushing his face towards hers in a threatening manner. 'I'll bet you couldn't wait to get in her ear after your best mate filled you in on what she saw, or should I say *thought* she saw.'

'Come on, Phil, even you can't wriggle out of that. You were seen kissing Abi's best friend. Are you going to deny it to my face?'

'I'll tell you what I would like to do to your face. I'd like to punch it in to get rid of that holier-than-thou expression,' he said, raising his hand as though he was about to carry out his threat.

Quicker than a heartbeat, Lucie grabbed his arm, twisted it behind his back and had him pressed up against the wall. Phil was stunned into silence.

'The first rule of combat, Phil, is to know your opponent. I might look like a fragile little Bible-thumper, but when I'm not singing in the choir or going to church services, I do martial arts so I can deal with idiots like you,' she said, forcing his arm further up his back to press home her advantage.

'All right, all right, you've made your point. You can stop now before you dislocate my shoulder.'

'Not until I hear you promise to stay away from Abi until she's had a chance to speak to Chloe about exactly what she saw.'

'I promise,' he said, 'just let go, you're hurting me.'

'Physical pain is nothing compared to the mental anguish Abi is going through,' Lucie said, digging her knee into the back of Phil's before releasing him and watching him fall to the floor. 'And, just for your information, it was Jamie who told Abi what had been going on, not me. I thought she'd already been through enough yesterday, but he wasn't of the same opinion. The police know about the bruising from the sex games, and I'm pretty sure Jamie will be falling over himself to incriminate you despite his pride being hurt because his girlfriend was cheating on him.' Lucie started to make her way towards the stairwell then stopped and turned back to face Phil. 'I'm off to church now, and I don't expect you to be here when I get back. If I were you, I'd get your story straight regarding your whereabouts late on Friday night, or you could find yourself in a spot of bother.'

'I was with Abi. We had dinner together when we got back from the hospital.'

'And according to her, she left your place at midnight so she'd be able to get up early the next morning to run with Hannah. I'm just wondering whether Chloe had rung you earlier in the day to tell you she was going to let your girlfriend know what she'd seen. Is that why you were so keen to stop Abi going to Velvet? Were you hoping to catch up with Hannah after work and ask her to lie for you? Did she refuse, and things turned violent?'

'That's not what happened,' Phil shouted, trying to get up from the floor but falling back in pain. 'Don't you dare go suggesting that to the police.'

'Or what, Phil? You'll strangle me to shut me up too? It's a shame that Chloe's gone home to Sheffield to nurse her mum, or we could have knocked on her door and asked her.'

'She doesn't know anything. All she saw was me kissing Hannah.'

'So, you admit you kissed your girlfriend's best mate. You really are a despicable human being. I hope you get everything that's coming to you.'

Lucie made her way down the stairs with Phil's words fading into the distance, 'I didn't kill Hannah… I swear on my mother's life…'

CHAPTER TWENTY-FOUR

As DCI Rachel Hart was gathering her notes for the 9 a.m. meeting, her phone rang.

'DCI Hart? It's Sam MacKenzie from the forensic team. I thought you should know that we've just discovered another body in the vicinity of where Hannah Longcross was found yesterday.'

Rachel's grip on the phone tightened. 'Is it another woman?'

'The clothing is female from what we can see. The body is face down in long grass. I'm about to get kitted up so that I can take a closer look, but I thought you'd want to know straight away.'

'Absolutely,' Rachel said, forcing herself not to jump to the conclusion that it must be Ruth as she had when Hannah's body had been discovered. 'I'm about to go into the morning meeting, but don't hesitate to call as soon as you've got something more concrete.'

On her way to the meeting, Rachel stopped by PC Eleanor Drake's desk.

'I forgot to ask DI Wilson if he managed to speak to Chloe at her mother's house last night,' she said. 'Do you know if he spoke to her?'

'He was going to bring it up in the morning meeting,' Eleanor said. 'He didn't speak to Chloe, but he did eventually get hold of her mother, Susan, when we were driving back from Anoushka's.

It seems she's undergoing treatment for breast cancer, and she was sleeping when he tried to call her earlier in the evening.'

'So, where was Chloe? Had she popped out?'

'Susan had no idea. She said she hadn't seen her daughter since Easter but was looking forward to the end of term so they could spend some precious time together.'

A tingling sensation started in Rachel's fingers and travelled quickly up her arms, causing her to shiver. It had seemed strange to Rachel that Chloe wasn't around to comfort Abi after her horrific ordeal, but maybe it wasn't by choice. *Could the second body be Chloe?* she wondered. *Was someone targeting the shot girls from Velvet?* She forced herself to pay attention to Eleanor, who was still speaking.

'DI Wilson got the impression from what she was saying that Susan might be terminal. He apologised for disturbing her and told her not to worry because he must have got his wires crossed. We both just assumed that Chloe had wanted the night off from Velvet, so had made up the excuse that she was visiting her sick mother. Is it important, Guv?' Eleanor asked.

'A second body has been discovered in the same area of the woods where Hannah was found,' she said. 'I'm just wondering if we've got a serial killer on our hands.'

Rachel wrote the words *Second Female Body* on the whiteboard and then turned to face her team.

'As you can see,' she said, indicating the words she had just written, 'a second body has been discovered by officers combing the area close to where Hannah Longcross's body was found yesterday. I'm only just in receipt of this information, so I have no further details at present and there's no way of knowing if the two incidents are connected. I am, however, concerned for one of Hannah's friends, Chloe Basset,' Rachel said, turning back to the board and writing Chloe's name followed by the words *possible victim*. 'She should have been working at Velvet last night but texted earlier in the day to say she wouldn't be in. The reason given has proved to be untrue, and despite our efforts to contact her regarding the Hannah Longcross murder, none of her close friends has seen or heard from her since Friday. Obviously, until we have more information on the identity of the second body, our primary focus should remain who killed Hannah, but I would also like to know Chloe's whereabouts, if possible. Who was tasked with monitoring Jamie Bolten's movements via the GPS on his phone?'

'Me, Guv,' PC Ahmet said.

'This could be another one for you, Ash. DI Wilson has Chloe's mobile phone number. I'll ask him to pass it on to you once he's back from interviewing Lloyd Tennant.'

There was a murmuring around the room.

'I see a few of you recognise the name. For those of you who don't, Lloyd Tennant is a former world champion boxer who got into a spot of bother a few years back. PC Drake, please elaborate on why Tennant is now a possible suspect,' Rachel said, turning back to the whiteboard and writing the boxer's name under the list of suspects.

Eleanor Drake stood up and moved to the front of the room. 'Lloyd Tennant was a customer at Velvet on Friday evening. We know from a witness statement that he had contact with Hannah Longcross. I'm looking for the relevant section of CCTV footage of their interaction in the club but haven't come across it yet. What is significant is that he was convicted of GBH four years ago after an assault on his then girlfriend that left her hospitalised. He had attempted to strangle her, which is consistent with the way Hannah met her death.'

'Thank you, Eleanor,' Rachel said. 'We'll know more when DI Wilson returns from interviewing Tennant about his movements after he left the club on Friday night. We also had a further interview with Hannah's boyfriend, Jamie Bolten, where he explained the historic bruising found on her wrists. It was a compelling story, but I'm not entirely convinced of its accuracy, which is why PC Ahmet is monitoring Jamie's movements via the GPS on his phone. What have you got for me, Ash?'

'When he left here last night, he appears to have driven around aimlessly for a while before heading to the university, more specifically to Hannah's building.'

Rachel raised her eyebrows. 'Why would he do that, I wonder? Her room is sealed for investigation. Nobody from forensics has reported it being broken into, have they?' Rachel asked, glancing around the room to be met with a lot of head shaking.

'He was in the vicinity of her room for around an hour before returning home, which is where he's been so far this morning.'

'It seems unlikely that he was just hanging around in the corridor all that time,' Rachel said.

'He might have gone there to talk to one of her friends,' PC Ash Ahmet offered.

'Possibly. Keep me posted when he's on the move again, and PC Leverette, perhaps you could ring Abi and Lucie to see if they've had contact with either Jamie or Chloe. Right, team, let's get this case solved.'

Once back in her office, DCI Hart rang DI Wilson to tell him about the discovery of the second body.

'Bloody hell, Guv,' Graham said, 'you don't think we've got a serial killer on our hands, do you?'

'My thoughts exactly,' Rachel replied, 'and I can't help wondering if this second body is Chloe.'

'Chloe? As in Hannah Longcross's friend? What makes you think that?'

'Eleanor told me that she wasn't at her mother's when you spoke to her last night, and Abi Wyett wasn't able to get hold of her on the phone to tell her about Hannah.'

'But Chloe sent that text message to Max Sullivan yesterday afternoon while you were at the club.'

'Did she, though? What if the text wasn't actually sent by her? It's been bugging me that neither Lucie nor Chloe was there to support Abi when they've been such a close-knit group of friends for so long, despite their obvious differences. Maybe Chloe couldn't be there for Abi because she was dead.'

'I see what you're getting at, Guv. The killer could have texted from Chloe's phone so that people wouldn't worry when she was a no-show at Velvet last night, meaning the killer knew her well enough to be aware of her sick mother.'

'Precisely. We already think that Hannah knew her killer, so it would be safe to assume it's someone who knew them both, either from university or Velvet,' Rachel said, thoughtfully tapping her fingers on her desk. 'Or, it was just luck that they used the "sick mother" excuse and the killer didn't know either of them personally. It could be someone with a grudge against shot girls.'

'A punter who felt cheated when they realised how much money they'd been persuaded to spend, maybe?' Graham asked.

'Or someone who didn't agree with exposing as much flesh as they do.'

'A religious nutter, do you mean?'

'I'm not sure I'd have put it quite like that, Graham,' Rachel said, surprised by her DI's blunt remark and thinking it sounded more like a comment Errol Green would make. 'People from different backgrounds have very firm views on the way women should dress.'

'But surely people who hold those sorts of views would stay away from nightclubs, where most of the women, customers and staff alike, are pretty scantily clad.'

'Unless these killings are a deliberate act to punish women for dressing provocatively, as they see it. Hannah and Chloe could have merely been in the wrong place at the wrong time.'

'We might be jumping the gun a bit here, Guv. We don't know that the second body *is* Chloe. For all we know she could be spending the weekend in Paris with a boyfriend.'

'Has she got a boyfriend?'

'Neither Abi nor Lucie mentioned one, but I can easily check with them when I'm done with Lloyd Tennant. If the second victim isn't Chloe, she could actually have sent the message because she fancied a night off work and knew Max wouldn't question the excuse she gave. It's possible we're barking up the wrong tree with the serial killer theory. There might not be a connection between these deaths.'

'Do you really think it's a coincidence that these two bodies were found less than twenty-four hours apart and within half a mile of each other? I'm sorry, Graham, but I find that hard to believe,' Rachel said, tapping her pen on her pad.

'What I find hard to believe,' he countered, 'is that any killer would dispose of a second body so close to a crime scene crawling with police. That's incredibly risky. Why not throw the body in the river where it might not wash up for days?'

'Because we *are* dealing with a serial killer who wanted the body to be found,' Rachel said with conviction. 'Imagine the adrenaline rush of dumping the second victim right under our noses and the perverse satisfaction of feeling like they have outwitted the police. It's what this type of personality thrives on.'

'I'm going to have to go, Guv,' Graham said, 'we're just pulling up at the gates to Lloyd Tennant's house.'

'Ring me when you're done with him,' Rachel said, ending the call. No sooner was the phone back in the cradle than it started to ring again. 'Rachel Hart speaking,' she said.

'Ah, good, just who I was after.'

For the second time in as many days, Rachel wondered who Toby Morrison from the lab was expecting to answer when he direct-dialled her number. 'Have you got something for me? Fingerprints, a rogue strand of hair, the attacker's DNA from under Hannah's fingernails?'

'Unfortunately, none of those. It's more what I haven't got, to be honest. It would appear that our attacker was wearing latex gloves. There's some residue of the powder used to make them easier to get on and off on Hannah's neck consistent with where the killer's hands would have been.'

'If the killer was wearing gloves it's more likely this was a premeditated attack rather than an accident,' Rachel said.

'My thoughts exactly. There were no skin or blood traces from under her fingernails,' Toby continued, 'which is quite surprising if she was fighting for her life. The only other thing I can give you at this point is that whoever did this is very strong. Although Hannah only weighed 50kg, she would have been a dead weight to lift up into the tree and drop from the branch.'

'And you're sure that's what happened? Couldn't the killer have hoisted Hannah up with the rope and then climbed the tree to secure the other end around the branch?' Rachel asked.

'Very good, DCI Hart. That was my other consideration, but judging by the way her neck was broken, Hannah was pushed from the branch. I can say with some certainty, though, that she was already dead at that point, so the drop didn't kill her.'

Rachel shuddered, picturing in her mind Hannah's final terrifying moments, as she would have struggled to inhale the tiniest amount of air, trying desperately to cling onto life. While anger could have fuelled the initial attack, squeezing the victim's windpipe until she lost consciousness and collapsed, maintaining the pressure was a deliberate action and could only mean one thing: the attacker wanted their victim to die. Along with the knowledge that the killer was wearing latex gloves, Rachel now knew they were looking for a murderer.

'Actually, Toby, I've got a question for you. Although we found Hannah's car in the Bath Street car park last evening, we couldn't locate her car keys. Has anybody reported finding them?'

'No. The team had a good look around but couldn't place them.'

That's odd, Rachel thought. *If I was in a car park on my own late at night, I would have had my keys in my hand ready to unlock my car and get into it as quickly as possible.*

'Was Hannah carrying another bag as well as the bumbag with the money in it? Maybe her keys were in there?'

'Only the nylon backpack where we found her purse. It had some boots and a belt in it, along with a bag of make-up, but definitely no keys.'

'And you checked her pockets?'

'I know how to do my job, DCI Hart,' Toby replied somewhat huffily.

'Of course, I wasn't suggesting otherwise. Listen, I appreciate you phoning this information through to me so quickly in advance of your full written report,' she said in an attempt to placate him. 'To be honest, I'm a bit surprised that you're in on a Sunday morning.'

'I wasn't planning on it, but as I'm here I thought I might as well ring this through to you while I was waiting for my next client to arrive.'

'Client? Oh, you mean the other body. Have you got any more information on that yet?'

'Not much. The team are just on their way back with it now. It seems this body has lain undiscovered for some time, and is quite badly decomposed.'

Rachel felt her throat tighten. 'Can you define some time?' she asked.

'Several weeks according to my colleagues at the scene, but I'll know more when I get her on the table.'

An icy fear crept through Rachel. She had all but convinced herself that the latest body was that of Chloe, but if it had lain undiscovered for weeks it couldn't be. 'I'm on my way,' she said, almost throwing the receiver back onto its cradle and rushing from the room.

Fifteen minutes later, Rachel swung her Audi into a parking space and noticed the forensics van already backed up against the entrance on the lower level where the lab was situated. She made her way up the front steps and signed in before taking the lift down to the basement and following the corridor around to the security door to the lab. She pressed the buzzer and waited for the door release to be activated. It wasn't, so she pressed the buzzer again, this time jabbing at the button repeatedly. A few minutes later Toby's voice crackled through the intercom.

'I presume that's you, DCI Hart?'

'You presume right. Can you let me in, please.'

'Not yet, I'm still prepping the body. I need you to give me a few minutes.'

'Don't be ridiculous,' Rachel said. 'You said it was fine for me to come straight over when we spoke on the phone.'

'Actually, I didn't. You announced you were coming over when I told you the second body was on the way and then you hung up on me before I could ask you to come a bit later,' he said.

'What difference can a few minutes make? Just buzz me in,' Rachel said, her tone becoming increasingly aggressive.

'I know you've got your job to do, DCI Hart, but I'm not appreciating your tone of voice. I suggest you go back to the station and let me do my job. I'll contact you as soon as I have anything concrete.'

'Am I missing something?' Rachel asked. She was almost shouting now. 'What could be more concrete than a dead body?' When there was no response, she continued, 'I'm sure you'd rather I didn't have to speak to your superior officer about keeping me waiting during a potential serial killer case.' Rachel knew she was being irrational and unfair, but she couldn't stop herself. *I have to know if it's Ruth*, she thought, taking some deep breaths to try and calm herself down. 'Look, Toby, I realise you're only doing your job,' she said, struggling to keep her emotions in check. 'If you can't let me in at the moment, could you just give me a few details?'

There was a short pause before Toby started speaking. 'I'm guessing from her clothing that our Jane Doe was in her late thirties or early forties.'

A prickling sensation started on Rachel's skin as she listened with a growing sense of foreboding.

'Mind you,' Toby continued, 'it's difficult to judge that type of thing these days as everybody seems to wear jeans.'

Rachel started to shiver, the blood in her veins turning to ice. *Ruth was wearing jeans when she walked out of Mountview.*

As he continued to deliver the few details he had, Toby was completely unaware of the effect his words were having on Rachel on the other side of the closed door. 'Her only recognisable feature is her hair, which is shoulder-length and brown in colour.'

A scream filled the air and Rachel began pummelling her fists against the unforgiving metal door. 'Let me in,' she shrieked. 'Let me see her, damn you!'

'DCI Hart, please, control yourself or I'll have to call security.'

But Rachel was unable to control herself. Her world had come crashing down. She continued hammering against the door and begging to be allowed in until the strength ebbed away from her and she sank to her knees sobbing. 'She can't be dead, not my Ruthie.'

CHAPTER TWENTY-FIVE

9.30 a.m. – Sunday

Graham checked his watch again as he and PC Harman sat side by side on the generously stuffed sofa in the plush living room of Lloyd Tennant's Marlow home. They'd already been kept waiting for fifteen minutes and it was starting to irritate the usually patient policeman. He was now wishing that he'd accepted the offer of tea for himself and his colleague from the former boxer's mother when they'd initially been let into the house. Since she'd gone off to rouse her son, they hadn't seen a soul.

Lloyd Tennant's mother wasn't very pleased to discover that the police wanted to talk to her son again.

'What's he done this time?' she had said after Graham had showed her his ID card.

'As far as we know, nothing. I just need to ask him a few questions about his whereabouts on Friday night and the early hours of Saturday morning.'

'He was probably out clubbing, pissing his money away as per usual. He seems to think it grows on trees,' she'd added, shaking her head.

'I don't suppose you know what time he got home, do you?' Graham asked, seizing the opportunity to double-check anything Tennant might say in his interview.

'I've no idea. I don't wait up for him when he's on a night out. I only know he's in when his keys are on the hook,' she said, indicating a key holder in the shape of a boxing world champion belt.

Graham couldn't help thinking how Tennant had thrown his career away. He'd used his strength to hurt his former girlfriend. *Could he be responsible for harming Hannah in the same way?* Graham wondered. *Perhaps this time it went too far.*

Mrs Tennant had shown Graham and PC Harman into the living room and offered the hot drinks before stomping off muttering about her son dragging the family name through the mud, again.

A smile played at the corners of Graham's mouth, as he'd exchanged a knowing look with his colleague. *He might be a former world champion boxer, but he's not above getting an earful from his mum.*

After a further five minutes, Tennant finally put in an appearance, his face almost as puffy as when he used to go twelve rounds in the boxing ring.

'What's all this about?' he demanded, taking a sip from the mug he was carrying.

Strong black coffee, Graham thought, *unless my nose deceives me, and boy, he looks like he could use it.*

'We're making enquiries about anyone who was at Velvet night-club on Friday night,' Graham said. 'I believe that includes you?'

Tennant narrowed his eyes. 'Yeah. What of it?'

'Our information is that you had words with one of the security guards after you touched one of the shot girls.'

'Are you kidding me? You make it sound as though I had my hand on her arse or something. I just put my hand on her arm when I asked her if she wanted to join my little party, and the next minute the goon was there acting all protective. It was something and nothing. What's the little bitch said?' Tennant demanded.

'Nothing. Have you seen the news over the past twelve hours?'

'Do I look like someone who sits in on a Saturday night watching the news? You'd be better off speaking to my mum if you're asking questions about what's been on the news.'

'I'm well aware of what's been on the news. The shot girl you were trying to chat up was found dead approximately six hours later.' Graham paused, waiting for the information to sink in before saying, 'She'd been strangled.'

'Wait a minute,' Tennant said, realisation dawning on his face, 'you can't think I had anything to do with that? You're not going to pin this on me.'

'We're not trying to pin anything on you, Mr Tennant, we just want to get to the truth. Can you tell me what happened at the end of the evening after Velvet closed?'

Lloyd Tennant's eyes flicked to the doorway where his mother was standing listening, then to the young police officer whose pencil was poised ready to take notes before returning his gaze to Graham. 'I left the club with a couple of girls.'

'And then what? Did you bring them back here? Or maybe you went home with them?'

'If you must know, we went to a hotel, not that it's any of your business.'

'We'll need to check that, sir,' PC Harman said. 'Do you have the names of the girls and the hotel?'

Tennant cleared his throat. 'I didn't catch their names.'

'For God's sake, Lloyd! What is wrong with you?' his mum said, turning on her heel and marching up the stairs.

'Thanks a bunch. I'm never gonna hear the end of this,' Tennant said.

Graham was about to repeat PC Harman's question when his phone started to ring. Glancing at the screen, he could see it was PC Drake.

'This had better be important, Eleanor,' Graham said after excusing himself and going into the hallway to take the call, 'we're in the middle of interviewing Lloyd Tennant.'

'It's the DCI, Guv,' Eleanor said, her voice high-pitched and worried. 'She's collapsed. You need to go to the hospital now.'

CHAPTER TWENTY-SIX

1.00 p.m. – Sunday

DCI Hart's face was as pale as the whiteboard on the wall of the incident room behind her and her legs felt as though they could barely support her weight. You could have heard a pin drop as the assembled officers sat waiting for her to speak. The rumour about the second dead body being her missing sister, Ruth, had spread like wildfire following the emergency phone call from Toby Morrison at the forensic lab.

Rachel cleared her throat and took a deep breath. 'As you're all aware, a second female body was found early this morning less than half a mile from where Hannah Longcross's body was discovered yesterday,' she said, struggling to keep her voice steady. 'Forensic evidence suggests this second female died between four and six weeks ago, but that is yet to be confirmed, along with the victim's identity,' she said, making eye contact with her DI, who was standing at the back of the room. She would be eternally grateful to Graham for backing her up at the hospital after the examining doctor had recommended she take some time off as he believed her collapse was stress-induced. 'I need to work, Graham,' she had said. 'Nothing's changed regarding Ruth and until it does, I need to keep busy. I'll go out of my mind with worry if I go home now.' Rachel was pretty sure that some subordinate officers would have seen it as an opportunity to take over as lead in an important case, but she knew her DI only had her best interests at heart. She took strength from the look of encouragement he gave her and continued, 'There is still a possibility that we are dealing with a serial killer, but obviously we now know that this latest body is not Chloe Basset. Until we receive more information from the lab on how our second female died, let's not jump to any conclusions and continue to work the leads we already have in the Hannah Longcross case. Speaking of which, how are you getting on with the CCTV footage from Velvet, PC Drake?'

'I've been concentrating on the cameras in the VIP area, and in particular looking at the interaction between Lloyd Tennant and the victim. To be honest, it didn't seem to be much of a big deal. Hannah looked across at our security man, Dave Etheridge, when Tennant touched her arm, but there was no further physical contact. Obviously, it's impossible to know what was said without a lip-reading expert examining the footage, but the moment Hannah finished pouring the second round of shots and moved away, Tennant went back to chatting up the girls he was buying drinks for.'

'Yes, DI Wilson,' Rachel said, responding to Graham's partially raised hand.

'That pretty much corroborates what he said in his interview this morning, Guv. He told us he didn't see Hannah again after she left the VIP area. He said he left the club at the end of the night with two girls.'

'I've been checking the front-of-house footage from closing time, Guv,' Eleanor Drake continued, 'and it shows him getting into a taxi with two girls, as he claims. Does that mean he's in the clear?'

'Not necessarily,' Rachel said. 'We need to trace the girls to find out where they all went in the taxi and whether Tennant stayed with them all night. He could just as easily have dropped them off and doubled back looking for Hannah.'

'Did he give you the girls' names?' Eleanor asked, turning to Graham, her pen poised over her notebook.

'Unfortunately not. He said he couldn't remember them,' Graham replied, struggling to disguise the look of distaste on his face.

What sort of bloke gets off with a couple of girls and doesn't even know their names when asked less than thirty-six hours later? Rachel wondered. 'It's possible these girls are regulars at the club, so we could ask around among the staff tonight. I need two volunteers to work late. Come and see me in my office at the end of the meeting. DS Green and PC Drake, you're both excused as you had late finishes last night. Are there any decent images of the girls leaving the club with Tennant that would be clear enough to print stills from?'

'I think so, Guv,' Eleanor said, 'but I'll check with the technical team. They've also been analysing the footage from the club and the surrounding area.'

'Does that include the car park footage?'

'No, Guv,' PC Jackie Leverette said. 'I've requested it again this morning, but still not received it as yet.'

'You need to stress the urgency when you speak to them,' Rachel said. 'Although the space where Hannah's car was found wasn't covered by CCTV cameras, the surrounding area is and might hold vital clues. We know she didn't leave the car park in her own vehicle, so as I see it, there are two possible scenarios,' she said, turning to write on the whiteboard. 'Either she was attacked in the car park and her body was moved in the killer's car,' Rachel explained, writing *car park* under the heading *Where Was Hannah Killed?* 'or, if she knew her attacker, as we strongly suspect she did, she got into his car willingly intending to return for her car at some other time,' she said, adding the word *elsewhere* beneath the heading. 'If the latter is the case, the car park cameras that monitor the exit barrier on Bath Street would have captured the car and hopefully the occupants, which is why we need that footage as our top priority. But we should check all the cameras that cover the pedestrian entrances on the side streets, too. If you experience any further delay, PC Leverette, refer them to me. I'm sure they won't want to be charged with perverting the course of justice by not complying with our request.'

'Yes, Guv,' PC Leverette said, her cheeks turning crimson.

Rachel didn't like to undermine any junior officer's ability to carry out the tasks they had been assigned, but sometimes it was necessary when time was of the essence.

'Regarding Hannah's car, have we had any information from the forensic team examining it yet, DS Green? When I spoke to Toby Morrison earlier,' Rachel said, a slight flush of colour creeping up her neck as she remembered her out-of-control behaviour at the lab, 'I asked him if they'd found her keys, but they hadn't at that stage and I'm guessing that's still the case.'

'They didn't mention keys when I checked with them just before the meeting,' Errol confirmed. 'In their words, the examination may take some time. While there are no obvious signs of a struggle on the exterior of the car, scratches, dents and the like, there are multiple sets of fingerprints on both the exterior and the interior.'

'Yes, PC Drake,' Rachel said, reacting to Eleanor's raised hand.

'After talking to some of her friends at the university yesterday, that's not altogether surprising. Hannah was often designated driver on nights out because she had stopped drinking since she started her Everest training. I shouldn't imagine many of her student friends will have been fingerprinted.'

'Actually, they've already identified one set of prints from our police database, Guv,' Errol continued, obvious irritation in his voice following the interruption. 'Jamie Bolten, Hannah's boyfriend, is an ex-policeman.' There was muttering around the room. 'He was sacked after allegedly roughing up a suspect in police custody.'

Rachel's mind flashed back to the interview she and Graham had conducted with Jamie the previous evening, specifically the explanation he had given for the bruising on Hannah's wrists and upper arms. *I wasn't convinced he was telling the truth and that was without having knowledge of his violent history*, she thought.

'Did you manage to speak to Abi or Lucie this morning, PC Leverette?'

'No, Guv, neither of them answered their phone when I called.'

'I can follow up on that, Guv,' Graham said, coming to the younger officer's aid before Rachel could quiz her as to why she hadn't kept trying. 'I'll do it as soon as the meeting's over.'

'You go, Graham, while I wrap up here,' Rachel said. She was concerned that Jamie might have confronted Abi or Lucie, assuming that one of them had spoken to the police about the bruising on Hannah's arms. *If he was responsible for Hannah's death, maybe after losing his temper with her, those girls could be in danger*, she thought. 'Let me know they're both okay, please,' she requested as Graham left the room.

'So, to summarise: we need to check Lloyd Tennant's alibi. I'll be in my office for anyone who doesn't mind giving up their Sunday evening to pay a visit to Velvet and try to track down and question the girls Tennant left with on Friday night. We also need to keep very close tabs on Jamie Bolten,' Rachel said, underlining his name. 'I want to know his every move, PC Ahmet.'

'Yes, Guv.'

'Have you had any luck in tracking down Chloe from her phone signal?'

'The phone is in her room at the university, but as she's not answering, I'm guessing she isn't. Maybe she left it there deliberately because she didn't want people to know where she was.'

'I wonder why she wouldn't want people to know where she is?' Rachel said. 'Unless we've got this completely wrong and she's not a victim,' she added, wiping Chloe's name away from beneath the heading *Second Female Body* and adding it to the list of potential suspects. 'Keep plugging away at that for me, Ash. I've always thought it odd that she wouldn't be around to support Abi. We also need to take a closer look at Dave Etheridge's movements in the early hours of Saturday morning in light of the Velvet CCTV footage that Eleanor viewed – it's turned out to be far less damning regarding Lloyd Tennant than he suggested. While I have no doubt Etheridge had genuine feelings for Hannah, the fact remains that he was the one who walked her to the car park from where she disappeared only to turn up dead a few hours later. We really need that car park CCTV as soon as possible, PC Leverette.'

'I'll ring them again as soon as the meeting finishes,' Jackie said without meeting her DCI's eyes.

'Remember, just refer them to me if they're being difficult. Are there any other questions? Right, let's get on with finding Hannah's killer.'

CHAPTER TWENTY-SEVEN

Although the sun was shining, a cold easterly breeze had picked up making it much cooler than the previous day. Abi wished she'd thought to bring a jumper with her to throw over her T-shirt and shorts, but that had been the last thing on her mind when Lucie had suggested going for a walk to get a breath of fresh air. Neither of them had wanted to walk in the woods, even away from the area within the police cordon, so they had headed towards the river instead. The cooler temperature hadn't been so noticeable while they walked along in near silence, each lost in their own thoughts. But now, sitting on the riverbank and gazing into the fast-flowing water below, Abi could feel the chill and shivered.

'Are you okay?' Lucie asked. 'At least, as okay as you can be under the circumstances.'

Abi nodded; she didn't trust herself to speak. She was far from okay. She had spent the past three years of her life basking in the glory of being Hannah Longcross's best friend, and had been completely devastated when it became apparent that the body she had stumbled across in the woods was Hannah. Those first few hours had passed by in a blur of shock and guilt, combined with the haziness brought on by the tranquillisers the doctor had prescribed her. Round and round in her head went the thought that if she had been with Hannah at Velvet as she should and could have been, her friend would still be alive. Hannah was so driven, not only in her desire to conquer the world's highest mountain but also in life generally. What Abi had to offer paled in comparison. She had found herself wishing that she could have taken her friend's place. Hannah was destined for great things, whereas Abi was happy to muddle along without a clear vision of what her future might hold. Thoughts of Hannah's parents grieving over the loss of their only child compounded Abi's misery. They might be divorced, but each loved their daughter in their own way.

After the police interviewed her the previous day, Abi had showered, desperate to wash away the guilt she was feeling. It hadn't worked, so she curled up in a ball willing sleep to overcome her, a sleep from which she fervently hoped she would never wake up, such was the depth of her despair. But she *had* woken up, and that was when her true nightmare had begun. Jamie's revelation about her friend sleeping with Phil might have made some people feel better, but it just made things worse for Abi. She found herself questioning whether anything about her friendship with Hannah had been genuine. She even considered the possibility that Phil had only asked her out in order to get closer to Hannah. She felt utterly crushed and worthless, unsure who to turn to. Lucie had stayed with her for several hours after Jamie left, offering words of comfort and reassurance that Abi had done nothing wrong and that, actually, she was the victim in this situation.

Abi assumed that Lucie must have crept out of her room the previous night once she had finally fallen asleep, because she wasn't there when Phil had woken her by hammering on her door earlier that morning. His attempt to absolve himself from all the blame for what had happened with Hannah had confused Abi still further. *What if he's telling the truth?* she had wondered. *What if Hannah deliberately got with him because she never really liked me at all and was just using me because I'm such a pushover? What if she was laughing at me behind my back? I need time to think.*

After she had sent Phil away, Abi sat on her bed with silent tears streaming down her cheeks. She had been betrayed by the two people she was closest to, and now she would never know for sure who the instigator of the betrayal was because one of them was dead.

Two hours later Lucie had returned from her Sunday morning church service to find Abi still sitting on the bed crying. Despite her best intentions, nothing she had said brought Abi any comfort. If Hannah was responsible for seducing Phil, it destroyed three years of memories; all the times they had laughed together and cried together would be rendered worthless. But if Phil had hit on Hannah, after he'd always insisted he hated her, the betrayal was even worse. Either way, a terrible thought lingered in Abi's head and just wouldn't go away: *once Hannah and Phil knew their secret had been discovered and one or other of them realised it had to end, had it caused an argument that got out of hand and resulted in Hannah's death?* Try as Abi might, she couldn't shake the thought.

'A penny for them,' Lucie said, snapping Abi back to the present.

'They're not worth that. My head is a complete mess.'

'That's understandable, Abs. You've had a traumatic couple of days. Your whole world has just been turned upside down,' she said, reaching for her friend's hand and giving it a gentle squeeze. 'It must have been horrifying when you realised it was Hannah hanging in that tree. Who would do such a terrible thing without giving any consideration to the person that would find her? There are some sick people in this word,' she added, shaking her head.

Abi shuddered. 'It was truly awful, Lucie. I didn't realise it was Hannah at first, but then I noticed the clothes and those bright green trainers. I keep having nightmares about it. Every time I close my eyes, I see her face and it's as though she's trying to tell me something or warn me about someone.'

'I said a little prayer for her at church this morning, and one for you too. You need to look after yourself, particularly since Jamie's thoughtlessness in telling you about Hannah and Phil.'

'I'm glad he did, I don't like secrets between friends,' Abi said, reproachfully. She paused. 'I'd rather have heard it from you though, if I'm being honest.'

'And I would have told you if I'd been absolutely sure Chloe was telling the truth, but I never got the chance to check it with her before all this happened,' Lucie said, spreading her hands. 'I'm sorry, Abs. I thought I was doing the right thing in not acting on hearsay.'

Abi reached her arms around Lucie and gave her a hug. 'I'm the one that should be sorry. You're not to blame. This is all down to Hannah and Phil.'

'What are you going to do about him, Abs?'

'What do you mean?' Abi asked, wondering whether Lucie had been having similar thoughts about Phil's possible involvement in Hannah's death.

'You are going to dump him, aren't you? Once a cheater, always a cheater. I know I'd never be able to trust him again.'

'Oh, that. Yes, of course. It doesn't really matter who seduced who, he barefaced lied to me time and again about how much he hated Hannah, when all the time he was screwing her behind my back.' Abi paused, wondering if she should voice her concerns to Lucie.

'Is there something you're not telling me?' Lucie asked.

'I've had time to think about things and—'

'What? Spit it out, Abs.'

'You don't think he had anything to do with Hannah's death, do you?' Abi felt Lucie tense up at her side. 'I – I don't mean intentionally. I just wondered if perhaps they'd argued, and things got out of hand and—'

'You know Phil better than I do,' Lucie said. 'Do *you* think that's what happened?'

'I don't know,' Abi said, burying her face in her hands and shaking her head. 'I don't know anything any more.'

'If you believe there's even the slightest possibility that Phil is responsible for Hannah's death, I think you should talk to the police about it,' Lucie said as she gazed out over the river. 'You wouldn't be accusing him as such, but if you're suspicious, you should tell them, like I did regarding Hannah's bruises, and let them investigate.'

Abi looked up at Lucie. 'Do you really think so?'

'Yes, I do, as much for your own peace of mind as anything else,' she said, turning to glance down at her friend, an encouraging smile on her lips. 'We could head there now, if you like.'

'You don't mind coming with me?'

'What are friends for?' Lucie said, helping Abi to her feet.

CHAPTER TWENTY-EIGHT

4.50 p.m. – Sunday

With ten minutes to go before their 5.00 p.m. meeting, DCI Hart was in her office collating the information gathered by her team during what had turned out to be a busy afternoon. Shortly after 2.00 p.m., she had received a phone call from Jamie Bolten revealing that Hannah had been unfaithful to him with her best friend's boyfriend, Phil Carter; this had been confirmed a little later in the afternoon when Abi Wyett and her friend Lucie had turned up at the station asking to speak to DI Wilson. Jamie had claimed that it was Phil who was responsible for any recent bruising on Hannah's wrists since he had refused to partake in her sex games. Rachel had wanted Jamie to come to the station to make a statement to that effect, but he'd asked if it would be possible to do it the following day. He had been unable to get out of travelling to Exeter for a Maguires gig in his role as head of security. Rachel had put her call with Jamie on hold to check his whereabouts with PC Ahmet; after his story checked out, she agreed to his request, albeit reluctantly.

She'd felt more comfortable with her decision once Abi Wyett had confirmed Jamie's claim about the affair during the course of her interview with DI Wilson. Although she'd given them nothing concrete to work on, it had presented both Hannah and Phil in a slightly different light and had resulted in Phil Carter's name being added to the list of suspects. If he had wanted to end the affair and Hannah didn't, Carter may have felt backed into a corner and taken drastic action. Rachel was anxious to bring him in for questioning, but no one had been home when they called at his flat earlier. She added a follow-up visit to Carter's home to her list of actions for the next day.

Rachel glanced at her watch. It was ten to five and they'd heard nothing from Toby Morrison all afternoon. She was still feeling embarrassed by the lack of control she had shown at the lab earlier, but she knew she would have to speak to Toby at some point to clear the air. *No time like the present*, she thought, reaching for her desk phone.

'Hello, Toby, it's DCI Hart here.'

'Ahh, DCI Hart, I hope you're feeling a bit better now?'

'Yes, thank you. I can only apologise for my behaviour earlier. It was totally unprofessional.'

'But understandable in the circumstances,' Toby said kindly. 'Think no more of it. Actually, I was just about to call you.'

Rachel gripped the phone tightly. 'Have you got a positive ID on the second body?' she asked, her voice sounding strained and tight.

'No ID as yet, but I can confirm how our second victim died. She was strangled.'

Rachel closed her eyes, trying to blank out the image of her sister Ruth that had come into her mind; the image she had seen in her nightmare on Friday night. 'Right,' was all she could manage in response.

'It's very difficult to say that it was in exactly the same manner as Hannah Longcross because of the decomposition in the soft tissue, but the windpipe was crushed, and lack of oxygen was definitely the cause of death.'

Rachel took a deep breath, filling her lungs to capacity, trying not to think what it must feel like to be prevented from inhaling the air you need to keep you alive.

'What I can tell you is that her neck wasn't broken, but of course we know that came post-mortem with Hannah.'

Rachel kept the meeting brief. She suddenly felt overwhelmingly tired and was looking forward to heading to Tim's for chilli con carne. After delivering the rest of the updates, she said, 'I've just got off the phone from speaking to Toby Morrison. The second female who was found this morning had also been strangled, which means there's a strong possibility that we do have a serial killer on our hands.' She looked around the room; nobody spoke, nobody moved. *They're all waiting to hear if the victim has been identified,* she thought, *but no one dares to ask.* 'As yet, the identity of the victim is still unknown. Toby said he'll let us know as soon as he does,' she added. 'I'm finishing for the day, so if there are any further developments, please report them to DI Wilson.'

After handing photographs of the two girls Lloyd Tennant had left Velvet with on Friday evening to the two volunteers, PC Harman and PC Millership, she concluded the meeting, fetched her jacket and handbag from her office and headed down towards the car park.

CHAPTER TWENTY-NINE

'Hey, how are you doing, sleepyhead?' Tim said, gently pushing Rachel's hair back off her face.

'How long was I sleeping?' Rachel asked as she wriggled herself into an upright position on his sofa.

'Only half an hour, but you obviously needed it. One minute we were talking about dinner and the next you were out for the count. Are you sure the doctor didn't give you a tranquilliser this morning? Or maybe my conversation isn't as interesting as I thought,' he said in an attempt to keep the mood light.

'I refused to take it,' Rachel said, smiling weakly. 'I need my wits about me for this latest case. Everyone we interview appears to have a motive of some description, which is weird because at the start of the investigation the victim seemed to be Little Miss Popular. Things are very rarely what they seem when you start scratching away at the surface.'

'It's the same in my business. We uncover things that the defendant would rather we didn't know and then try to bury them deep enough in the hope that the prosecution won't dig them up. I sometimes have to question my own integrity.'

'I think I may have restored a little of mine with Toby Morrison. He must have thought I was some kind of crazy woman, wailing like a banshee and trying to hammer his door down.'

'Don't think about any of that stuff now,' Tim said, lifting Rachel's legs down to the floor and sitting next to her on the sofa, draping his arm across her shoulders.

She rested her head on his chest. The softness of his cashmere sweater felt comforting against her cheek. 'I was so certain that the second body was another of the shot girls from Velvet that I hadn't given a thought to the possibility of it being Ruth. When Toby said the body had been deceased for over a month it hit me like a ton of bricks. And then at the lab when he mentioned the victim's dark, shoulder-length hair, I – I just lost it, I guess.'

'You don't know that it's Ruth,' Tim said, pulling her even closer into his side. 'It could just be an awful coincidence, and then you'll have got yourself upset for nothing. You must have read the text message she sent you on the day she disappeared a hundred times or more, and after each time you've always said she didn't sound as though she was about to do anything stupid. Try and hold onto that positive feeling,' he said, entwining his fingers through Rachel's. 'Ruth must have had her reasons for running away, but she'll be back, I'm sure of it.'

'Do you mean that? You're not just saying it to make me feel better?' Rachel asked, lifting her face up so that she could search Tim's eyes for the truth.

'I'm not just saying it, I promise. It won't be too long before the lab will have a positive ID through dental records or something, and until then we have to believe it's not Ruth. Okay?'

'I don't know how you've put up with me these past few weeks,' Rachel said. 'I can't have been easy to be around, especially in the early days when I was placing all the blame for Ruth running away on your shoulders. I don't know why you didn't just walk out on me.'

'Because I love you, Rachel. I don't know how many times I have to tell you that for you to believe me. My life had no purpose before I met you. I never want to let you go.'

Rachel wanted to say those three elusive words that she knew
he wanted to hear. She had come close on a couple of occasions,
but her head wouldn't let her express what her heart was feeling.
Instead, she snuggled closer into his chest and pulled her knees
up under her.

'We should spend more time here. The view is amazing,' she
said, looking out of the full-length glass windows over the River
Kennet and the town to the countryside in the distance.

'Actually, I've been meaning to tell you something, but it never
seemed to be the right moment, particularly since the trauma of
Ruth going missing.'

'What?' she said. 'You've mentioned it now, so you'll have to
tell me.'

'I've given two months' notice on this place.'

'Why? You've always said how much you like being in the centre
of things, and you couldn't get much more central than this.'

'I guess I just decided it was time I stopped living the life of
a single man in my penthouse bachelor pad and put down some
proper roots. I've bought a house, a house that I hope we can
share one day.'

Rachel was stunned. Although they'd been seeing each other for
the past seven months, there had never been the slightest hint that
things were getting quite that serious. For a moment, she thought
he might be about to present her with a diamond engagement
ring. *How would I feel about that?* she wondered.

'It's nothing flash, in fact it was a bit of a wreck when I bought it,
but I've been doing it up and it's looking pretty good now. Maybe
we can go and see it after dinner. If you feel up to it, of course.'

She could hear the hope in his voice, and although it was the
last thing she felt like doing, she heard herself agreeing to go.

'Brilliant. I've hated keeping it a secret from you, but I wanted
your first impression of it to be once it was finished.'

His excitement was almost childlike.

'Whereabouts is it?' Rachel asked.

'The location is top secret,' he said, placing his finger vertically across his lips. 'In fact, I might even get you to wear a blindfold and reveal all once we're inside, like those home makeover programmes on TV.'

'You're not serious?'

'Yes, why not? Come on, Rachel, it would be fun, and you've had precious little fun in your life lately.'

'We'll see. It might depend on how much red wine you ply me with first,' she said, smiling up at him as he got up off the sofa and walked into the kitchen to retrieve a bottle of Malbec from the wine rack.

'We'll let it breathe for a few minutes while I make a start on dinner. Are you still up for chilli?' he asked.

'Absolutely. You know the way to this woman's heart.'

'Do I?' he asked, his eyes locking onto hers.

Rachel held his gaze for a few moments, wondering what was holding her back from committing fully to this perfect man. He was funny, thoughtful, clever, kind and undeniably handsome. *Say it, Rachel*, a voice nagged at the back of her head. *Tell him you love him*, but before she could speak, Tim's phone pinged with a message. He picked it up off the work surface and scanned it briefly before making a big show of turning it off.

'No phones tonight,' he said. 'I turned yours off earlier so it wouldn't disturb you while you were sleeping. You don't mind, do you?' he asked, responding to her frown.

'No, of course not. I was going to ring Graham to see if there are any new leads, but I'm officially finished for the day and I'm sure he can handle anything that comes up.'

'That's my girl,' Tim said, reaching into the fridge for the plastic bag containing minced beef and slapping it down on the quartz worktop next to the chopping board. 'Do you want to watch the maestro at work, or would you like the television on?' he said, getting out a pair of latex gloves and pulling them onto his hands.

'What on earth are you doing?' she asked.

'My secret weapon against this little monster,' he said, holding up a bright red chilli. 'I remember when I first started cooking properly, rather than punching holes in cellophane and popping trays in the microwave.'

'Is that a dig at me?'

'Maybe,' he replied, laughing. 'Do you want to hear this story or not?'

'Fire away, although I think I might know what's coming.'

'Nobody had ever told me that you need to wash your hands very thoroughly after chopping chilli,' he said, expertly cutting the down the length of the red-hot pepper and scraping out the seeds before wiping the knife on the edge of the chopping board to clean them off the blade. 'Once I'd got everything in the saucepan, I must have rubbed my eyes and the next thing, the burning started. I thought I was going blind. Why are you laughing? It wasn't funny, I was terrified.'

'I'm sure, but imagine how much worse it would have been if you'd gone for a pee!' she said, dissolving into fits of laughter.

'And I expected sympathy,' he said, peeling off the latex gloves and putting them straight in the bin. 'Maybe I don't know you as well as I thought I did.'

CHAPTER THIRTY

6.30 p.m. – Sunday

Graham could hear laughter as he closed his front door and hung his jacket over the newel post at the bottom of the bannister. It was just the tonic he needed after the day he'd had. He knew exactly where his boys would be. Having had their tea at half past five, they would have been allowed thirty minutes of playtime before their bath. He took the stairs two at a time and stood leaning against the wall on the landing outside the bathroom door listening to his boys having fun.

'Don't splash so hard, you're soaking me,' his wife Rosie squealed.

Bath time was one of his favourite times of the day, that and reading his boys a bedtime story, and he hated missing them both when his job required him to work late. He reached for the bathroom door handle and flung the door open. 'Surprise!' he said.

'Daddeee!' two small foam-clad boys cried out in excitement, reaching their arms towards him, their fingers wiggling, to entice him in for a cuddle.

'Mummy first,' Graham said, wrapping his arms around Rosie and giving her a brief kiss on the lips. 'Only good boys get a daddy hug. Have they been good, Mummy?'

'Not bad,' she said, smiling, but before he could lean in, he felt his phone vibrating in his pocket.

'Sorry,' he said, giving Rosie an apologetic look, 'I need to take this. I'll be right back boys,' he added, heading out of the bathroom to a chorus of disapproval.

'This had better be important, Eleanor,' he said, answering the call.

'Sorry to bother you at home, Guv, but I've just taken a call from Toby Morrison and we have a positive ID on the second victim. I tried to call the DCI first, but she didn't pick up.'

Graham gripped the phone tightly. *Why did Eleanor ring Rachel?* he wondered. *Please don't let it be Ruth.* He took a deep breath. 'And?'

'Well, the good news is that it's not the DCI's sister.'

Graham breathed a huge sigh of relief.

'This lady is one Brenda Diment, reported missing five weeks ago by, and I'm quoting Toby Morrison here,' Eleanor said, '"a fellow lady of the night".'

'Are you trying to tell me she was a prostitute?'

'That's right, Guv.'

Graham was wondering what possible connection there could be between Hannah Longcross and a prostitute. *Maybe we're wrong and this isn't the work of a serial killer,* he thought. 'Thanks for letting me know, Eleanor. I'll keep trying DCI Hart throughout the evening to pass on the good news that it's not Ruth.'

'Before you go, Guv, there's one other thing I wanted to run by you.'

Graham raised his eyebrows. 'Go on, Eleanor, but make it snappy. My boys are starting to get cold in the bath.'

'I've been going through the footage from Velvet's exterior CCTV camera. It's to do with the amount of time that Dave Etheridge is away from the club. He told us he walked Hannah to the bottom of the stairs of the multistorey car park and then came straight back, but according to the time code he was gone for almost twenty minutes. I'm going to check the camera near the Canal Street pedestrian entrance to the car park next to try and establish how long Dave was actually in the car park.'

'Do you know what time it is, Eleanor?'

'About half past six?'

'It's twenty to seven to be precise. You're to finish what you are doing by 7.00 p.m. at the latest, handing over any leads that are still pending to the night team. I don't expect you to ignore this direct order under any circumstances. Do I make myself clear?'

'Yes, Guv,' Eleanor said, sounding suitably chastised.

'You were a bit harsh,' Rosie said as they each lifted a squirming little boy out of the bathtub and carried them through to their bedroom to dry them off.

'I need to be with Drake. She's a workaholic, that one.'

'It takes one to know one,' Rosie said, giving the merest shake of her head.

CHAPTER THIRTY-ONE

7.40 p.m. – Sunday

'Mind your step,' Tim said, helping Rachel out of the car.

'Can I take the blindfold off now? I feel really silly and a bit unsteady,' Rachel said, gripping on tightly to his arm as she heard the sturdy clunk of the Jaguar door closing and the beep as Tim locked it from his key fob. 'It's a good job you haven't had as much wine as me, or I'd have to nick you for drink-driving.'

'Nearly there. Hold tight, we just need to cross the road.'

Rachel did as she was instructed. She stood next to Tim on what she presumed must be the front doorstep, acutely aware of the jangling of keys. He took her by the elbow to guide her into the house.

'It had better be worth all this cloak-and-dagger stuff,' Rachel said, stepping forward onto what felt like a wooden floor. She smiled. She loved wooden floors. It had been the first thing she had altered when she had moved into her house in Sonning. She loved the comfort of carpet underfoot in a bedroom, but, in her opinion, nothing could beat a wooden floor and a tasteful rug in a living room. She felt a pang of sadness at the thought of moving out of the home she had lovingly created, but the thought of sharing her life with another person, particularly someone as kind and attentive as Tim, made up for it.

'Right,' he said. 'Are you ready for the big reveal?'

She could feel him fumbling to undo the knot in the silk scarf he had wrapped around her head once they were in his car. She kept her eyes closed momentarily as she felt the gentle pressure release, before gingerly opening them, expecting light to flood in.

'I've kept the shutters half closed so that it wouldn't be too bright for you until your eyes adjust,' Tim said.

She smiled at him. *He's always so thoughtful.*

'What do you think?'

She was standing in the middle of a medium-sized room that was decorated in a subtle shade of taupe. Not too brown, not too grey; it was a bit like Goldilocks' third bowl of porridge – perfect. On one wall was a fireplace housing a log burner, something Rachel had always wanted. She tried to remember if she'd ever mentioned it to Tim. There were two comfy sofas facing each other across a glass coffee table, not dissimilar to the one she had at home, under which was a pop art-style rug in shades of dusky rose. Because the shutters were partly closed, Tim had switched on a lamp in the corner, its tendril-like arms culminating in crystal globes. She turned to face him.

'Wow. It's like you've read my mind and then brought my vision of a beautiful home to fruition. It's gorgeous, I love it.'

'Phew!' he said, pulling Rachel into a hug and planting a kiss on her lips. 'What do you want to see next? The kitchen and family room, or do you want to go upstairs? I only finished painting the spare room yesterday, so we won't go in there. It still smells of paint and there's no carpet in there yet, but our room is finished.'

Rachel raised her eyebrows.

'What? Oh, sorry, I'm jumping the gun a bit. Our room *if* you want it to be,' he said, taking her hand and leading her out into the hallway. 'Which is it to be, upstairs or downstairs?'

Tim's obvious excitement in showing off what he had achieved was infectious. Rachel wasn't a particular fan of kitchens as she spent so little time in them, so she said, 'Let's go up.'

She slipped her feet out of her ballerina pumps and followed Tim up the stairs, appreciating the feel of quality wool carpet underfoot.

'I feel like I want to sweep you off your feet and carry you over the threshold of the bedroom,' he said, 'but I guess we can wait until we're married for that special moment.'

Rachel's heart started to thump in her chest. *Was that Tim's idea of a proposal?* she wondered, but the thought disappeared as he flung open the door.

'Ta-da!' he said.

Nothing could have prepared Rachel for what she was looking at. Again, the shutters at the windows were partially closed, but the Tiffany-style bedside lights were turned on and cast a warm, rosy glow. She felt a different carpet underfoot, deep and plush, as she took a couple of steps into the room. The bed was huge, and she could feel a blush starting at the thought of the pleasure to be had in it. Tim had walked over to a door in the far corner and was beckoning her over.

'Oh my God, Tim, this is amazing,' Rachel said, standing at the door to an ultra-modern en suite bathroom, tiled from floor to ceiling in slate grey. 'I'm speechless. I couldn't love it any more if I tried.'

'Do you love it more than you love me?'

'Don't be silly, of course I don't,' she said, turning to face him.

'So you do love me, then?' he asked, tilting Rachel's chin upwards so that she was looking into his eyes. 'Only you've never actually said it.'

Rachel knew this moment had been coming for weeks. It had taken her such a long time to find someone she could trust with all her heart. She knew once she said those three little words there would be no going back. The blood was pulsing in her veins. She raised up on her tiptoes and kissed Tim passionately on the mouth before pulling away from him. 'I love you, Tim Berwick.'

He swept her up in his arms and carried her over to the bed, where the passionate kissing continued.

*

Rachel realised she must have dozed off snuggled into Tim. She could hear him in the bathroom taking a shower. She reached for the towelling robe he had thoughtfully left on the end of the bed and wrapped it around herself. *It's funny*, she thought, *I didn't notice the paint smell when we first came up here, but it's quite overpowering. I wonder if Tim has got the window open in there?* She padded across the landing and pushed the door to the spare room open. Like the other rooms there were shutters at the windows, but here they were fully closed. She picked her way carefully across the bare floorboards, hoping that Tim hadn't spilled too much paint when he had been decorating the room the previous day.

Who knew he had such a hidden talent for interior decoration? she thought, unfastening the bar on the shutters and pulling them inwards so that she would be able to access the window to open it and let some fresh air in. She was humming to herself as she stuck her head out of the window and took a deep breath of delicately fragranced air. It was sweet without being overpowering and seemed vaguely familiar. Although the sun was about to set, there was still just enough light to get a flavour of the surrounding area. Beyond the gardens of the row of houses that Tim's was part of was what looked like a new housing development. *I'm so glad he bought a more traditional house rather than a new build,* she thought, *it has so much more character.* She adjusted her gaze to look out over the rear gardens with their various outbuildings and plants, wondering where the pungent aroma was coming from. There wasn't much in Tim's garden from what she could see, apart from a large tree near the bottom of it. She was straining her eyes, trying to decide if it was a cherry tree and if that's where the perfume was emanating from. Despite the warmth of the evening air, she shivered.

'What the hell are you doing?'

Rachel spun round to see Tim, fresh from his shower, standing in the doorway in a matching towelling robe to the one she was wearing.

'Sorry, I know you said not to come in here, but the smell of paint was making me feel a bit queasy. I thought if I let some air in it would help to get rid of it.'

'You weren't supposed to see it yet,' he said, marching across the room and pulling the windows closed with a bang.

'The garden? I couldn't really see much, it's getting dark already,' Rachel said, struggling to understand why Tim was so cross with her.

'Not the garden, the tree,' he said, taking hold of her shoulders and shaking her.

The light from the window highlighted the green in his eyes as he glowered down at her. A hint of the blossom aroma lingered in the room and suddenly everything started to fall into place. It wasn't cherry blossom; it was apple blossom. Rachel began to shake uncontrollably.

'You know, don't you? I had it all planned out, but you had to disobey my instruction, just like you disobeyed your mother when you were a child. You've spoiled everything now,' he said, moving his thumbs to either side of her windpipe and applying pressure.

As she was sinking into the darkness, Rachel realised what her sister Ruth had seen on the day she had met Tim: he had the same eyes as the man who had abducted them thirty years previously.

CHAPTER THIRTY-TWO

9.45 p.m. – Sunday

The sense of relief that Abi had felt after her interview with DI Graham Wilson earlier in the day was soon overshadowed by a sense of loss. Phil might not have been the best boyfriend in the world, but throughout their fifteen-month relationship he had said and done some pretty thoughtful things.

Abi kept racking her brain trying to remember whether she had noticed a change in Phil's attitude towards her that would correspond with the time he had started seeing Hannah, but she genuinely couldn't. He hadn't made any attempt to contact her since Lucie had warned him to stay away, something for which she was very grateful. *It's all very well sticking to my guns from the other side of a locked door,* she thought, *but would I stay strong if I could see him?* He'd been able to win his way back into Abi's affections after the whole row about her working as a shot girl, so there was no reason to suspect that he would be any less successful if he could convince her that he was Hannah's victim.

A thought occurred to Abi: *had Hannah started seeing Phil after that row? Was she mad at me for being so weak?* she wondered. *Or maybe she was just stringing him along with the intention of exposing him for the gutless wonder he is? Perhaps, in her own weird way, Hannah thought she was being kind because she didn't think Phil was good enough for me.* The more Abi thought about it, the more she wanted to believe that revealing Phil's weakness was Hannah's intention. *Hannah was a good friend to me*, she thought, *no matter what Lucie thinks.*

Lucie and Abi had gone for a pizza after their interviews at the police station earlier that afternoon, but although Lucie had hungrily devoured her quattro formaggi, Abi had barely touched her goat's cheese leggera. *I'm paying the price for it now*, she thought, as her stomach started to grumble. *I wonder if there's any bread in the kitchen for me to have a piece of toast?* The more Abi thought about melted butter oozing through the crunchy surface of toast and into the doughy softness beneath, the more her stomach protested. Eventually, just after ten o'clock, she gave in to her craving, grabbed her door key and crossed the corridor to the communal kitchen. Abi's eyes were well adjusted to the gloom as she'd been sitting in her room as dusk turned to darkness, so she didn't bother with the lights. Reaching into the bread bin, her fingers made contact with the plastic covering of the thick-sliced loaf. She removed two slices of bread from the packet and dropped them in the toaster before going over to the fridge for the butter that they had started to keep in there since the weather had turned warmer. She pulled open the door, which cast a panel of light across the tiled floor and illuminated the table in front of the window. She gasped.

'Jesus! Chloe! You scared the life out of me. Where have you been? We've been worried about you.'

Chloe raised her tear-stained face. 'Really? I find that hard to believe.'

Abi flicked the kitchen light on, causing them both to blink in the harsh brightness, before walking over to the table. 'We have, I promise,' she said, pulling out a chair to sit on, 'especially after the police told us you weren't at your mum's, like you told Max. Where were you?'

'I couldn't face any of you after what happened to Hannah. It's my fault. I let my dislike of her colour my judgement, and now she's dead. I'm just a wicked person,' she said, dropping her face into her hands again.

'Don't say that,' Abi said, reaching her arm around the other girl's heaving shoulders. Although she didn't particularly like Chloe, she couldn't bear to see anyone so upset without trying to comfort them. 'Whatever your motivation was, all you did was tell Phil and Hannah that you had seen them together. They were in the wrong, not you. Come on, stop crying, please.'

'I didn't need to tell Hannah. She saw me that afternoon when they kissed. I think she wanted me to tell you, but I wanted to ask Phil what was going on first.'

'What did he say?' Abi said, her heart pounding in her chest. She had told the police earlier in the day about her suspicions that Phil and Hannah may have got into an argument, with devastating consequences.

'Nothing. I never got to see him. I was going to speak to him on Thursday before my shift at Velvet, but he was injured at rugby, so he was in the hospital.'

Why didn't I think of that when I was telling the police my suspicions? Abi thought. *If Phil didn't know he'd been seen, he'd have had no reason to go in search of Hannah to have it out with her.*

The sound of the toast popping out of the toaster startled Abi and Chloe.

'I'm sorry,' Abi said, 'you've lost me. If you didn't tell either Phil or Hannah that you'd seen them together, then how is what happened to Hannah your fault?'

'I told Big Dave.'

Abi's skin began to tingle. 'What exactly did you tell him?'

'He was having a go at me, basically telling me that if I was nicer to the punters like his precious Hannah, I might make a bit more money.'

'And?'

'And so I just said she's not as nice as you think. Nice people don't screw their best friend's boyfriend.'

Abi winced. 'How did Dave react?'

'He told me to shut my filthy mouth or he'd shut it for me. That's why I didn't want to go to work last night. He scares me.'

'When?'

'When what?'

'When did you tell him about Hannah?'

'On Thursday night after I'd spoken to Lucie about confronting Phil and Hannah before telling you.'

'You're coming with me,' Abi said, grasping Chloe by the forearm and dragging her up from the kitchen chair.

'Where are we going?' Chloe asked, fear evident in her voice.

'It's too late to go to the police station now. We'll go first thing in the morning, but tonight I'm not letting you out of my sight. I think we'll both be safer if we stick together in my room.'

CHAPTER THIRTY-THREE

8.05 a.m. – Monday

Graham had barely sat down behind his desk with his first coffee of the day when there was a knock at his office door.

'Come in, Eleanor,' he said without looking up.

'How did you know it was me, Guv?'

Does she really need to ask? Graham thought. 'Just a lucky guess. Did you knock off at seven o'clock last night, as instructed?'

'Yes, although it meant I had to come in super-early this morning to finish what I was doing.'

Graham raised his gaze to look questioningly at her.

'Only joking, Guv. I just got in fifteen minutes ago, although I've now finished what I started last night and there's something I think you need to see,' she said.

'What is it, Eleanor?' Graham said, sensing a degree of urgency in her voice.

'I need to show you on my computer. You know I've been going through the multistorey car park footage from the Canal Street entrance looking for any sightings of Dave Etheridge? Well, I decided to extend my search to the exit barrier cameras in case they'd picked him up.'

'And had they?' he asked, following Eleanor through the open-plan office on the way to her desk.

'No, but I spotted something else.'

'Not Hannah?'

'No.'

'Then what, Eleanor?' Graham asked, starting to feel agitated.

Eleanor slid behind her desk and started tapping keys. 'I recognised someone in one of the cars and I thought it was a bit odd seeing him in that location on his own at that time of night.'

'Get to the point, Eleanor.'

'I am,' she said, pulling up a still of a car at the exit barrier of the car park.

Graham peered at the screen. 'That looks a bit like Tim Berwick's car and unless I'm very much mistaken, that's him at the steering wheel.'

'It is his car,' Eleanor confirmed. 'I've already checked it with the DVLA database. And I think we can be fairly confident it's him driving.'

'I can see why you might think it's slightly unusual for him to be out on his own at that time in the morning,' Graham said, noting the time code on the footage, 'but there's no law against it.'

'No, of course not. A dozen or more cars exited the car park in the thirty-minute time frame after Hannah entered it and we're running checks on all of them, but it wasn't just the car park footage that captured my attention.'

'Go on.'

'I've been going back over some of the Velvet interior footage, too, to see if I recognised any of the car drivers as being customers in the club. I'd concentrated mostly on the Lloyd Tennant incident in the VIP area, but when I checked some of the other cameras, I spotted this,' she said, changing the image to one next to a bar on the first floor of the club.

The footage showed a rear view of Hannah engaged in conversation with someone for several minutes. Her body prevented a clear view of the other person until she moved away. Eleanor froze the image on screen... it was Tim. Graham inadvertently sucked in his breath.

'I know, Guv. That was my reaction.'

'The fact that he was talking to Hannah in the club doesn't mean anything, of course. She probably speaks to a hundred or more customers on a good night, but I think it justifies some further investigation,' he said, noticing the pulsing of the vein in his neck that always happened when something in a case concerned him. 'See if you can find any connection between the two of them and report it to me, no matter how tenuous the link may seem. And can you get me Tim Berwick's home address, please?' he said, heading back to his office.

Tim's failure to respond to the text message he'd sent the previous evening asking if Rachel was okay because she wasn't answering her phone hadn't unduly concerned him at the time. *But that's before I knew about Tim chatting to Hannah Longcross in Velvet on the night she died*, Graham thought, pushing his office door open with unnecessary force and causing it to crash against the filing cabinet. *I wonder why he didn't mention that he'd spent several minutes talking to her when the subject of her murder came up at the hospital yesterday morning?*

Graham had rung Tim to tell him that Rachel had been rushed to hospital, and he was waiting in the corridor for him when he arrived twenty minutes later.

'What the hell happened?' Tim had demanded as they stood outside the private room where Rachel was undergoing an examination.

Graham had struggled to find words that wouldn't give anything away about an ongoing investigation. In the end he had simply said, 'There's a possibility we may have found Ruth.'

'Ruth? Is she okay?' Tim had asked, a look of concern on his face.

'I'm sorry, Tim. I can't give you any more information at this stage. Rachel asked me to call you to let you know what happened, but she's pretty adamant that she wants to go back to work with me.'

'We'll see about that. I don't think it's a good idea. She's so bloody fragile at the moment. What's so important that she thinks you can't manage without her?' Tim had asked, sounding exasperated.

'We're in the middle of a murder inquiry.'

'Oh yes, of course, the nightclub girl. I saw it on the news. Terribly sad, she had her whole life ahead of her.'

It would have been the most natural thing in the world for Tim to say how shocked he was that he'd had a conversation with Hannah in Velvet and to comment about his perception of her, Graham thought. *By hiding the fact that he'd spoken to her, Tim had made his behaviour seem suspicious.*

Graham snatched his phone from his desk to check whether Rachel had messaged while he'd been with Eleanor; there was still no word from her. *Relax*, he thought, *it's still early*, but something approaching panic was gnawing away at his stomach. He tried Rachel's number, but it was going straight to voicemail. He reread the text message he'd eventually received from Rachel the previous evening:

Hi Graham, Tim told me you've been trying to get hold of me. Sorry, my phone was off earlier. Tim thought it would be best for us to have a quiet night in front of the TV at his place with no phone interruptions, so I'll be turning mine off again when I've sent this. I just wanted you to know I'm feeling a bit better, although I'm not sure if I'll be up to coming in tomorrow – a few days off might do me good. I'll let you know in the morning.

The surge of relief Graham had immediately felt when he'd seen who the message was from hadn't lasted long. Something about the way it was written hadn't felt very Rachel. Despite the enormous emotional strain she had been under since Ruth's disappearance, Rachel had insisted on returning to the office with him the previous day, such was her commitment to the Hannah Longcross case. It made her comment about taking a few days off seem even more out of character. Graham had been thinking about it all evening, but finally, as he and Rosie were climbing into bed, he realised what else had been bothering him about the message. In the three and a half years he had worked alongside Rachel, she had never started a text message to him with the word 'Hi'. He had broken his own rules of never talking shop with his wife and asked, 'Do you think it's odd that Rachel Hart started a text message to me with the words *Hi Graham*? She's never done that before. It's always just *Graham*.' Yawning, Rosie's answer had been non-committal; she suggested that perhaps Rachel had been confused and thought she was texting her boyfriend. It had satisfied Graham at the time, however that was before he knew that Tim had not only been in Velvet nightclub but also the Bath Street car park on the night that Hannah Longcross died. *Something isn't right. I'm not so sure that Rachel sent that message and, if she didn't, why would Tim want me to think she did?* He decided to text Tim again as he'd had the response, seemingly from Rachel, after messaging him the previous evening.

Sorry to bother you again, Tim. I was just wondering if Rachel is intending to come in to work today. Could one of you let us know one way or the other so I can make alternate plans if necessary? Thanks, Graham.

He was tapping his fingers on the desk waiting impatiently for some kind of response when Eleanor stuck her head round the door.

'Tim Berwick's address, Guv,' she said, crossing the office and handing him a piece of paper. 'Would you like me to go over there?'

Graham's heart was thudding against his ribcage as he glanced down. Marchment Towers was only ten minutes away from the police station by car. *I could drive over there, check on Rachel and be back behind my desk by nine*, he thought. 'That's all right, Eleanor, I'll go myself,' he said, getting up and reaching for his jacket. 'It's not really official police business, just me checking on a colleague. Plus, she still doesn't know the good news that the second body is definitely not her sister Ruth,' he added, striding purposefully across the room as his desk phone started to ring. 'Answer that for me, Eleanor, and call me on the mobile if it's important.'

As Graham headed for the stairs down to the car park, Eleanor scurried across the room and snatched up the receiver, 'DI Wilson's phone.'

'There are two young ladies at the front desk who are anxious to talk to DI Wilson. Is he there?' the desk sergeant said. 'They say it's urgent.'

'He's popped out for a few minutes,' Eleanor replied, remembering what her DI had said about the trip to Tim's flat not being official business. 'Do you have their names?'

'Abi Wyett and Chloe Basset. Should I send them up?'

Eleanor caught her breath. Chloe hadn't been seen by any of her university friends for three days, and at one point during the previous day there had been a possibility that she could be the second body found in the woods. 'I'll come down and collect them and put them in an interview room until DI Wilson gets back.' She debated calling her DI but decided against it. *It won't hurt to have an off-the-record chat with them over a cup of tea if he's a bit longer than expected*, she decided.

Graham was at Marchment Towers for a total of fifteen minutes. There had been no reply when he pressed the buzzer for the penthouse, so he'd tried every other apartment until someone answered and buzzed him in once they knew he was a police officer. He took the lift up to the top floor and rang the doorbell to Tim's apartment several times, but again there was no reply. He got back in the lift and went down to the underground car park. There was no sign of Tim's Jaguar in its allocated parking space.

Graham couldn't pin down why he felt so uneasy about finding nobody home. There was a strong possibility that both Rachel and Tim had already left for their respective jobs. Although Rachel was normally in at 8.00 a.m., perhaps his DCI had allowed herself a short lie-in after the trauma of the day before, particularly as she hadn't texted to say she wouldn't be in. As he walked up the ramp heading for his car, he tried Rachel's mobile again; it went to voicemail. Keeping his voice as neutral as possible, he left her a short message telling her that he had news on the identity of the second body. He deliberately didn't elaborate, knowing that she'd be desperate to find out if it was Ruth, and would call or text if she was in a position to. Then he called PC Drake. She picked up on the second ring.

Dispensing with any pleasantries, he said, 'Is the DCI in yet?'

'No,' Eleanor replied, sounding surprised. 'I thought that's why you'd gone to Tim Berwick's?'

'Neither of them is here. Can you ring Tim Berwick's workplace and find out if he's there, then call me straight back?'

'It's a bit early for lawyers, but I'll give it a try. Are you on your way back?'

'Yes, I'm just leaving now,' he said, opening his car door and lowering himself into the driver's seat.

'Good, because you'll never guess who walked into the police station with Abi Wyett just after you left.'

'I'm not in the mood for guessing games, PC Drake.'

'Sorry, Guv. It's Chloe Basset.'

'Did she give a reason for lying to her boss and causing me to worry her terminally sick mother?' he snapped, swinging his car out of the parking space into the slow-moving stream of traffic.

'I did try to ask her, but she doesn't want to talk to anyone but you. Do you want to put the morning meeting back by thirty minutes so you can speak to them first, or will you just make them wait?'

'Put the meeting back and let the rest of the team know. And get straight back to me with the information on whether Tim Berwick showed up for work this morning,' Graham said, aware not only of the vein throbbing in his neck, but also of how short he had been with Eleanor.

CHAPTER THIRTY-FOUR

9.35 a.m. – Monday

'I'm sorry to have kept you waiting,' Graham said, addressing the gathered officers in the incident room. 'We've got a very busy morning ahead if the first hour of today is anything to go by. There was a fairly major development overnight. We have a positive ID on the second body, and I'm sure you'll all be relieved to hear that it's not DCI Hart's sister.'

Graham allowed the muttering that followed his announcement to die down before he continued. 'The victim is Brenda Diment, and according to Toby Morrison she's a known prostitute who was reported missing five weeks ago. PC Leverette, I'd like you and PC Millership to go to the victim's home to deliver the news.'

'Yes, Guv,' Jackie Leverette responded, making eye contact with her young counterpart.

Both Graham and his DCI had noted Leverette's compassionate manner when dealing with victims' families, and had suggested she might think about choosing the career path of Family Liaison Officer, feeling she was better suited to that type of police work.

'And already this morning we've had another development. I've just finished interviewing Chloe Basset. She came to the police station first thing this morning with her friend Abi Wyett. Far from being a suspect in this case,' he said, wiping her name off the suspect list, 'she was afraid of becoming a victim.'

*

It hadn't taken long for Graham to establish why Chloe Basset had been so elusive over the previous few days. When asked why she hadn't offered her support to Abi following the discovery of Hannah's body, she had simply said, 'I didn't know anything about it. I got on a train to Bath first thing on Friday morning because I was frightened.'

'Frightened of what?' Graham asked.

'More like who. I completely underestimated Dave Etheridge's reaction when I told him about Hannah cheating on her boyfriend,' she said. 'We all knew he was absolutely besotted with her, but it was like a pistol going off in his head. I was really scared waiting for my taxi home because he was standing just inside the front entrance, and I could almost feel his eyes boring into my back like lasers.'

'Did he physically threaten you?' Graham asked.

Chloe cast a sidelong glance at Abi.

'Go on, Chloe. You'd better tell DI Wilson what you told me,' Abi urged.

'He said I should shut my filthy mouth or he'd shut it for me,' Chloe said.

'I'd certainly say that was a threat.'

Graham excused himself from the interview and went straight to Eleanor Drake's desk.

'Finished already?' she'd asked. 'It obviously wasn't that important.'

'On the contrary, Eleanor, it might be very important indeed. I just wondered if you'd managed to go through all the CCTV footage from the area around the Bath Street multistorey between the times Dave Etheridge was visible on the Velvet exterior cameras?'

'I'm just finishing the exit barrier footage now. I broke off to look at the Velvet interior footage when I spotted Tim Berwick in the car park, so I'm a bit behind.'

'And?' he said.

'There were no sightings of Etheridge on those cameras. He might have showed up somewhere on one of the parking levels, but we haven't had that footage yet. Jackie seems to think that maybe the cameras weren't turned on and that's why they've been stalling.'

'So the only images of Etheridge are on the Canal Street cameras?'

'Yes. He entered the stairwell with Hannah and then there are no visuals of him until he exited some eighteen minutes later. The footage shows him holding the door open for her to go in, but he comes out alone.'

'Would you say Hannah looked scared of Etheridge?'

'You must be joking. She looked completely at ease. In fact, she even gave a cheeky little wave to the camera as she went in.'

Graham had swallowed hard at that piece of information. It was the last sighting of Hannah alive: a young woman with an incredible joie de vivre. It had made him want to wrap his own two boys up in cotton wool to protect them from the outside world, but he knew that was no way for anyone to live.

'Why do you ask?'

'Chloe Basset has been in hiding for the past three days, only returning to Reading last night,' Graham said. 'According to her, Etheridge threatened her after she told him about Hannah cheating on Jamie. I just wondered if maybe he broached the subject with Hannah and then lost control if she laughed it off or told him it was none of his business. How did he appear when he exited the car park? Did he look agitated?'

'It's difficult to say because he had his head down, but he did appear to be in a hurry.'

'This new evidence throws a different light on things. Rather than trusting that Etheridge will turn up for his interview at half past eleven, I think DS Green should go to his house and pick him up. I need to get back to Chloe and Abi. Can I leave you to organise that, Eleanor?'

'Chloe's statement points the finger of suspicion in Dave Etheridge's direction,' DI Wilson explained to the team. 'We already knew he was at the car park with Hannah and one of the last people to see her alive, but now it looks like he might have been *the* last person to see her alive because he killed her. Etheridge is due here at 11.30 a.m. for an interview, so hopefully we'll get a clearer picture of what happened in the car park then. That said, we can't afford to rule out any of our other suspects. Current whereabouts of Jamie Bolten, PC Ahmet?'

'He's still in Exeter, but due back late this afternoon,' Ash replied.

'Okay, make sure you keep an eye on him. What about Phil Carter? Have we been able to get in touch with him yet?' Graham asked. When there was no response, he continued, 'He hasn't been seen since turning up uninvited at Abi's yesterday morning and she sent him packing. I checked with her at the end of the interview with Chloe and she confirmed that she hasn't seen him since, and we've no reason to believe otherwise. We need to keep on top of that, please. If we haven't spoken to his rugby teammates already that might be a good avenue to go down. PC Drake, I'll leave that in your hands as a matter of priority.'

'Yes, Guv.'

'Have we had any joy identifying the two girls Lloyd Tennant left Velvet with on Friday night?'

'Yes, Guv,' PC Millership said. 'One of them, Sally Durham,' she said, consulting her notebook, 'was in the club last night. She said she and her friend, Stacy Gold, went to a local hotel with Tennant and he left at around 5.30 a.m. after giving them some cash to pay the bill.'

Graham fleetingly thought of the dead prostitute, Brenda Diment. The only difference between her and the two girls Tennant had taken back to a hotel was motivation. Brenda probably did it to keep food on the table, whereas Sally and Stacy were after another celebrity notch on their bedpost. *I'd stake my life that he left them with more money than just the cost of the room*, he thought, *which basically means they were being paid for sex.* 'Well, that rules him out then,' Graham said, wiping Lloyd's name off the shortening suspect list. 'Has anyone got anything else?' Graham asked, glancing around the room. 'No? Then let's try and solve this case.'

CHAPTER THIRTY-FIVE

'Well, that was a piece of piss,' Jack said, clutching a parcel of his meagre belongings while following his lawyer across the car park. 'If I'd known it'd be that easy, I'd have behaved better years ago. To think of all the time I've wasted in this stinking hole,' he said, turning back to look at the Victorian prison where he had been incarcerated for a huge chunk of his sentence.

'This is it,' Tim said, unlocking the doors of a silver Toyota Prius.

'Bloody hell! I would have thought you lawyer types could have afforded something a bit classier than this. It looks like a bloody tank.'

Tim toyed with the idea of telling Jack his Jaguar was in the garage for a service and the Prius was just a loan vehicle, but he couldn't be bothered to lie. 'It's free transport, Jack. It will get us to where we're going.'

'I suppose,' Jack said ungraciously as he slumped in the front seat of the car. 'How long will it take?'

'It depends on the traffic, but we should be there in a couple of hours. How does it feel to be free?'

'I'll let you know when I actually am free. At the moment I've got you as a babysitter.'

Tim clamped his jaws together. What he wanted to say was, 'you should be grateful' and 'make the most of it', but he said neither as he shifted the gearstick to drive and they silently started moving towards the barrier of the prison car park.

Just under two hours later, Tim pulled into a parking space opposite his house and shook Jack's shoulder to wake him. He'd fallen asleep about ten minutes into the journey, something Tim was immeasurably thankful for as he had been dreading the drive back with Jack's constant sniping and criticism.

'We're here,' he said as Jack stirred.

'It hasn't really changed much, apart from the colour of the front door. We'll have to change that. I hate red.'

Unbelievable, Tim thought. *He's not even properly awake and he's already complaining.* 'I wouldn't worry about it, Jack,' he said, 'it's only paint.' He didn't add that it was irrelevant as Jack wouldn't be seeing much of it. 'Come on, let's get you inside and settled in.'

As the two of them crossed the road, Jack's eyes wandered to the adjoining property. 'Nice neighbours?' he asked with a glint in his eye.

Tim couldn't bring himself to answer, instead concentrating on unlocking the front door then stepping aside to let Jack pass. He locked it behind them and put the bunch of keys in his pocket. He'd made sure that all the doors and windows could only be opened with keys for added security, and he'd removed all the keys from the window locks following the mishap with Rachel. *That's something I can't allow to happen again*, he thought grimly.

'It's a bit bloody different in here,' Jack said, his disapproval evident. 'Where's the door to the kitchen gone?'

'I had it blocked up when I had the extension built to create an open-plan kitchen/family room. Nobody wants poky little kitchens any more. It's the modern way of living, but I don't expect you know too much about that. Times have changed, Jack.'

'Don't treat me like an idiot, boy. I've seen stuff on television, I just didn't expect *my* house to be like it,' he said, opening the door and sticking his head round it. 'Very fancy,' he added, crossing the room to the window. For the first time since he had left the prison, he smiled. 'I see you've kept the apple tree.'

'You asked me to, although I'm not sure why. I'd have thought you'd want to forget what finally got you caught and locked up.'

'Memories, my boy. Happy memories that kept me going all through my time in prison.'

Tim had to turn his back on Jack to stop him from seeing the look of revulsion on his face. *Now I know I've made the right decision*, he thought.

'So, are you going to show me the rest of the house? Then maybe we can go to the pub for lunch? Is The Grapes still on the corner?'

'No.' Tim's one-word response was to all three of Jack's questions.

'What's through there?' Jack asked, indicating a door under the stairs, seemingly oblivious to Tim's cool response. 'Is it still the basement? Can I have a look, for old time's sake?'

Tim pulled the bunch of keys out of his pocket. 'That's exactly what I was going to suggest.'

CHAPTER THIRTY-SIX

Can I get you anything, Guv? A cup of tea, maybe?' PC Eleanor Drake asked.

Graham was about to refuse, but on seeing the genuine look of concern on Eleanor's face he changed his mind. 'Thanks, Eleanor, that would be much appreciated. I'm sorry if I've been a bit short with you this morning.'

'That's okay. It must be difficult picking up the reins on a big case like this and worrying about DCI Hart at the same time. Still no news?'

'No. I'm just going to try her number again,' Graham replied, picking up his phone while Eleanor went to make his tea. It still went straight to voicemail. He was desperate to put Rachel out of her misery and tell her that the second body discovered in the woods wasn't her missing twin sister, but he needed to locate her first. He scrolled through the numbers on his phone and selected the personal number for Colin, his former colleague in the traffic division.

'All right, mate? It's Graham Wilson here.'

'I know, your name came up,' Colin said. 'I haven't deleted you from my contacts just because we no longer work together. What can I do for you? I presume you're after a favour again, that's the only time you ever call.'

'Sorry, mate. Things have been pretty full on lately with my Guv taking some extended leave, and when I'm not at work, I'm trying to keep Rosie and the boys happy. Once I've got this latest case sorted, maybe we could meet up for a beer.'

'Sounds good. So, back to my question: what can I do for you?'

'I'm trying to find the whereabouts of a white Jaguar XF, registration plate RV67MSX. It's pretty urgent, if you get my drift.'

'Okay, let me check it out. I'll get back to you as soon as I can.'

'Thanks, Colin, and I mean it – let's meet up for a beer soon,' Graham reiterated, ending the call as Eleanor Drake appeared in his doorway with a cup of tea in an actual cup and saucer with a chocolate biscuit on the side. 'I hope you're not trying to bribe me when it comes to your recommendation for detective training, Eleanor,' he said, doing his best to keep a straight face.

'Of course not, Guv, I just thought…' Eleanor started saying before realising he was pulling her leg. 'Well, it's good to see you smile. Just to let you know that Dave Etheridge is in interview room one with DS Green when you're ready,' she said, crossing the room and handing him his hot drink.

'He's early. I'll let him stew for a few minutes while I enjoy this in peace,' he said.

Ten minutes later Graham was sat across the interview room table from Dave Etheridge, the bouncer from Velvet nightclub. He nodded his head towards DS Green for him to activate the recording equipment.

'Am I under arrest?' Dave asked.

'Not at the moment. You're being questioned under caution, but your interview is being recorded. For the record, please can you confirm that you've waived your right to have a lawyer present?'

'I don't know any lawyers,' Dave said. 'I've never needed one.'

'We can appoint one for you, if you'd like?'

Dave shook his head. 'No, I just want to get this over with.'

'Good, then let's get started. Can you describe to me the events that took place in the early hours of Saturday morning, after Velvet nightclub closed, specifically any contact you had with Hannah Longcross?'

'Hannah was on her own that night because Abi hadn't come in to work,' Dave explained tentatively. 'I don't like the shot girls leaving the club on their own at the end of the night because they're carrying a fair amount of money in cash. I offered to walk Hannah to her car, which was parked in the multistorey car park at the end of the street, and at first she said no, but then she changed her mind.'

Graham couldn't help thinking that Etheridge's speech sounded rehearsed, as though he knew the police would bring him in for further questioning sooner or later. 'What time was this?'

'I don't know for sure, but it would probably have been around 2.45 a.m.'

Although Graham knew the exact time that Hannah and Dave had walked out of the front entrance of Velvet together because of the club's CCTV footage, he decided to keep it to himself for the time being. 'So, what happened next?' he prompted.

'We walked along Canal Street to the pedestrian entrance and, like I told the police lady, I held the door open for Hannah and we both went inside. She said I didn't need to go up to her car with her as she was parked near the stairs, so I just said good night and went back to the club.'

'You went straight back to the club?' Graham asked.

'Yes.'

'Are you sure about that, Dave, because we have the exterior footage from the car park CCTV cameras that indicates you were inside for a total of eighteen minutes,' Graham said, carefully watching the bouncer for his reaction.

He coloured up and appeared flustered before he started to speak again. 'Erm, well, actually, that's not quite the whole truth,' he admitted. 'I wanted to make sure that Hannah was safe, so I went where I could see the exit barriers. I waited for what seemed like ages and although a few vehicles left, Hannah's wasn't one of them. I was starting to worry, so I went back into the stairwell and up to the first level that I could get out into the parking areas from.'

'That would be level two?' Graham checked for confirmation.

'Yes. Hannah didn't tell me exactly where she'd parked her car, but she said it was near the stairwell exit, so I started looking around for it.'

'Did you call out to her at all?' Graham asked, thinking that would be what he would have done in similar circumstances.

'No. I didn't want Hannah to think I was stalking her.'

'Stalking her? That's a bit extreme, isn't it? You were just showing concern for a friend.'

Dave started to pick at his cuticles. 'She knew I was fond of her,' he said. 'I never made a move on her because she had a boyfriend. And anyway,' he added sadly, 'she was far too good for me.'

Graham felt some sympathy for the man sat opposite him. He had clearly placed Hannah on a pedestal, content to worship her from afar. *But maybe something happened in those few minutes in the car park that changed everything*, Graham thought. 'Did you find Hannah's car?'

'Eventually, yes. I'd been all the way up to the top floor looking on the even level numbers around the stairwell, which is where the girls try to park if there are any spaces because quite often the security cameras aren't working.'

Graham nodded. He knew Dave was telling the truth about the cameras because most of them hadn't been working on the night Hannah died. When the footage had eventually come through, it was only from the two pedestrian entrances and the vehicle exit barriers.

Dave continued, 'I couldn't see it, so I came back down checking the odd level numbers and there it was on the third level, but there was no sign of Hannah. I was going to call out to her then because I was getting increasingly concerned, but I decided against it. For all I knew, she might have been meeting her boyfriend and they could have been in his car or something. Maybe that's why she didn't want me to walk her to her car.'

'And you're absolutely sure you didn't see Hannah again after she left you at the bottom of the stairwell?' Graham said.

'Absolutely certain. You do believe me, don't you?'

'I want to, Dave, but I'm just wondering why you didn't tell DCI Hart this when she interviewed you originally. DS Green was at Velvet when she spoke to all the staff,' Graham said, turning to his colleague. 'Which version of events did Mr Etheridge offer to the DCI, Errol?'

'The first one, where he said he stayed in the stairwell,' Errol replied.

'So, you can see my dilemma, Dave. How do I know you're telling me the truth now?'

Dave shook his head as though at a loss for words.

'Anyway, we'll come back to that in a minute. Can you remember what you and Hannah were talking about as you walked along the street?'

'Not really, probably just general stuff about her evening.'

'Did you mention the incident with Lloyd Tennant?'

'I don't think so. Why would I? It was something and nothing. A good-looking girl like Hannah has to fend off unwanted attention all the time.'

'*Had* to, Dave, in the past tense. Hannah's dead, remember.'

'I don't need to be reminded. I've thought of nothing else since I found out on Saturday. I can't believe it. I keep hoping there's some mistake, even though I know there isn't. It's just so awful,' he added, a big fat tear rolling off the end of his nose and dropping onto his equally well-proportioned hands.

Hands that would have had no trouble in squeezing the life out of someone, Graham thought.

'Here's another suggestion for what you might have been talking about,' Graham said, sensing that Dave's emotional state would more than likely elicit a truthful answer. 'Did you mention what Chloe Basset had revealed to you the previous evening?'

Dave gripped the arms of his chair. 'Of course not. Why would I when I knew Chloe was lying?'

For a brief moment, Graham felt quite sorry for the bouncer and his unconditional love for Hannah. Chloe had been telling the truth, and yet Dave was so blinded by his feelings that he would never accept it. He contemplated telling Dave that Chloe's accusation was true but couldn't see the point in upsetting him further, especially as he was trying to uncover vital information about the last minutes of Hannah's life.

'She's always been jealous of every aspect of Hannah's life, even something as unimportant as me preferring Hannah to her,' Dave said, clenching his fists. 'She's a malicious little liar, and I told her as much.'

'Weren't your actual words, "shut your mouth or I'll shut it for you"? Graham said, referring to his notepad.

'What difference does it make what I said to her? I just wanted her to stop spreading rumours about Hannah. As if she'd look twice at Abi's idiot of a boyfriend,' Dave growled.

My thoughts exactly from having met him and what others have said about him, Graham thought, *but she did, for whatever reason.* 'So, you were absolutely sure that Chloe was lying, and you definitely didn't mention it to Hannah.'

'That's what I said, isn't it?'

'Yes, you did, but as all of us know,' Graham said, indicating the three of them around the table, 'you've already been economical with the truth.' He paused to allow the impact of his words to sink in. 'I'm just wondering if you followed Hannah to her car after plucking up the courage to ask her if she'd been sleeping with Abi's boyfriend. Maybe you didn't like the answer she gave you and you momentarily lost control – a crime of passion, it's sometimes called.'

Dave's jaw dropped open in shock. 'Are you seriously accusing me of killing Hannah?' he asked. 'Not in a million years. I would have killed to protect her, but I would never have harmed a hair on her head and that's the truth,' he said, folding his arms as though to signal the end of his cooperation.

'Well, obviously our investigations still have a long way to go. We may need to bring you back in for further questioning, so I'd request that you don't attempt to leave the country.'

Dave grunted.

'Just before we let you go, are you absolutely sure you didn't see or hear anything in the car park while you were searching for Hannah's car?'

'You didn't ask me that. All your questions were about Hannah.'

Graham was immediately alert. 'Are you saying you did see something?'

'I saw a girl when I was on the sixth level, who I think was in the club earlier. She was clearly drunk and staggering towards the stairwell entrance on the corner of Albemarle Street. Normally I'd have offered to help her, but I was concentrating on trying to find Hannah's car. The girl's all right, isn't she?' Dave asked, his voice full of concern, but Graham had stopped paying attention.

Has anyone looked at that footage yet? he wondered. *Because it was so late coming in, our focus has been on the Canal Street entrance, the one nearest to Velvet.*

'I guess she must have been,' Dave continued when he got no response from DI Wilson, "cos I thought I heard running footsteps a few minutes later, although she must have taken her shoes off because I couldn't hear the click-clacking of her heels against the concrete surface any more. She wouldn't have been able to run if she was as drunk as she appeared,' he said, almost as though he was trying to reassure himself.

Graham was already on his feet. 'Thanks for agreeing to come in for questioning, Mr Etheridge, you've been most helpful. We'll see to it that you get home all right,' he said, hurrying from the room. As he passed PC Drake's desk he said, 'Eleanor, I need to see you in my office now.'

'What is it, Guv?' Eleanor Drake asked moments later as she stood in front of DI Wilson's desk. 'Did Dave Etheridge confess?'

'Far from it, Eleanor. Although he'd lied to us about the amount of time he was in the car park, he gave a reasonable explanation of why he was there. It's what he said as he was about to leave that we need to follow up on. Has anyone been looking at the CCTV footage from the Albemarle Street pedestrian entrance to Bath Street car park?'

'Not yet. I'm going to make a start on it once I've put out a few more feelers for the elusive Mr Carter.'

'Is Jackie Leverette not back yet?'

'No, Guv.'

'Well, as soon as she is, report where you're at with Phil Carter to me and then you get on with the car park footage and Jackie can pursue our missing student.'

'Am I looking for anything in particular?'

'A drunken female, possibly carrying her shoes. Dave Etheridge says he saw one shortly after he escorted Hannah to the car park,' Graham said, in response to Eleanor's raised eyebrows. 'We need to know if she exists both to corroborate his story and to interview, although it's highly unlikely she'll remember anything if she was in half the state Etheridge claims she was.'

'You don't think he's making the girl up to throw us off the scent, do you?' Eleanor asked.

'Maybe, but until we know otherwise, we shouldn't assume he's telling the truth.'

As Eleanor left his office, Graham leaned forward onto his elbows, his head resting in his hands and his DCI's voice filling his mind. 'Don't assume anything in this business, Graham.' Rachel had voiced concerns about Dave Etheridge and his devotion to Hannah, without knowing that Chloe had told him Hannah wasn't the angel he believed her to be. *Did that information trigger him to do something terrible? If only Rachel was here to talk this through,* Graham thought, reaching for his phone to check for messages. There were still none. At that moment Rachel's concerns about Etheridge paled into insignificance compared to his own regarding the whereabouts of his boss.

CHAPTER THIRTY-SEVEN

12.05 p.m. – Monday

Rachel thought she could hear voices. They seemed to be coming from a long way off. At first she wondered if she was dreaming, but as she gradually dragged herself into consciousness, she realised they were real. Her head was pounding and her neck felt tender and sore, reminiscent of when she and Ruth had the mumps as children. *Why does it feel like this now?* she thought. Suddenly, fragments of what had happened the previous evening started to piece together.

Tim, her Tim, the man to whom she had finally said those three little words, 'I love you', had tried to strangle her. *Why would he try to kill me? And why was he so angry that I opened the window?* Then she remembered the apple tree, the same tree she and Ruth had picked fruit from the day they had been abducted. She began to shiver uncontrollably, fearful of opening her eyes. She didn't need to. Instinct told her that she was back in the house where the innocence of her and Ruth's childhood had come to an abrupt end. *Strange*, she thought, *I can almost smell her fragrance, but of course she didn't wear perfume when she was a child.*

The voices were getting louder. Rachel could distinctly hear two men and one of them sounded like Tim. *He tried to kill me. I need to get away from him*, she thought, struggling to sit up. That's when she became aware of the straps across her chest and thighs securing her to the bed on which she was lying. She opened her eyes. It wasn't what she was expecting. She had been visualising the dingy cellar in which she and Ruth had been held captive, but this was a beautifully decorated room. As well as the bed on which she was lying, there was a leather sofa positioned in front of a flat-screen television, beyond which was a small kitchen area. In the other corner was a doorway and she could just make out a shower cubicle. *Where am I? Did Tim drive me somewhere after I blacked out?* Rachel wondered.

The sound of keys jangling was coming from somewhere above her head. She tried to twist around but didn't have enough freedom of movement. Her pulse was racing as she heard a door open followed by footsteps on stone treads. The sound was horribly familiar, even though it had been buried deep in her memory for thirty years. Back then he hadn't bothered to lock the door behind him, but she heard him do so now.

'Who's there?' Rachel called out as a shadow fell across her.

'Don't you remember me?' a gruff voice replied. 'I remember you. It was the thought of getting out and coming to find you that kept me going all those years in prison. I'll never forget my little Ruth.'

Rachel screamed, 'Help! Somebody, help me!'

A hand closed across her mouth. 'Shhh, there's no need for that. Nobody's going to hurt you if you just stay quiet.' Tim knelt down at the side of the bed. 'Trust me, okay?'

Rachel was staring up at the green eyes she had looked into so many times without seeing the family resemblance, but it was clear to her now. Snippets of overheard conversations from the period after their next-door neighbour had been arrested for abducting and sexually assaulting her and Ruth danced around her mind. 'What'll happen to his son?'... 'Do you think the mother will come back for him?'... 'He'll probably have to go into care'... They jostled alongside the version of his childhood that Tim had given her, where he'd said his mother had abandoned him and his father couldn't cope so he'd been brought up in a series of foster homes. She'd felt so sorry for him, but now she wondered if it was all lies.

'If I take my hand away, do you promise not to scream again?' Tim said.

'Yeah, we wouldn't want to disturb the neighbours,' Jack said, chuckling.

It was only a fleeting look of contempt in Tim's eyes, but Rachel spotted it. She had no idea what was about to happen, but of the two men she felt less threatened by Tim. She nodded her head in agreement and he removed his hand.

'Here, let me undo the straps. It was only for your own protection. I had to drug you while I went to fetch Jack from prison. I didn't want you falling and hurting yourself,' Tim said, an unsettling gentleness in his tone.

Rachel lay very still while Tim undid the straps and then slowly sat up, her head spinning slightly.

'You've turned into a beautiful woman, Ruth. I always knew you would,' Jack said, taking a step towards her.

'I'm not Ruth. I'm the other sister, the one you rejected,' Rachel blurted out.

'What's going on here, boy? You promised me Ruth would be here. Have you been lying to me?' Jack said, approaching Tim in a menacing way.

'She was supposed to be here too, but she ran away when I told her my plan. I don't think Ruth trusted me once she figured out who I was. Not surprising, really, after what you did to her,' Tim said, throwing a contemptuous glance in Jack's direction before returning his attention to Rachel. 'It spoiled things a bit, just like when you looked out of the window, Rachel, and saw the apple tree. I wanted to show you the tree in my own time, so that you could finally rid yourself of your awful memories.'

Tim paused, as though waiting for a reaction from Rachel, but she was shocked into silence.

'I've brought him here,' Tim said, nodding his head in Jack's direction, 'to make it up to us: all of us. You weren't the only one he rejected, Rachel. He sent me away to boarding school when you and Ruth were babies and never let me come back home even in the school holidays. I was five years old. That's how I knew how you felt. Rejection is a terrible thing, and he rejected us both, but it's our turn now. We're going to make him pay.'

'You're not making any sense, Tim,' Rachel said.

'No, you're not, boy. You'd better start explaining yourself pretty damn quick.'

'Or else what, Jack? I'm in charge now. This is my house, not yours, bought with money I earned after I made a success of my life. My house, my rules. Get it?'

'Why, you scheming little shit. I'm not taking orders from you. You can keep the house. I'm off.'

'Really, Jack?' Tim said, dangling the bunch of keys just out of his reach. 'And how do you think you're going to get out? Every door and window in this house has a lock on it and I have all the keys. You've exchanged one prison cell for another. This is your home for the rest of your life, locked away from decent people. They deserve better than to have scum like you living in their midst. You know, I started off thinking I was doing the right thing in helping to secure your release from prison. I thought you'd learned your lesson and paid your debt to society. But when I realised I was wrong, I couldn't risk you abusing some other young girl. I knew you'd get out of prison eventually with or without my help, so the next best thing was for me to become your new jailer.'

Jack lunged towards Tim, knocking him off balance, shouting, 'Give me those keys!' Tim responded with an upwards blow to Jack's jaw that sent him flying backwards across the room. He stayed down like a dog licking its wounds after a kicking.

'What was the rest of your plan, Tim?' Rachel ventured. 'The one you shared with Ruth that frightened her enough to make her leave her place of sanctuary?'

'I hadn't planned to tell her that day,' Tim said, sitting beside Rachel on the bed. 'I didn't expect her to see the resemblance to my father as quickly as she did, particularly as you'd never noticed it. But then I guess you were never close enough to look him in the eye because he rejected you just like he rejected me.'

He stroked Rachel's face and she had to fight the desire to pull away from him.

'I knew Ruth would piece together who I was eventually, so over lunch I told her that Jack, my father and her abuser, was up for parole and would most likely be released. He'd always told me he would go looking for Ruth if he ever got out,' Tim said, scowling at Jack, who hadn't moved from his position on the floor. 'When I told her that, she got really scared even though I promised her that I had a plan to keep you both safe. I told her I'd bought his old house for us all to live in, but he would be locked away in the basement so we would always know where he was and we wouldn't have to live in fear of him and what he might do.'

Rachel was incredulous. *How could Tim ever believe in his wildest dreams that Ruth and I would agree to live under the same roof as his father, even if he was locked up?* She could completely understand why Ruth had been spooked and run away, but it had obviously surprised Tim that she wanted no part of his weird plan. *I need to play this carefully,* she thought. *At the moment I'm as much of a prisoner as Jack is.*

'So why did Ruth run away?' she asked, feigning surprise.

'I honestly don't know. I thought she trusted me, but maybe she was just pretending to. I don't know if she dropped her phone accidentally or if she did it deliberately so that the police couldn't trace it. Whatever happened,' he said, shrugging his shoulders, 'I found it outside Mountview. I sent the text message pretending to be her so that you wouldn't feel rejected again.'

Rachel stifled a gasp. 'So all this time I was holding onto the belief that Ruth cared enough about me to send that message, and now you're saying it wasn't her? Don't you think that's a bit cruel?'

'Cruel?' Tim said, confusion in his voice. 'I was trying to protect you.'

'By lying to me? I don't know if I believe a word of this. If you repeatedly lied to me about who sent the text message, how do I know you're not lying to me now? For all I know you could have brought Ruth here because she wouldn't go along with your plan and was threatening to tell me all about it. Oh my God,' Rachel said as though a veil had lifted from her eyes. 'Is that what happened? Did you strangle my sister like you tried to strangle me? That body in the morgue is Ruth, isn't it? Tell me the truth,' she shrieked, raising her fists and pummelling them into his chest.

'It's not Ruth. I swear it's not. Everything happened exactly as I've told you. You know I would never do anything to hurt you, Rachel. I love you, for God's sake,' Tim said, taking hold of Rachel's wrists and looking deep into her eyes.

The relief she felt was short-lived as Tim continued. 'When Ruth disappeared and made no attempt to contact you, I began to wonder if she'd come up with a plan of her own, one that involved revenge. I couldn't allow that to happen,' Tim said, shaking his head. 'I grant you, Jack's not much of a father but he's the only one I've got. I had to be prepared to deal with her if she showed up and tried to hurt him.'

'What do you mean, *deal* with her?' Rachel said, her heart pounding against her ribcage.

Tim frowned. 'I couldn't let her ruin everything I've worked so hard for. One of your clever colleagues might have come up with some theory connecting me to her death.'

Rachel felt the blood draining from her face. 'So she *is* dead. You have killed her.'

Tim dropped to his knees in front of Rachel. 'You're not listening,' he said patiently. 'You're letting your emotions get the better of you. I said I had to be prepared to kill her *if* it became necessary. I had to set up a cover story that wouldn't link me to her death. That's when I came up with the idea of a serial killer,' Tim said, a smug expression on his face. 'The dead woman in the morgue is a hooker. You and your team were supposed to find her weeks ago, but obviously I hid her body too well, so I had to give you a clue.'

Rachel started to shake even before she realised the full enormity of his words. Tim, her kind, considerate boyfriend, had killed an innocent woman as part of some warped plan to protect himself should it become necessary to kill her sister Ruth. Then, almost in slow motion, the final part of his sentence sank in. *Oh my God, he's talking about Hannah Longcross*, she thought. 'What kind of monster are you?' she demanded before she could stop herself. 'Hannah was only twenty years old. She had her whole life ahead of her.'

'I didn't kill Hannah,' Tim said with a look of surprise on his face, 'how could you believe that of me? I liked her when we chatted in Velvet, and she was telling me about her Everest attempt. I admire women with drive and determination. In fact, she reminded me a bit of you.'

Rachel fought back the bile that was rising in her throat. *What was Tim doing in Velvet?* 'Then what did you mean about giving us a clue? Did you kill Hannah and string her up so that we couldn't fail to see her, knowing it would lead us to discover the other body?'

'Now you're thinking like a DCI. That's exactly what I did, apart from the killing bit.'

'What do you mean?'

'I'd been in the club in search of my next victim. I was looking for someone who was falling down drunk, not hard to find in nightclubs these days. Honestly, girls should have more thought for their safety before allowing themselves to get in such a state,' Tim said, a look of distaste on his face. 'I'd walked a girl back to my car and she was just about to get in when we heard shouting. It sobered the girl up pretty damn quickly, and she said I should go and see if someone needed help. That's when I found Hannah Longcross. She was lying dead at the side of her car. For all I knew, someone had already called your lot and I didn't want to get involved, so I went back up to the sixth floor where I was parked only to find the girl had done a runner. I was annoyed at first,' he said, irritation obvious in his voice, 'until I realised fate had been kind to me.'

Rachel was feeling queasy. *How could Tim be so nonchalant about finding a young girl dead?* It made her skin crawl to hear him speak about it in that way.

'I just took advantage of the situation,' he continued. 'Actually, I was quite relieved that I wasn't going to have to commit another murder. The look in that prostitute's eyes as I squeezed the life out of her gave me nightmares for days. Do you remember that patch where I couldn't sleep?'

'Yes,' Rachel murmured, trying desperately to control the shaking that was threatening to engulf her entire body. She had been sympathetic at the time, offering Tim lavender pillow spray and camomile tea… how inadequate those natural remedies seemed now that she knew the reason for his insomnia.

'Well, that was why. I'm so glad I only had to kill once, well, unless Ruth proves troublesome, of course.'

His tone of voice is so matter-of-fact, Rachel thought. *He's talking to me about murdering my sister as though he's asking me what I want for dinner.* Memories of all the dinner dates they had shared and the previous evening where she had felt so close to him that she had told him she loved him were making her feel nauseous.

Tim continued, apparently oblivious to the distress he was causing, 'I drove my car down to the third floor, loaded Hannah's body into the boot and drove out to the woods, it was as easy as that. Mind you, it's a good thing she had a slight build or I'd have struggled to haul her up into that tree, what with her being a dead weight, excuse the pun,' Tim said, flashing Rachel the goofy smile that she had become so accustomed to when he cracked one of his lame jokes.

Before she could respond, Jack, who had been lying quite still on the floor, rushed across the room and launched himself at Tim's back. There was a sickening sound as heads collided and Rachel fell back onto the pillow with Tim spreadeagled across her.

CHAPTER THIRTY-EIGHT

12.25 p.m. – Monday

'It seems Phil Carter went on a bit of a bender on Sunday, Guv,' PC Drake said. She was in DI Wilson's office bringing him up to speed with what little information she had gleaned from Phil's rugby teammates. 'Apparently, he was very drunk when he left The Monkey's Forehead at around nine thirty, as in only just able to walk.'

'That's the pub on the river, not far from the university, isn't it?' Graham asked.

'Yes. A lot of the students drink there, so much so that the locals give it a wide berth,' Eleanor said with an expression of distaste.

'Did he leave alone?'

Before she could answer, Graham's phone began to ring. Glancing down at the screen, he could see it was his friend Colin from the traffic division.

'I'm sorry, Eleanor, I need to take this,' he said. 'Colin, thanks for getting back to me so quickly. Have you got any information on the Jag?'

'Indeed I have, it was picked up by CCTV cameras earlier this morning turning into a private lane off Grove Street after being parked on the roadside overnight. We don't have CCTV coverage of the lane, but it's a dead end that leads to a row of garages that are probably allocated to the properties on Grove Street, as they have no private parking.'

'So, it looks like he was just moving his car to a more secure parking place. I don't suppose the cameras saw which house he went into after he'd moved it, did they?'

'Well, that's the thing, nobody came out of the lane on foot, but a few minutes after the Jag turned in, a grey Toyota Prius pulled out. I think your Jaguar driver parked up in one of the garages and changed vehicle for whatever reason. A bit of a downgrade, if you ask me.'

Why would Tim do that? Graham wondered. *Perhaps he was trying to keep his whereabouts secret by keeping his vehicle out of sight. And what was he doing on Grove Street when he lives twenty minutes away in Marchment Towers?* A thought struck Graham. *What if Tim and Rachel had rowed the previous evening and she'd gone back to her house in Sonning? Maybe he'd been cheating on her with whoever lived in the house on Grove Street. That would explain why she wasn't at Tim's when I called around earlier; maybe she was so upset that she forgot to text to say she wouldn't be in.*

'Hold on a minute, Colin,' Graham said, putting his hand over the mouthpiece. 'Eleanor, can you try DCI Hart's home number, and if there's no reply get someone in the area to go and knock on her door.' In answer to Eleanor's puzzled expression he added, 'Maybe she wasn't feeling well and went back to hers, which would explain why she wasn't at Tim's. Sorry about that, Colin,' he said as Eleanor left his office, 'you were saying?'

'I thought you might be interested to know where the Prius was going, so we tracked it with the cameras. It drove out to Randlesham Prison and was there for just under an hour before returning to Grove Street.'

'Is it still there?'

'Yes, parked outside number 42, although the occupants crossed over the road and went into number 37.'

'Hang on, did you say occupants, plural?' Graham asked.

'Yes. It looks like the driver picked up an inmate who was being released.'

'Interesting,' Graham replied, making a note on his pad to check if any prisoners had been released from Randlesham Prison that morning. 'Thanks so much for this, Colin. I really appreciate you going the extra mile. We'll definitely have that beer soon, and I'll be buying,' he said, replacing the receiver as Eleanor reappeared in his office doorway.

'The DCI didn't pick up her home phone, Guv. I tried three times, but it went straight to answerphone. PC Harman was the closest to Sonning, so he's heading to her home now. I told him to persevere if she didn't answer straight away.'

'You know, I may just drive there myself. I know where she keeps her spare key and, in the circumstances, I think it's appropriate to let myself in and check that she's okay. Have we finished all the stuff you've got on Phil Carter?'

'Yes, Guv. None of his friends has seen him since he left the pub last night.'

'Good work, Eleanor. Can you make a start on the Albemarle Street CCTV now? Oh, and could you also check the names of any prisoners released from Randlesham Prison today?' Graham asked, hurriedly pulling his jacket off the back of his chair and picking up his car keys. 'Hopefully I won't be too long. Is everything all right, Jackie?'

PC Leverette was standing in the doorway to Graham's office, her face as white as a sheet.

'I've just taken a 999 call put through from the emergency services requesting a team to go to a house on Grove Street in response to a suspected kidnap. The caller claimed to be Ruth Hart, and she alleged that DCI Hart is the kidnap victim.'

CHAPTER THIRTY-NINE

12.59 p.m. – Monday

Jack only had a matter of seconds to try and make good his escape before his son regained consciousness following the clash of heads with Rachel Hart. He wrenched the keys out of Tim's back pocket and hurried over to the stone steps leading up to the main part of the house. He kept checking over his shoulder as he tried the different keys before eventually finding the right one. He turned it in the lock and yanked the door towards him. A brilliant flash dazzled him; it caused him to take a step backwards and almost lose his footing on the smooth stone of the top step. As he regained his balance, Jack realised the flash was daylight glinting off the blade of a knife. 'What the hell are you doing here?' he said to the woman blocking his path to freedom.

Confronted with her abuser, Ruth Hart was struggling to keep control of her emotions. She had spent the previous weeks trying to imagine how this moment would feel, but nothing could have prepared her for the rush of revulsion coursing through her body. The steeliness in her voice when she spoke belied the fragility she felt. 'You're not going anywhere, Jack. You may have served your time in prison, but you'll never fully pay for what you did to me and my sister and all those other young girls you abused.'

A slow smile spread across Jack's face. 'You haven't aged as well as your sister, and you smell a bit, but I still would,' he leered. 'Why don't you put that knife down? You know you don't really want to hurt me, Ruthie. I was your first, so I'll always have a special place in your heart, just as you have in mine,' he said in a thin and whiny voice, casting another anxious glance over his shoulder.

Ruth could barely believe what she was hearing. *How can he possibly think I feel anything for him but loathing?* 'You disgusting pervert,' she said, kicking out at Jack, her foot making contact with his groin. He doubled over in pain and staggered back down the staircase, collapsing in a heap at the bottom. She turned to close and lock the cellar door before following him down the steps. Jack was still writhing in agony on the floor, and Tim was hauling himself into an upright position on the bed next to where Rachel lay prone.

'Is she all right?' Ruth asked, resisting the urge to rush over to her sister. 'I'll kill you both if you've done anything to her.'

'Ruth,' Tim said, rubbing his forehead. 'What are you doing here?'

'I'm rescuing my sister from a psychopath. Move away from her, Tim, and take him with you,' Ruth said, indicating Jack with her foot. 'I won't hesitate in using this if you don't do as I say,' she added, sounding braver than she felt and making small jabbing movements in his direction with the chef's knife she had taken from the kitchen drawer minutes earlier. 'Go and sit on the floor against the far wall with your backs against it.'

Tim rose gingerly from the bed and lifted Jack by the elbow, helping him across to the other side of the room. 'He's not a psychopath, Ruth, he's a paedophile.'

'I wasn't talking about him,' Ruth said, edging towards her sister while still holding the knife and never taking her eyes off the two men. 'He's a pervert but you're the crazy one, Tim. Crazy to think that Rachel and I would agree to live in the house where we were held prisoner and abused as children, no matter how beautifully you'd done it up, with the man who took us prisoner living in the basement. It was never going to work and, deep down, I think you knew it. Is that why you brought Rachel here with a blindfold over her eyes?' she said, perching on the edge of the bed to check Rachel's wrist for a pulse before gently stroking the hair back off her forehead.

'You've been spying on me,' Tim said in an accusatory tone.

'I suppose you could call it that. It wasn't that difficult. After all, I knew where the house was, we used to live next door,' Ruth said, a shiver running down her spine.

'But why?'

'Once you'd told me your crazy plan and given me the idea of how I could escape from Mountview by passing myself off as my sister, I had to disappear so that I could keep a very close eye on you. I knew Rachel wouldn't accept your plan either, and I was afraid of what you might do to her when she told you as much.'

'Then why didn't you just tell her what I was planning instead of running away from Mountview?' Tim asked. 'You've caused my love so much unnecessary heartache.'

Ruth flinched on hearing Tim refer to Rachel as his 'love'. 'It broke my heart, but it had to be this way because of him,' she said, directing the point of the knife at Jack. 'In some ways I could see the logic of what you were trying to do. You wanted to keep Rachel and me safe from *him* once he was released, but she would never have agreed to what you were proposing. If I'd told Rachel your crazy idea, Jack would still have been allowed to go free because you coached him on what to say to the parole board to secure his release. He would have been out in the community, and my sister and I would have forever been looking over our shoulders, unable to live a normal life. *We* would have become the prisoners, trapped by the fear that he would come looking for us again. I couldn't let that happen. So I had to be patient. I had to wait and watch and come up with a plan of my own.'

'What plan? What's she talking about, Tim?' Jack said.

'How should I know?' Tim replied. 'I'm not a bloody mind reader.'

'You don't need to be one to work out that she's got something not very pleasant in mind for me. What are you planning, you little bitch?' he demanded, turning his attention back to Ruth. 'I preferred you as a five-year-old when you were too scared to fight back.'

Ruth swallowed hard. 'You really have no understanding or remorse for what you did, do you, Jack? You forced yourself on a terrified child,' she said, referring to herself in the third person to remove herself from the acute pain of the memory. Despite her effort to remain emotionally detached, tears were coursing down Ruth's cheeks. 'I can't let you do that to another young girl, Jack. I'd never be able to live with that on my conscience.'

'Ruth?' Rachel said groggily. 'Ruth, is it really you?'

'Yes, it's me. Thank God you're okay,' Ruth said, relief flooding through her. 'Try and sit up,' she urged, still keeping her eyes firmly fixed on the two men against the far wall.

'Where have you been, Ruth?' Rachel asked, struggling into an upright position. 'I've been so worried about you.'

'I know, and I'm so sorry for causing you all that pain, but I had to leave Mountview so that I could keep watch on your boyfriend once I knew what he was planning. I didn't know what he might be capable of if you chose not to go along with it, and I was pretty sure you would refuse.'

'He's capable of murder,' Rachel said, her voice trembling.

Ruth gasped. 'What? Who?'

'A prostitute. She was randomly selected to start building the case that there was a serial killer at large in the event that he had to kill you. You shouldn't have come here – you've put yourself in danger.'

'I had no choice. Tim told me he was certain Jack's parole appeal would be accepted. He's an animal, Rachel, we both know that, and yet the law can't protect us from him because in their eyes he's paid his dues. I've got no life anyway, thanks to him,' she said, again waving the knife towards Jack, 'so it's best for everybody if I kill him and go to prison for it. After all, it will just be a less luxurious version of Mountview, and you won't have to pay an extortionate amount of money to keep me there.'

'Don't say that, Ruthie. I was trying to do what I thought was best for you. You can come and live with me when this is all over. We'll work it out somehow,' Rachel implored.

'But it won't be over, will it?' Ruth said. 'Tim will go to prison for murdering the prostitute, but the paedo will still be free.'

'She's right, my boy. You'll be sent down for killing that tart. You should never have admitted it to your piece of skirt. Rookie error,' Jack said, shaking his head. 'Trust me, you don't want to go to prison, you'd never survive it. You're not made of the same stuff as me. Come on, we can easily overpower these girls.'

'I thought you loved me, Rachel,' Tim said, appearing to ignore Jack. 'I did all of this for you… for us. I wanted to make you feel loved and needed instead of the rejection we both suffered at his hands. We can still be happy, just the two of us, if we get rid of them.'

Rachel shook her head. 'No, Tim, the killing has to stop. I loved the person I thought you were, not the murderer of innocent women.'

'Woman!' he shouted. 'Singular! I told you the girl was already dead. Don't try and pin that on me as well, just so that smart DCI Rachel Hart can say she solved Hannah Longcross's murder.'

It was like a switch had flicked in Tim's demeanour and Jack grasped the opportunity. 'She's been using you, boy,' he said, his voice low and persuasive. 'They both have, just to get at me. I think they've been scheming together all along, and you played right into their treacherous hands. Let's rush them and get out of here.'

Tim was staring at Rachel almost as if he were in a trance, a confused look on his face. Ruth was fairly sure Jack was right. The two men acting together would easily overpower the sisters. *I can't let that happen*, she thought, *I can't*. Her heart was trying to escape the confines of her chest and her right hand, still tightly gripping the knife, was shaking. She tried not to think about the physical feeling of plunging the blade into Jack's chest. There would be blood on her hands in more ways than one, but it was something she had to do. Without warning she rushed forward, relying on the element of surprise to counterbalance Jack's superior strength.

It took a split second for Rachel to realise Ruth's intention. *I can't let her do it*, she thought, *I can't risk losing her all over again*. Rachel had thought she was imagining things on hearing Ruth's voice as she started to come round after the clash of heads with Tim. She could hardly believe her eyes when she saw her sister, who she had feared dead, sitting by her side stroking her forehead in a reversal of the roles they had held as children locked up in that same basement. The overwhelming feeling of relief she had experienced on seeing her sister alive was quickly replaced by fear when Jack made his remark about overpowering the two of them. There would only be one opportunity for the element of surprise to work, but Rachel couldn't allow her sister to take it. She couldn't let her sister become a killer; there had to be another way.

'Nooo!' Rachel shrieked. 'Don't do it, Ruth, he's not worth it.'

The cry distracted Ruth. She tripped, the knife falling from her tenuous grip and landing at Tim's feet. He reached to pick it up.

'Well done, boy, that's more like it,' Jack said, still wincing with pain from Ruth's well-aimed kick earlier as he scrambled to his feet. 'Now who's calling the shots?' he said, towering over her as she started to back away. 'Let's tie them up and slit their throats. I don't want anything more to do with either of these bitches.'

Tim didn't move.

'What are you waiting for, boy?' Jack demanded. 'Don't go soft on me now. It's not as though you haven't killed before, is it?' Tim still didn't move, so Jack softened his tone. 'Look, lad, they're the only witnesses to your confession of killing that prostitute. With them out of the way we'll be free to go our separate ways, if that's what you want.'

'Don't trust him, Tim,' Rachel said, her police negotiating skills eventually kicking in. 'Even if you kill Ruth and me, Jack will know what you did. He'll always have that hold over you, the threat of handing you in to the police if you don't do what he wants. In your heart you know he's a vile human being, or why would you have wanted to keep him locked up down here?'

Tim's gaze flicked from Rachel to Jack.

'Kill her first,' Jack ordered. 'She was always the less appealing one.'

Ruth had shuffled her way backwards across the floor and was clinging to Rachel's legs. 'I'm sorry I messed it up.'

'I'm not,' Rachel said, gently stroking the hair back off Ruth's face as she had done every time her twin sister had been returned to the basement after Jack had pleasured himself. 'You thought you wanted to kill Jack for what he did to us, but then he'd be winning. He'd have succeeded in turning you into someone who could commit a terrible crime. Trust me, Ruthie, it wouldn't have given you the closure you were seeking,' she added, cupping her sister's upturned face in her hands and looking deep into her eyes. 'If this is the end for us, at least we'll go together, the same way we came into the world.'

'Very touching,' Jack snarled. 'Give me the damn knife if you're too much of a coward to do it,' he said, trying to goad Tim into action.

'I'm so sorry, Rachel, it wasn't meant to happen like this. I really do love you,' Tim said, plunging the knife deep into flesh.

CHAPTER FORTY

1.15 p.m. – Monday

The midday traffic in central Reading had been heavier than usual, and DI Wilson could feel the pulsing of the vein in his neck as they tried to force their way through it with blue lights flashing. Within five minutes of receiving the information from PC Leverette that DCI Hart was the victim of a kidnap, Graham had four vehicles on their way to the Grove Street address where she was allegedly being held. All were under strict instructions not to have their sirens wailing, so as not to alert the kidnapper and force them into any desperate action. Eventually, DS Green was able to speed up as they moved further away from the town centre, throwing the car around corners and running red lights.

The woman who had made the 999 call, claiming to be Rachel Hart's missing sister, said she would be inside the property herself and would leave the front door unlocked for the police to gain access. There was no further information to go on, but Graham suspected he knew who the perpetrator was; it was the motive he didn't understand.

DS Green pulled the car to a screeching halt outside number 37 and Graham jumped out and directed one of the three approaching vehicles to reverse back and block one end of Grove Street, while sending another car to block the far end.

'Is everybody wearing their stab vests?' he queried as the officers gathered outside the smartest-looking house on the street.

'Yes, Guv,' came the chorused reply.

'Right, let's get in there,' Graham said, approaching the front door which had been left ajar. He held his finger up to his lips to signal that they should keep as quiet as possible and stepped inside. Indicating for the other two officers to head upstairs, he and Errol Green started checking the ground floor. He pushed the door to the front room open, waited for a moment and then entered with Errol close behind him. The room was empty and, despite the circumstances, Graham couldn't help but be impressed by the way it looked. The two of them made their way along the hallway leading towards another door. Flattening his back against the wall, Errol used his foot to open the door into an open-plan kitchen and family room that also looked as though it had come straight from the pages of an interiors magazine. They checked the large space thoroughly; again, it was empty, but Graham spotted that the door leading outside was open. Silently signalling Errol, they moved quickly towards it and out into the garden where there was an imposing, blossom-laden apple tree. A quick glance was all that was needed to ascertain that no one was there either, so they headed back inside as their colleagues were descending the stairs.

'There's no one up there, Guv,' PC Harman whispered, 'although there are some women's clothes on the bed in the front room.'

'Wait here and keep your eyes open,' Graham said, taking the stairs two at a time, fearing what he might find. It was the jacket that gave it away. Not usually one for noticing what his female detective colleagues wore to work, he'd remarked on the light blue jacket Rachel had worn into the office the previous day because his wife Rosie had a similar one. Graham's mouth felt dry and the pulsing vein on his neck went into overdrive. *If Rachel's clothes are here*, he thought, *where the hell is she?*

'Guv,' he heard Errol's voice call softly up the stairs, 'there's another door off the hallway and it's locked. It might lead down to a cellar.'

Leaving Rachel's clothes where they were for the forensic team to examine later, should it become necessary, Graham was halfway down the stairs when muffled screaming cut through the silence. There was the sound of wood splintering as, without waiting to be told, Errol raised his foot and kicked the door in. The hysterical screaming became instantly louder, but it was the words that terrified Graham as he rushed headlong down the stone steps.

'Stop screaming and help me, Ruth,' a woman's voice shouted; a voice he immediately recognised as belonging to Rachel Hart.

The scene that greeted DI Wilson and the other police officers at the bottom of the stone staircase leading to the basement was like something from a horror film. A man was lying on his back with multiple stab wounds to his chest and neck, and another man, who Graham thought might be Tim Berwick, was lying across him crying huge, racking sobs. DCI Rachel Hart, wearing only a white towelling robe splattered with bright red, was standing over the two men holding a knife dripping with blood. Ruth Hart was curled into a foetal position, clinging to one of Rachel's legs.

'Graham,' Rachel said, her shoulders slumping forward, the knife she had been holding in an attacking position falling down by her side, 'thank God you're here.'

'What the hell happened, Rachel?' he asked, pulling the cuff of his shirt down over his hand so that he could remove the weapon from her without compromising any forensic evidence.

'I don't know, it all happened so fast. Tim had the knife and I thought he was going to kill me and then suddenly he turned on his father and started driving it into his chest. It was horrific.'

'Hey, take it easy,' Graham said. 'It's over now. Are either of you hurt?'

'No,' Rachel said, shaking her head, 'not physically, anyway.'

'Okay. Errol,' he said, turning to his shocked-looking sergeant, 'we need an ambulance, and you'd better give Toby Morrison a call to get a team down here.' Returning his attention to Rachel, he said, 'I think we need to get you out of here. Are you all right to walk, Ruth?' he asked, dropping to his haunches to offer her support.

'Thank you for coming,' Ruth said, looking up into Graham's kind brown eyes. 'I was so scared you were going to be too late after I dropped the knife.'

Graham looked up at Rachel questioningly.

'I'm not really sure how Ruth got into the house or how she appeared holding a knife; I'm just glad she did, or my life might have ended down here,' Rachel said, the merest hint of a tremor in her voice.

'Your very clever boyfriend isn't as smart as he thinks he is,' Ruth said.

Tim's sobbing had subsided and he raised his head to fix Ruth with a stare.

She glared back at him, seeming to gain strength from his confrontational look. 'While he was decorating the upstairs rooms, he used to leave his keys on the kitchen worktop, presumably thinking no one could force their way through the overgrown jungle that was the back garden. It was worth the scratches from the brambles to take them and have duplicates cut so that I'd be able to get into the house whenever I wanted. It was risky, but I figured he would have assumed it was an opportunist burglar if I couldn't get them back in time.'

'I should have killed you when I had the chance. You've always been the spanner in the works. I wanted Rachel, not you, but I couldn't have one of you without the other. Now look what you've made me do, you evil bitch,' Tim said, getting to his feet and starting to move towards Ruth, 'you've made me kill my own father.'

Two burly policemen stepped in to block his path and restrain him.

'Come on, Ruth,' Rachel said, lifting her sister to her feet with Graham's help, 'we need to get you away from here.' As they reached the bottom of the steps, Rachel turned back to look at Tim, her emotions swinging between pity and loathing. 'Ruth's right, you're not as smart as you think you are. You've said far too much without your lawyer present. You've just confessed to murder.'

Graham watched as the police car carrying the two Hart sisters pulled away from the kerb heading for the police station. He knew they should have been travelling in different vehicles to avoid compromising their witness statements, but Ruth had become hysterical at the suggestion that she should be separated from her sister. Graham had agreed that Ruth and Rachel could travel together if PC Harman sat between them and noted down any conversation. Rachel was still wearing the bloodied towelling robe, so he had offered to drop by her house and pick up some clean clothes. Her keys were in her handbag, which she had left at Tim's flat, but he knew where she kept her spare key in case she ever locked herself out. 'You'll have to find a new place for it now, Guv,' he'd said, and was rewarded with a weak smile and the words, 'I think I can trust you, Graham.' He was about to start his car when his phone began to ring. It was PC Drake.

'Errol let us all know that the DCI is safe. How's she doing?'

Graham could hear the concern in Eleanor's voice. 'She and her sister are both a bit shaken, but otherwise fine, thankfully.'

'That's a relief. As requested, I did a bit of digging on the prisoner who was released into Tim Berwick's care this morning. His name's Jack Duggan, and you'll never believe this – he was convicted of abducting the DCI and her twin sister thirty years ago, Guv. Did you know about it?'

'Yes, I did. It's not something DCI Hart wanted to be common knowledge, so I'd appreciate it if you could keep this piece of information to yourself for now.'

'Of course. But I was thinking, it can't just be a coincidence. Do you think the kidnap was planned as some kind of payback for getting him sent down, and that Tim Berwick deliberately got to know DCI Hart so that he could help this prisoner for some reason?'

'Your instincts are pretty good, Eleanor. The one vital connection you're missing is that Jack Duggan was Tim Berwick's father.' He heard the gasp on the other end of the phone. 'We'll get a fuller picture once the DCI and her sister have given statements, but for the moment let's try and avoid office gossip by keeping this between the two of us.'

'Of course, Guv. Are you on your way back?'

'Via DCI Hart's home in Sonning. I volunteered to pick up some clothes for her as the ones she was wearing yesterday are part of a crime scene investigation. I'll see you in about an hour.'

CHAPTER FORTY-ONE

2.45 p.m. – Monday

By the time Graham arrived back at the police station with a change of clothes for his DCI, Ruth Hart was already in the process of giving her witness statement to DS Errol Green and PC Jackie Leverette. Rachel had not been permitted to sit in the room, despite her sister's pleas, but when she'd explained that it could compromise Tim's conviction, Ruth had reluctantly agreed to do the interview on her own. She'd begun in a faltering way, explaining the reason for her disappearance and that she had been watching the house belonging to Tim Berwick where he'd previously told her he planned to keep his father as a prisoner in the basement. She admitted to taking the knife from the kitchen drawer and threatening Jack with it. Ruth had closed her eyes when she recounted the frenzied attack Tim had made on his father. She said she remembered screaming repeatedly moments before the door was kicked in. Because she had stuck to the basic facts, the interview was over in twenty minutes, after which Jackie Leverette took her to the cafeteria to get her a cup of tea away from all the police activity.

Rachel had quickly showered and changed into the fresh clothes Graham had brought from her house. Looking at herself in the mirror of the women's washrooms, she permitted herself a smile. *Graham might be an excellent policeman, but he has absolutely no fashion sense*, she thought, observing the coral shirt he'd selected to go with a pair of royal-blue trousers that had been an impulse buy she had regretted. The label with the price tag might have been a clue that it wasn't a favourite from her wardrobe, but clearly Graham hadn't noticed. Leopard-print kitten heels completed the look, with Bridget Jones-style pants and her TV-watching bra as undergarments. Graham had blushed slightly as he'd handed everything over, and Rachel couldn't help thinking that he probably wished he'd sent a female officer to her house instead of volunteering to go himself. Graham had asked Rachel to join him in the incident room when she was changed, and as she pushed the door open, every officer got to their feet and applauded. She could feel the prickle of tears at the back of her eyes, but she refused to succumb to them.

'Carry on, Graham,' she said, starting to take a seat at the back of the room.

'I'm sorry, Guv, but you need to go and give your statement and then make sure your sister is okay. I can handle things here and bring you up to speed in the morning.'

Rachel was about to protest before realising the futility of it. 'Yes, boss,' she said instead, a smile on her face. As she walked along the corridor to the interview room she thought, *it's good to see Graham taking control, even though that might mean I'll lose him as my second in command before too long.*

Once the door had closed behind Rachel, Graham got straight down to business, letting the rest of the team know that Tim Berwick had not only admitted killing the prostitute, Brenda Diment, but was also responsible for removing Hannah Longcross's body from the Bath Street car park, claiming she was already dead when he found her.

'He strung Hannah's body up in the tree because he wanted it and Brenda's body to be discovered so we would think we had a serial killer on our hands.'

'Why did he want us to think that?' Eleanor Drake asked.

Graham shot her a warning look. 'Let's just say he wanted to cover his tracks if it became necessary to commit another murder. It will all become clear once we've charged Tim Berwick. The point is, he's adamant that when he came across Hannah at the side of her car she was already dead. If that's true, and Berwick would have no reason to lie about it, having already confessed to murder, it means her killer is still at large. That is where we need to focus our attention so we can bring whoever did kill Hannah to justice.' He turned to the whiteboard. 'As it stands, we have three main suspects: Dave Etheridge, Jamie Bolten and Phil Carter. Have you got any further with tracing Carter, Eleanor?'

'No, Guv. I did a quick ring around of the friends he was drinking with yesterday before I came into the meeting, but nobody's seen him at all today.'

'Keep plugging away at it. He can't just have disappeared into thin air.'

'Will do. I've also made a start on the Albemarle Street entrance footage. I should have finished going through it by the end of the day, so we'll be able to confirm Dave Etheridge's account of events.'

'Which leaves us with Jamie Bolten,' Graham said, indicating his name on the board. 'What time is he due here for his interview, Ash?'

'He was supposed to be coming in at 4.00 p.m., but he called to say the band's van has broken down and he's still in Exeter. I checked, and he is. He asked if it would be all right to come in the morning instead. I couldn't very well say no.'

'If he makes any more excuses, we'll send a car to fetch him.'

'Yes, Guv.'

Graham stopped by PC Drake's desk on his way out of the building. It was half past five, and for once he decided to finish on time.

'How's it going, Eleanor? Are you almost done?'

'I was just about to drop by your office. Part of Etheridge's story checks out, the bit about the very drunk female clubber. She staggers out of the exit, but she's still wearing her high-heeled shoes. I ran the footage on a bit and a couple of minutes later another figure pushes past her, almost knocking her over.'

'Male or female?'

'It's hard to say, Guv. I've run it several times, but they're wearing jeans and a hoodie that's completely obscuring their face. The only distinctive thing about them is the bright green trainers. Wasn't Hannah wearing green trainers when she was discovered?'

'Yes, she was.'

'A bit of a coincidence, wouldn't you say?'

'I'm not sure I believe in coincidences,' Graham said, fleetingly wondering if perhaps Hannah and her boyfriend had matching trainers. 'Get the footage over to the techie boys to see if they can enhance the image at all. And when you've done that, you're to go home,' he said, heading for the stairs.

CHAPTER FORTY-TWO

5.35 p.m. – Monday

Abi and Chloe had spent the afternoon in the garden of The Monkey's Forehead. The girls hadn't had breakfast before going to the police station, and so had decided to go for brunch at a nearby cafe after their interview had finished. Brunch had stretched almost to lunchtime. As they were waiting for their bill, Abi had asked Chloe why she hadn't told any of the group about her mum's illness. Shrugging her shoulders, Chloe had said, 'I didn't think any of you liked me enough to care. Even Lucie's been a bit off with me since I started at Velvet.' Abi had assured her that she did care, and said if she wanted to talk things through about her mum's cancer, her door was always open. 'Can we talk now?' Chloe had asked. 'I don't have any brothers or sisters, and this has been a huge burden to carry on my own.'

'Of course,' Abi had said, 'why don't we head down to The Monkey and sit outside? We could both do with the fresh air.'

It was a beautifully warm spring day, and after ordering a cider each Abi and Chloe carried them out to one of the wooden trestle tables overlooking the river. They sat in companionable silence watching the swirl of the current as it meandered past, until Chloe started to speak.

'I know you're fragile yourself after what happened with Hannah, so I really appreciate you taking the time to listen to what's going on with Mum.'

'It's the least I can do, Chloe, and to be honest you're doing me a favour because I hate being on my own at the moment.'

'When I found out back in November that Mum's cancer had spread to her bones, I was devastated. She'd battled breast cancer so bravely and it seemed liked all the chemo was working, but the sad fact is it doesn't work for everybody, and she's one of the unlucky ones.' A tear trickled down Chloe's cheek as she spoke.

Abi reached into her pocket for a tissue and silently handed it over.

Chloe gave Abi a watery smile and dabbed at her tears. 'I couldn't believe it when Mum's consultant gave her a best-case prognosis of six to nine months, and I still can't get my head around the fact that she's dying. She's been my world since my dad walked out on us when I was little. I just want her to make it to Graduation Day,' Chloe continued.

Abi reached her hand out and placed it on top of Chloe's, giving it a gentle squeeze.

'I'm the first person in my entire family to go to university, and Mum was so proud of me when I got a place here. She said she'd die happy when she's seen the photographs of me throwing my mortar board into the air,' she added, biting her lip.

'She'll make it, Chloe. She wants it so badly she'll hang on.'

'Do you really think so? You're not just saying it because you think it's what I want to hear?'

'You hear of things like that all the time. You know, I wish you'd felt able to share this with us,' Abi said. 'We'd have all rallied around to help.'

'Well, you and Lucie might have. I'm not so sure about Hannah, though.'

'I know you and Hannah weren't exactly best pals, but she might have been a bit kinder to you if she'd known that you took the job at Velvet to be able to pay for private carers for your mum.'

'I'm not sure I agree with you on that. I think Hannah and I were too different to ever really get on. She came from a place of privilege – her perfect life was handed to her on a plate, while I had an uphill struggle to try and make something of my life.'

'It wasn't all perfect, you know,' Abi said quietly. 'Yes, her parents are wealthy, but I don't think her home life was particularly happy. She was jealous of her mum's good looks, I think.'

'Don't be ridiculous. She was drop-dead gorgeous herself.'

Abi flinched, but Chloe seemed oblivious to the insensitivity of her remark.

'Hannah had self-esteem issues. That's why she was always striving to be the best at everything. I think she also felt guilty for the breakdown of her parents' marriage. For some reason she seemed to think it was her fault.'

'It's funny, you think you'd know someone quite well after living with them for three years, and yet she hardly told me anything about her home life.'

'Look who's talking,' Abi said. 'On the subject of which, it might be a good idea to tell Lucie what's going on with your mum. After all, you two have known each other since primary school. She might be a bit upset that you've told me and not her. You could do it when we get back, if she's in,' Abi said. 'We probably should be making a move anyway.'

'It's a big ask, I know, but would you come in with me?'

Abi hesitated. 'Don't you think maybe you should tell Lucie on your own? It'll be easier for you to talk about it now you've told me.'

'I suppose you're right,' Chloe said, frowning.

'Look, once you've told her, why don't we all grab dinner together later? Like I said earlier, I'm not a fan of my own company at the moment.'

'I'll suggest it to Lucie,' Chloe said as the two of them got up off the wooden bench seats and headed for the bridge to cross the river, 'but I'm definitely up for it.'

CHAPTER FORTY-THREE

Rachel hadn't slept well, despite feeling exhausted from the drama of the past twenty-four hours. When she'd returned home the previous evening after making sure Ruth was settled back into her room at Mountview Hospital, she had gone upstairs intending to go straight to bed. She'd opened the door to her bedroom but had found herself unable to set foot in the room where she and Tim had been so intimate. She'd stood frozen in the doorway, the tears she had been holding back while staying strong for her sister now streaming down her face. Images of herself with Tim, the man she had allowed herself to fall in love with, had filled her mind and the physical pain in her chest felt as though her heart was breaking. Not trusting herself to walk, she'd sunk to the floor and sat hugging her knees while she rocked gently backwards and forwards until she felt she had no more tears left to cry. Shortly before midnight, she'd hauled herself to her feet before crawling under the duvet of the bed in the spare room, fully clothed, and falling into a restless sleep.

The light filtering through the flimsy curtains woke Rachel shortly after 5 a.m. Drained from her outpouring of emotion the previous night, she lay on her back staring up at the ceiling, trying to process what had happened. *Was the initial meeting with Tim coincidental?* she wondered. He'd been assigned to defend a woman in a case Rachel was investigating, but had he volunteered to represent the suspect in order to get close to her? Rachel turned it over and over in her mind for the best part of two hours before finally realising that she would never really know the true answer. The only person who knew for sure was Tim. Once she'd reached that conclusion, it was like a weight had lifted from her. The sadness and feelings of betrayal were still there, but she could do nothing to change what had happened.

Rachel knew from past experience that the best way for her to move forward from unhappiness was to bury herself in her work, and there was still plenty to do to bring Hannah Longcross's killer to justice. She pushed back the duvet and stripped off her clothes from the day before, then forced herself to walk through her own bedroom to her en suite shower where all her toiletries were.

Fifteen minutes later, she selected an outfit from her wardrobe and made her way downstairs to prepare breakfast, having realised while she was showering that she hadn't eaten since the chilli con carne at Tim's on Sunday evening. *How my world has changed since then*, she thought, running some warm water into the sink to rinse her plate and coffee mug. *But Ruth is back safe and well, and that is the most important thing.*

Despite taking her time with a leisurely shower and cooking eggs for breakfast rather than just toast, Rachel was still ready to leave by eight. She was walking out of her front door when her phone started to ring.

'I know I'm already five minutes late, Graham,' she said, her phone precariously balanced between her shoulder and her jaw while she locked the door, 'but I would have thought you could have cut me some slack in the circumstances.'

'I would have, Guv, but we've just taken a call about another dead body and it's in your neck of the woods. If you haven't left yet, I thought you might want to drop by the crime scene.'

Rachel was instantly in work mode. 'You thought right. What's the exact location?'

'The riverbank, just upstream from the bridge. A man walking his dog this morning was alerted when the animal started barking at something and went to investigate. He called it in at about 6.30 a.m.'

'It will only take me a few minutes to get there on foot. Knowing the village, there's probably already traffic backed up to the High Street.'

'While you're walking, I might as well bring you up to speed on a development in the Hannah Longcross case that happened after you left yesterday afternoon.'

'Go for it,' Rachel said, setting off at a brisk pace.

The area next to the riverbank in Sonning where the body had washed up was already cordoned off when Rachel arrived five minutes later. A tent had been erected to prevent onlookers and the news crews who were already on the scene from seeing the body. She dipped under the tape, showing her ID card, and strode over to the tent where Toby Morrison and his team were kitted out in protective clothing.

'No closer, DCI Hart,' he said, 'unless you want to get yourself a set of these.'

'It's all right, Toby. I need to get to the station, but I live in the area, so I thought I'd drop in on my way to see what you've got.'

'It's another strangulation, judging by the marks on the neck,' Toby said, 'although it's impossible to say at this stage whether the victim died from that or drowning.'

'So, a similar MO to Hannah Longcross. Do you think they're linked? Perhaps we have got a serial killer on our hands after all.'

'Maybe, but it's quite unusual for a serial killer to target different sexes. They normally pick one or the other and stick with it.'

'Hold on, so you're saying our latest victim is male?'

'Yes, sorry, I should have said straight away. Of course, I never take anything for granted when it comes to identification from items a victim is carrying, my methods are much more accurate,' he said, smiling. 'But if the contents of his wallet are to be believed, this chap is one Philip Carter and he's a university student.'

That would explain why Eleanor Drake wasn't able to locate him, Rachel thought. 'Any idea how long he's been dead?'

'Impossible to say with any accuracy at this early stage, but I'd guess at less than twenty-four hours. I'll be able to let you know more when I get him on my table.'

Rachel was just turning away when something lying next to the body caught her eye. At first glance, it appeared to be a shoe covered in mud and weeds from the river. 'What's that?' she asked, pointing at it.

'One of his trainers. This one was hanging off his foot and the other must have washed away completely. I think that's how he was spotted, actually. A dog walker saw the flash of bright green when he came down here to try and find out what his dog was barking at. Not a very pleasant discovery first thing on a Tuesday morning, or any morning for that matter.'

Rachel had stopped listening. Graham had just been telling her about the shadowy figure from the car park who they were currently trying to identify; the person had been wearing green trainers. *Is it possible that Phil Carter is our mystery figure, and was responsible for killing Hannah?* she wondered. *But if that's the case, who murdered Phil?*

Rachel pushed her way through the gathering crowd and headed towards the small car park where she had left her car. As she walked, she dialled her DI's number. He picked up on the second ring.

'You're never going to believe this, Graham, but everything points towards the body fished out of the river being Phil Carter.'

'You're joking.'

'You know me better than that. It's not the sort of thing I'd joke about.'

'Is it suicide? Did he throw himself in?'

'No. He was strangled in a similar manner to Hannah Longcross, from what Toby can tell at this early stage. And there's something else: he could well be our mystery figure from the car park.'

'What makes you say that, Guv?'

'He was wearing green trainers, well, one green trainer to be precise, one of them had washed away in the river.'

'Shit! If he hadn't been strangled, I'd have guessed at him accidentally killing Hannah and then feeling so overcome with remorse that he chucked himself in the Thames, but that can't be what happened. What are you thinking, Guv?'

'I'm thinking perhaps someone saw him kill Hannah and make a run for it. Maybe this is punishment for what he did? We know Dave Etheridge was in the car park, and we also know he held Phil in very low regard.'

'Or Etheridge might have killed them both,' Graham said. 'Hannah's death could have been accidental, but he wanted to punish Phil for being the cause of the accident.'

'Who else might want to punish both Hannah and Phil?' Rachel asked, unlocking her car and climbing into the driving seat.

'The wronged parties – Jamie and Abi,' Graham replied.

'Exactly, but Abi didn't know about the affair until after Hannah's death, which brings us back to Jamie Bolten,' Rachel said. 'Do we know where he is?'

'Hold on a second, Guv, while I check with Ash.' Moments later Graham was back on the line. 'It looks like he's at the university, close to Abi's building.'

'Then I think we should pay Mr Bolten a visit and ask him what he's doing there,' Rachel said, backing out of the parking space and turning in the opposite direction to the traffic jam by the bridge. 'My satnav is saying twenty-five minutes. I'll meet you there.'

CHAPTER FORTY-FOUR

Abi knocked on Lucie's door and waited for her to answer. Lucie had been terribly upset the previous day when Chloe, her friend since childhood, had stopped by to tell her the dreadful news about her mum's terminal cancer, but she was utterly devastated that Chloe had chosen to confide in Abi rather than her. Chloe had invited Lucie to have dinner with them, but she had refused, saying she had other plans.

'She'll get over it eventually,' Chloe had said as she and Abi shared a takeaway pizza in her room. That was when Abi had come up with the idea of taking Lucie out for breakfast the next morning to try and smooth things over. Chloe was drying her hair when Abi had knocked, so Abi volunteered to go down to Lucie's room and wave the olive branch.

'Oh, it's you,' Lucie said when she opened the door. 'Is your new best friend with you?'

'Don't be like that, Lucie. Chloe only told me about her mum first because we'd been at the police station together. I think she was feeling emotional and it all just came pouring out. I'm sorry if it caused friction between you, but you're her best friend and you always will be. Friends?' Abi asked, holding her arms out for a hug.

Lucie waited a moment before leaning towards Abi and allowing her arms to wrap around her, but she didn't return the hug.

'It's just, I would have thought she would come to me with something as huge as this, after all, we've known each other most of our lives, but I'm not one to hold grudges,' Lucie said. 'Do you want to come in, and I'll make us a cup of tea or something? Mint or ordinary?'

'Just ordinary, thanks,' Abi said, deciding to wait until Chloe arrived before mentioning going out for breakfast. *It might be better if the idea seems to come from her*, Abi thought, kicking her shoes off and climbing onto Lucie's bed. She leaned back against the headboard and closed her eyes. 'It's pretty shocking about Chloe's mum, isn't it? It makes me want to call mine, but she's on holiday somewhere in the depths of the Welsh countryside with my dad and the mobile signal is so bad, they don't even bother to have their phones switched on most of the time.'

'Mrs Basset has had a hard life,' Lucie said. 'She didn't deserve this. Still, at least she may never have to hear about how Chloe disgraced her family by working as a shot girl.'

Abi's eyes snapped open. 'That's a bit harsh, Lucie. She was only doing it so that she could afford a private carer for her mum. And you forget, I've been working as a shot girl, too.'

'Yes, but I forgive *you*, because you were conned into it by Hannah. You were just being a supportive friend, whereas both she and Chloe did it willingly for the money,' Lucie said, turning her nose up in distaste. 'It's not much better than being a hooker, really.'

Alarm bells were ringing in Abi's head. Lucie was behaving very strangely. *What does she mean, she forgives me?* she wondered, accepting the mug of tea Lucie was handing to her. 'I'm not sure I like this topic of conversation, can we change it?'

'That's the trouble with you, Abi. You stick your head in the sand even when the truth is staring you in the face. Take the situation with Phil and Hannah. You would never in your wildest dreams have thought that they deserved to be punished – you're far too nice for that. In fact, I'll bet you even considered giving Phil yet another chance.'

Abi felt her cheeks colouring up. To try and disguise it, she dropped her head and took a sip of tea.

'I'm right, aren't I? But he didn't deserve another chance. Neither of them did. They messed up, so they had to face the consequences.'

Abi was starting to feel really uncomfortable. She'd always liked Lucie, but something about the way she was talking had a menacing edge to it.

A slow smile spread across Lucie's face. 'I take it you haven't seen the breaking news? A man's body washed up on the riverbank in Sonning earlier. He must have fallen in, or maybe he jumped or maybe he was pushed... I guess we'll never know.'

'That's awful. Have they identified the body?' Abi asked.

'Who cares?' Lucie said, shrugging her shoulders. 'Whoever it is got no more than they deserved.'

Abi shivered. She was almost too afraid to ask her next question. 'Is – is it Phil?' she whispered, unable to keep the fear from her voice. 'It is, isn't it? What have you done, Lucie?'

'He was responsible for Hannah's death. He couldn't be allowed to get away with that. And now you're free of him, Abi. You can go home to Telford for a fresh start and forget about Phil and the whole degrading shot girl episode. Your secret's safe with me.'

Abi was shaking so violently that the tea she had been sipping moments earlier was slopping over the rim of the mug and onto the thin fabric of her dress. She was aware of it but couldn't feel the heat of it against her skin.

'Be careful, you're spilling your tea,' Lucie said, reaching for the mug, but Abi's grip on the handle was tight. 'Let go of it,' she ordered.

I need to get out of here, Abi thought, *and I might only get one chance*. She jerked her hand upwards and the hot tea flew through the air, almost in slow motion, into Lucie's face. She staggered backwards, allowing Abi a moment to squirm beneath her and make a dash for the door. In her haste, Abi knocked against the table and dislodged Lucie's pot of pens, which spilled its contents onto the floor; her bare foot made contact with a set of keys, making her cry out in pain. She glanced down to the offending keys and her heart missed a beat. They were on a distinctive mountain boot key ring: the same key ring Abi had bought for Hannah when she had first announced her intention to climb Mount Everest.

'You should have just given me the mug,' Lucie said, an icy edge to her voice. She regained her balance and moved swiftly across the room to pin Abi against the wall. Lucie's eyes were as black as coal, the pupils fully dilated as Abi looked into them.

'W-why have you got Hannah's keys?' Abi stammered.

'I think you know,' Lucie said as her thumbs caressed Abi's throat. 'I suppose you want to know why she died?'

Abi could feel hot tears pricking the backs of her eyes. She said nothing.

'Hannah was so full of herself that night in the car park. I'd gone there to ask her why she'd betrayed your friendship by sleeping with Phil. She laughed in my face. Your precious Hannah laughed in my face and said, "If she'd kept him satisfied in the bedroom he wouldn't have needed to turn to me. Just keep your nose out of things you don't understand". She started to unlock her car door, then turned back to face me. "Have you ever actually had sex, Lucie?" she asked. How bloody dare she take that attitude with me just because I'm not some tart that sleeps around?' Lucie said, barely controlling her anger and slowly increasing the pressure on Abi's neck. 'I might have spared her if she hadn't said that.'

Tears were streaming down Abi's cheeks. She was trying to take in air through her nose as her windpipe was being gradually crushed. She knew Chloe was on her way, but would she arrive in time? *I just have to stay alive until she knocks at the door*, she thought. *Please don't be too long, Chloe.* With a tremendous effort

Abi managed to force out the words, 'But why take Hannah's keys? And why hide them in your room rather than dumping them somewhere?'

'And risk the police finding her keys with my DNA on them? You must think I'm stupid. The bitch scratched me with them as I was squeezing the life out of her,' Lucie said, releasing her grip with her left hand and touching an angry scratch on her right arm.

It was the chance Abi needed. With an almighty effort she twisted her head away from Lucie's right hand, causing her grip to slacken and screamed, 'Help me!'

CHAPTER FORTY-FIVE

9.15 a.m. – Tuesday

Rachel sped towards the university campus, blue lights flashing and, unusually for her, the radio tuned to a music station on full volume. She needed to keep her mind clear from thinking about Tim, and concentrating on listening to lyrics was helping. Her music was so loud she almost missed a call from Toby Morrison.

'Have you got a moment, DCI Hart?' he asked.

'Fire away, Toby. Have you got a positive ID on the body? Is it definitely Philip Carter?'

'It's early days for that, I'm afraid, but I have found something interesting about the body I thought you should know straight away. I was doing some preliminary measurements, his feet to be precise, and discovered something a bit odd. He's a size seven.'

Rachel threw her Audi around a corner, tyres squealing against tarmac, waiting for Toby to explain the relevance. *Granted it's quite a small shoe size for a man*, she thought, *but I'm not sure it warrants a phone call.*

'And?' she prompted.

'Oh, right, well, it's the trainer, you see,' Toby continued. 'No wonder one got lost in the water and the one we have was hanging off his foot. It's a size nine. Why would someone be wearing trainers two sizes too big for them?'

'Why indeed,' Rachel echoed, 'unless they weren't actually his trainers, but someone wanted us to think they were.'

'My thoughts exactly,' Toby said.

'Thanks for ringing that through, it could turn out to be crucial information. Let me know as soon as you have a positive ID,' she said, ending the call and immediately ringing PC Drake back at the station.

'Morning, Eleanor.'

'Morning, Guv. It's good to have you back on the case. Are you feeling a bit better today?'

Rachel bit her lip to prevent an emotional response to her young PC's comment. 'Graham told me about the mystery figure you spotted when you were going through the Albemarle Street CCTV footage after I left yesterday. Have you been able to determine who it is yet?'

'Unfortunately not. I've viewed it with the techie boys, and despite their best efforts the person clearly didn't want their face to be seen. They were able to establish that the figure is tall, probably about 5 ft 11 in, and had fairly large feet, which kind of suggests a male.'

'Size nine,' Rachel said.

'I'm sorry, Guv, they weren't that precise.'

'It wasn't a question, Eleanor. Green trainers aren't that common, but the body that washed up on the riverbank, who we're assuming is Philip Carter, was wearing one green trainer and it was a size nine. The thing is, the body has size seven feet, so they probably weren't his shoes.'

'So someone deliberately put the shoes on Phil Carter's feet to make it look as though he was the person in the car park and to point the finger of blame at him for Hannah's death. Are you thinking it's Dave Etheridge?' Eleanor asked.

'That was my initial thought, but for some reason my gut's telling me it's not him.'

'Well, if it's not him and Phil Carter is dead, there's only one other suspect left on our list: Jamie Bolten.'

'Precisely. We know he's a tough cookie after being chucked out of the force for violent conduct, and he knew both of our victims, so getting close enough to them to strangle them wouldn't be a problem. And let's face it, he had more reason for wanting them both dead than anyone else. DI Wilson and I are meeting at the university because that's where Ash says Bolten is.'

'Do you need back-up, Guv?'

'We won't know until we get there. Ring me if there's a break-through on our mystery figure from the car park,' Rachel said, ending the call and bringing her car to a screeching halt moments before Graham parked his car beside her.

They climbed out of their cars in tandem and ran in the direction of Bowater House. Although the door was meant to be on a security buzzer, someone had propped it open with the fire extinguisher.

'You'd think the students would be more vigilant about security after what happened to Hannah,' Graham remarked as they rushed inside.

'It's young people,' Rachel responded, 'they seem to think they're invincible.'

They headed up the stairs to the first floor and immediately became aware of loud knocking. At the far end of the corridor they could see Jamie Bolten outside Abi's door.

'Move away from the door, Jamie!' Rachel shouted, running along the corridor towards him with Graham in hot pursuit.

Jamie turned in their direction, a look of confusion on his face. 'What's wrong?' he asked. 'I've just come to see if Abi's okay. I heard on the news about Phil's body washing up on the riverbank. After all she's been through these past couple of days, she shouldn't be alone when she finds out.'

'How do you know it's Phil?' Rachel asked. 'We haven't had a confirmed identification yet.'

'The female presenter on the radio was interviewing the man who found the body. He'd looked in the corpse's wallet for ID before he reported the incident to the police,' Jamie said.

We'll need to check that, Rachel thought. *He could just be bluffing because he's realised that he's made a big mistake in knowing that Phil is dead.*

'You're supposed to be at the police station this morning for your interview, Jamie,' Graham said. 'Did you forget?'

'No. I was going to come once I'd checked on Abi. Like I said, I thought she should have someone with her, and you guys didn't seem to be in that much of a hurry to interview me.'

'Well, we're quite keen to interview you now, if you wouldn't mind accompanying us to the station,' Graham said.

'Okay. I've got nothing to hide, but what about Abi? The fact remains that she shouldn't be alone when she finds out about Phil.'

'Did you try either of her friends' rooms when you couldn't get a reply from her?' Rachel asked.

'No, I was about to when you turned up.'

'Let's try Chloe first,' Graham said, 'her room is only a few doors down.'

Keeping Jamie between them, they walked along the corridor and knocked on Chloe's door. A few moments later, she answered.

'Hello,' Chloe said, her expression turning from surprise to concern as she recognised Jamie first and then the policeman she had spoken to the previous day with Abi. 'Is something wrong?'

Before either of the police officers could speak, Jamie said, 'Have you seen Abi this morning?'

'Yes, about ten minutes ago. We're taking Lucie out for breakfast, but I needed to finish drying my hair first, so Abi went on ahead. Why do you ask?'

Jamie looked at Rachel before saying, 'I take it you haven't seen the news this morning?'

Chloe shook her head.

'Phil's body washed up on the riverbank in Sonning this morning,' he said.

Chloe gasped.

'It's believed to be Phil's body,' Rachel corrected, glaring at Jamie. 'We're still awaiting positive identification.'

'Oh my God, I need to get to Abi,' Chloe said, rummaging in her cupboard and pulling out the first pair of shoes she laid hands on. Rachel and Graham exchanged a look as she did up the laces of the green trainers.

'Aren't they the same trainers Hannah had?' Rachel asked.

'What?' Chloe asked, looking down, seeming to notice what she was putting on her feet for the first time. 'Oh, yes. We all had the same trainers from when we went to a fancy-dress party as the Teenage Mutant Ninja Turtles, but I don't wear mine much, they're a bit bright for me.'

'When you say "all", who exactly do you mean?' Rachel demanded.

'Me, Abi, Hannah and Lucie. I was Donatello, the purple one,' Chloe said, dropping her gaze momentarily so she could fasten her other shoe. When she looked up, Jamie and the police officers were already halfway down the corridor at a run. Chloe got to her feet and set off after them; as she reached the top of the stairs a voice screamed, 'HELP ME!'

There was the sound of wood splintering as Jamie's shoulder made contact with Lucie's door and it crashed inwards.

'Stay back, Jamie, this is police business,' Rachel ordered.

'What the hell is going on?' Jamie said, looking into the room to see Abi collapsed on the floor with a startled-looking Lucie towering over her.

'Cuff her, Graham,' Rachel said, indicating Lucie, 'while I call an ambulance.'

'Let me past,' Jamie said, 'I'm a trained first-aider. Let me take a look, it could save her life.'

'Oh my God, Lucie,' Chloe said as she arrived in the doorway, 'what have you done?'

CHAPTER FORTY-SIX

Rachel stood a short distance away from the friends and family gathered at Hannah's graveside. She had wanted to attend the funeral to pay her final respects to a young woman she had never known in life but who she had come to know through the tragic circumstances of her death. The last thing she wanted was for her presence to upset anyone, particularly Hannah's parents, who were standing next to each other but were not touching. *How sad to see the two people who created such a beautiful, driven human being unable to put aside their differences even to mourn her passing.* Instead of being supported by her ex-husband, Miranda was leaning heavily on Anoushka, who had her arm around her friend's shoulders. *At least Rupert was considerate and didn't bring his girlfriend*, Rachel thought. *That just wouldn't have been right.*

Rachel had arrived at the small village church of St Peter's half an hour before the service was due to start and had made herself as inconspicuous as possible by taking a seat on the end of the back pew furthest from the aisle. She had wanted to spend a few quiet minutes in reflection before the church started to fill up. She was acutely aware that, but for Tim's last-minute change of heart, this could have been a different church with her friends and police colleagues gathering to mourn the death of their DCI and her sister. The shiver that ran through her body could not only be attributed to the cool interior of the church. She was still finding it hard to believe that Tim was so psychologically disturbed after his experiences as a young child that he thought it excused the terrible things he had done.

It was the second funeral in as many days that Rachel had attended.

Brenda Diment had been cremated the previous day, following a church service with fewer than a dozen people in attendance. Rachel had felt compelled to be there, reasoning that if it hadn't been for Tim's warped plan, the woman would still be alive. It had been a sombre occasion with everyone dressed in black, in contrast to the people who were beginning to crowd into St Peter's. Not one person wore black, and Rachel couldn't help thinking it was exactly what Hannah would have wanted. Everything about Hannah had been vibrant and colourful, not least her dress sense, which made it even more difficult to accept that her life had been cut tragically short by someone who had misguidedly thought they were doing the right thing.

Lucie had made no attempt to run from the scene; in fact, she'd seemed almost surprised to see Abi collapsed at her feet when the door to her room had been forced open and the two plain-clothes police officers had rushed in. It wasn't until Chloe had blurted out, 'Lucie, what have you done?' that she had seemed to emerge from a trance-like state.

'Why are you all in my room?' she'd asked. Graham had pulled her hands behind her back and applied the handcuffs before walking her out of the room into the corridor to give Jamie more space to attend to Abi. Rachel had noticed him flinch at the sight of the cuffs, before he bent over Abi's limp body, trying to detect a pulse.

'You're not to blame, Jamie,' she'd said quietly. 'It isn't your fault that Hannah needed something different from your relationship than you did.'

Without raising his gaze to meet Rachel's, he'd replied, 'I disagree. I should have been strong enough to let her go, no matter how much I loved her, when I realised I couldn't give her what she wanted. If I had, none of this would have happened.'

Jamie had sat next to Abi during the ceremony that celebrated the life of a bright and popular young woman rather than dwelling on the tragedy of her death. He was still at her side at the graveside as the polished-wood coffin was being lowered into the ground.

The breeze carried Miranda's noisy sobs in Rachel's direction. For a moment, Rachel visualised her own mother standing beside an open grave with two child-sized coffins waiting to be laid to rest. She shivered, pulling her lightweight mustard-coloured jacket closer around her. Her and Ruth's nightmare was finally over, but Miranda Longcross's was just beginning. Rachel dropped her chin forward as the final prayer was said and then watched as Hannah's university friends and work colleagues from Velvet each dropped single yellow roses into the yawning hole, among them Dave Etheridge, who looked utterly devastated. Rachel turned away and started to walk back to her car, but was stopped in her tracks by someone calling her name. She turned back to see Abi approaching with Chloe and Jamie close behind.

'I just wanted to thank you,' Abi said. 'If you hadn't been at the university that morning, I wouldn't be here now.'

Although it was true, Rachel felt a pang of guilt for not having considered that Lucie could have been responsible for the killings. It was pure luck that they had been in the right place at the right time.

'I can't take the credit for that, I'm afraid. It's Jamie you should be thanking,' Rachel said, nodding in his direction. 'If he hadn't gone to the university to check that you were all right after hearing about Phil's death on the radio, we wouldn't have been there. Not only that, but the paramedic team said he saved your life with the mouth-to-mouth resuscitation he gave you.' *From prime suspect to hero*, Rachel reflected. *Who'd have thought it?*

Abi blushed.

'I only did what anyone would have done in the circumstances,' Jamie said. 'I guess it's just lucky that I had to be first-aid trained to work with the Maguires. Speaking of which, I'm going to have to make a move, I'm afraid.'

'Are you not coming back to Hannah's house?' Abi asked, disappointment obvious in her voice.

'I can't. The Maguires are very needy, if you get my drift. They've got a gig in Southampton tonight, and it was all I could do to get the morning off. Stay in touch, Abi, and let me know if you girls ever want any concert tickets,' Jamie said, heading off down the path towards the church car park.

'I can't believe I was ever scared of him,' Abi said, her gaze following him as he walked away. 'Now that I've got to know him a bit better, I can see why Hannah liked him so much. He's a really caring person.'

'Lucky for you that he is,' Rachel said, reminding Abi of her earlier remark, 'or we might not be standing here having this conversation.'

'What will happen to Lucie?' Abi asked.

'She'll have to have a psychological assessment before we'll know how to proceed with the case,' Rachel said. 'In fact, I need to get back to the office to process the paperwork.'

'Aren't you coming back to Hannah's house either?' Abi asked.

'No, I don't think it's appropriate. Look after yourselves, girls.'

As Rachel walked away, she couldn't help thinking that although her sister Ruth was the one who had been incarcerated for years with mental health issues, it was impossible to know what was going on inside anyone's mind.

CHAPTER FORTY-SEVEN

Rachel loaded the breakfast things onto a wooden tray to carry upstairs to her bedroom. Despite Ruth's protestations, Rachel had insisted that her sister should have her room because it had an en suite bathroom, saying it would make it feel more like her room at Mountview. That was only part of the reason: Rachel had been unable to sleep in the bed that she had shared with Tim since the day she had found out who his father was. *No amount of fresh linen will ever make that bed feel clean enough for me*, she thought, climbing the stairs.

'Hey, wake up, sleepyhead,' Rachel said, gently tapping on the door of her bedroom before pushing it open with her free hand. In the other she was carefully balancing the tray with coffee and a plate of hot buttered toast. She stopped abruptly. The bed was empty. She experienced a mild flutter of panic before she heard the toilet flush and Ruth emerged from the en suite looking as though she had just woken up.

'Morning,' Ruth said, the croakiness of sleep not quite cleared from her voice. 'Is that for me?' she asked, indicating the tray. 'I could get used to this.'

So could I, Rachel thought. Ruth had returned to Mountview after the ordeal in the basement of Tim's house, but had refused any medication other than a mild sedative on the first night to help her sleep. Rachel had been visiting every evening after work, but they both knew that wouldn't be able to continue long-term because of Rachel's job. They'd decided on a trial weekend of Ruth staying at her sister's house, which Rachel was hoping might turn into a more permanent state of affairs.

'It's for both of us, actually,' Rachel said. 'There are two mugs of coffee and half a loaf of bread's worth of toast. Even the biggest of appetites wouldn't be able to manage all that.'

'That's not a challenge, is it?' Ruth asked, reaching for a piece of thick-cut toast and crunching into it. 'You know me, always up for a challenge.'

Both women fell silent for a moment. Rachel was remembering the fateful day when she had challenged her sister to climb over their neighbour's fence and pick apples, and she was pretty sure Ruth was thinking the same thing.

'It's over now, Ruthie,' she said gently. 'It really is finished once and for all. Jack can never hurt anyone again.'

'I know. Thank you for stopping me from killing him. You were right when you said it wouldn't have brought me closure. My motivation for leaving the safe haven of Mountview was never revenge – all I wanted was to protect you,' Ruth said, wiping a dribble of melted butter from her chin and licking it off her finger. 'You've had the burden of caring for me since... since I tried to commit suicide, and I wanted to repay that by doing something for you. You know, I was terrified when I set foot outside the hospital that night, but I knew I had to get away.'

'Where did you go, Ruth?' Rachel had wanted to ask her sister everything about the six weeks she was missing, but she'd decided it was best to wait until Ruth broached the subject. 'It was like you disappeared off the face of the earth. I had alerts out for you and everything, but the only reported sightings were of me – people getting confused because we're so alike.'

'I remembered hearing one of the cleaners at Mountview ages ago talking to one of the male nurses about his motorhome. A friend allows him to park it on the industrial estate near the Madejski Stadium without the owner of the site knowing. He said he had to leave the keys under the rear wheel arch in case his friend ever needed to move it in a hurry. It was a perfect hideaway for me, and it beat sleeping rough, which I'm not sure I could have survived.'

'We'd have found you if you had,' Rachel said, taking a sip of black coffee. 'We visited every single rough sleepers' location every day for a couple of weeks after you disappeared. We even had a couple of our police informants on the lookout for you. That's why I was so convinced you were dead,' she said, reaching for Ruth's hand, needing the tangible reassurance that her sister really was sitting in her bed eating toast and not lying dead in an alleyway somewhere. 'I couldn't believe you'd be able to stay so well hidden in these days of CCTV. What did you do for food, though? You must have had to go into shops.'

'I only risked it once. I bought a load of non-perishable stuff: crisps, biscuits, tins of tuna and bread with a sell-by date you wouldn't believe – all the healthy stuff! It makes you wonder what they put in some bread to keep it fresh for several weeks,' Ruth said, pulling a face. 'That's why this tastes so good,' she added, helping herself to another slice. 'I crept out just before the industrial park closed for the day and then I waited until it was dark before attempting to get back in. I threw the bags of shopping over the metal fence before following them. I hadn't heard any guard dogs the previous night, but I was still petrified until I got back inside the van and locked the door.'

'What did you use for money? You've never really needed any at Mountview apart from the few pounds I give you each week for stuff from the café or magazines from the shop…' Rachel raised her eyebrows at the guilty look on Ruth's face. 'You squirrelled that away?' she asked. 'But why? You know you can always ask me for more.'

'I don't like to. I've always felt like a child being handed my pocket money. I hid it away, promising myself that I would give it all back to you if I ever felt well enough to leave Mountview. I had almost £600: imagine all the weekends of pocket money that equates to. I'm so sorry, Rachel. I never wanted to steal away your life just because I couldn't cope with mine.'

'You didn't. I'm high up in the police force, don't you know,' Rachel said, putting on a posh voice and trying to make light of things.

'You know what I mean. Having to visit every weekend and deal with me being ungrateful or, worse still, jealous if you ever mentioned a boyfriend. I'm not sure I would have been as good a sister to you if the roles were reversed.'

'Yes, you would,' Rachel said, moving the tray from the bed to the floor and reaching her arms around Ruth for a hug. 'Just look at what you did for me. You risked your life for your stupid sister who'd allowed herself to get involved with the wrong man.'

'You weren't to know that. I only met Tim that one time at Mountview, and before I figured out who he was he came across as charming and kind and attentive, all the things you'd look for in the perfect man. You shouldn't blame yourself for being taken in by him,' Ruth said.

'I guess you're right, but I've always been so careful not to get emotionally involved with boyfriends, even the ones I really liked, and the one time I let my guard down, it turns out he had an ulterior motive. I'm not sure I'll ever be able to trust another man.'

'For what it's worth, judging by the way Tim spoke about you at Mountview and when we were all in the cellar together, I think he'd actually fallen in love with you too, whatever his initial reasons for starting to date you were. It must have been the rejection by his father that created his issues. He's a very disturbed human being, even crazier than me. What will happen to him, do you think?'

'He'll stand trial, both for holding me prisoner and for murdering the prostitute. I can't believe he could do that to a random stranger,' Rachel said, shuddering. 'It was a cold-blooded and calculated killing. As for stabbing his father, it will most likely be a manslaughter charge, as I don't think he intended to do it. No doubt he'll instruct his lawyer to plead diminished responsibility. He'll have to have a psychological assessment, and they may decide to send him to a secure unit like Broadmoor.'

'Without you, I might have ended up in a nuthouse somewhere. Don't frown at my choice of words, I know I'm a bit bonkers,' Ruth said, pulling a crazy face.

'I wouldn't have put it quite like that, but you do have your moments,' Rachel replied, laughing and ducking out of the way of the pillow Ruth launched in her direction, narrowly missing the breakfast tray. It felt so good to have such a normal interaction with her sister. *I hope this is just the start of things to come for us*, she thought.

'You know,' Ruth said, 'the strange thing is, I actually feel better for not being on medication. The first few days after leaving Mountview were horrendous when I guess I was going cold turkey. But once I got past that and I had snooping on Tim to keep me occupied, I started to feel more in control somehow.'

'I think it's amazing the way you've coped without your meds. It does beg the question whether you actually needed as much medication as you were on, or whether Mountview just found it easier to cope with patients who were sedated.' Rachel paused. 'Have you given any more thought to not going back there and staying here with me instead?' They had talked about it the previous evening over dinner, but Ruth had been non-committal.

'I like the idea of being here, but I'm not sure how I'd cope on my own for long periods while you're at work. And before you say anything heroic about giving up work, I won't hear of it.'

'I wasn't going to,' Rachel said. 'I like my job and I'd be miserable, not to mention poor, without it. No, I've got another suggestion,' she said, taking Ruth's hands in hers. 'Do you remember me mentioning my friend Maddy to you? I met her at Mountview, when her daughter was a patient there.'

'Yes, I think so.'

'I rang her last night after you'd gone to bed and asked her to call in and see us this morning with Bella, the Portuguese nurse who looked after you a couple of times.'

'I definitely remember her. I liked her a lot,' Ruth said, smiling.

'Well, she's decided to move to England permanently, and Maddy has offered her a home, right here in Sonning.'

'I think I know where you're going with this, at least I hope I do,' Ruth added.

Right on cue, the doorbell rang.

'That's probably them now. Do you want to throw some clothes on and come down when you're ready?' Rachel said, getting up off the bed and heading towards the stairs.

A few minutes later, Ruth made her way downstairs to be met by Maddy and Bella, each holding a bunch of flowers. Bella got to her feet and offered Ruth the bunch of blousy hydrangeas she was holding, saying, 'These are for you.'

'*Obrigada*,' Ruth said shyly.

'You remembered,' Bella replied, clearly delighted.

'Yes. And I also remember you promised to teach me some more Portuguese.'

Maddy had followed Rachel into the kitchen area where she was searching for vases to put the flowers in. 'I think this is going to work out just fine,' she whispered.

'I think you could be right,' Rachel replied.

A LETTER FROM J.G. ROBERTS

I want to say a huge thank you for choosing to read *Why She Died*. I really hope you enjoyed it and if you did, and want to keep up to date with all my latest releases, just sign up at the following link. Your email address will never be shared and you can unsubscribe at any time.

www.bookouture.com/jg-roberts

I'm not going to lie, it has been quite challenging to get this book finished on time as I broke my wrist during the editing stages. I'm not the quickest at typing anyway, but the added hindrance of working one-handed slowed me up even more. That said, I've really enjoyed writing *Why She Died* and explaining the mystery of Ruth's disappearance from the end of *What He Did*. I hope I kept you guessing 'who did it' until near the end of the book, and that you were happy with the concluding chapter.

If you enjoyed reading *Why She Died*, I would be very grateful if you could spread the word among your friends and also write a review. I love hearing your thoughts on my books, and it makes such a difference helping new readers to discover my writing for the first time.

I also love to interact with my readers – you can get in touch on my Facebook page, through Twitter, Goodreads or my website.

Thanks,
Julia Roberts

JuliaRobertsTV

@JuliaRobertsTV

www.juliarobertsauthor.com

@juliagroberts

ACKNOWLEDGEMENTS

Turning an idea into a book is a fairly lengthy process and not just in terms of the hours an author dedicates to sitting in front of a computer screen. It's a team effort, and I'm very grateful to every member of 'Team Julia' for their work on *Why She Died*.

As with *What He Did*, the previous book in this DCI Rachel Hart series, my editor is Ruth Tross and once again she has been a pleasure to work with, providing feedback at every stage and a professional guiding hand. Between the structural edit and line edit phase for *Why She Died*, I had ankle surgery and Ruth was very mindful that I might need extra time to complete the line edit if I was struggling with pain. I was determined to meet my deadline even after I fell off my crutches and broke my wrist, something I kept from her until I was certain I was going to be able to complete the line edit one-handed. She is also tremendously supportive, enthusiastic and honest, all vital attributes for an editor, in my opinion. I feel very fortunate to be working closely with Ruth.

I've also worked with my copyeditor Lucy Cowie on the previous Rachel Hart books and appreciate her input tremendously. She is seeing things with fresh eyes and often picks up on little things that I've missed because I 'know' the story intimately and sometimes forget other people do not.

I love the title of this latest book, too – I wonder if you noticed that I snuck it into the pages of the book? Ruth liked that! And the cover designer Stuart Bache has worked magic, in my opinion.

Once again I'd like to thank the Bookouture publicity team, headed up by Kim Nash. It's no good writing a book if people don't know about it, and thanks to Kim and her team, lots of people know about Rachel Hart and her police colleagues now.

I always thank my family for the part they play in each new book. They are the ones who see the hours spent at the computer throughout each stage of the process, and have to put up with me vaguely nodding my head during conversations at the dinner table when my mind is clearly elsewhere working out a new twist in the plot. I'm pleased to say both my son and his girlfriend have read and enjoyed the Rachel Hart series so far, along with my daughter, my mum and mother-in-law, my sister and my nieces – as you can see, I have a very supportive family!

But a book wouldn't be a success if it was only read by a handful of family members. I want to thank you, my readers, for the wonderful response to the DCI Rachel Hart series so far. I've been blown away by the amazing reviews for both books, and really appreciate you taking the time to write them. I hope you've loved *Why She Died* as much – thanks for reading it.

Printed in Great Britain
by Amazon